The BALLAD of JAYCE:

Not your Mothers LitRPG

Lluew Grey

Formatted for print and eBook by Inicio Press
https://www.iniciopress.com/
The Ballad of Jayce:
Not your Mothers LitRPG

ISBN: 978-1-998315-19-2
978-1-998315-20-8

Dedication

Always and Forever to my wife!

To quote Madmartigan: "You are my sun, my moon, my starlit sky, without you I dwell in darkness. I love you."

Also to:

My Brother Jason, who got me addicted to LitRPG.

My Friend Ryan, who is one of the most supportive people I have ever met and always cheers me up.

My Friends John, Marshall, and Harley: Keep on Rockin' my friends, you are awesome!

My Friends TJ, Seth, and Tony. More musicians and awesome people!

Chapter One

Still laughing, Jason stepped outside and started to shut the door. This monthly *D&D* was the best because it guaranteed he would set aside time to spend with his cousin Jared and his best and only real friend TJ; the rest of the players were cool too, but they were really TJ's friends. And stepping out of himself to play a character was always a good time. It always got his creative juices flowing and helped him while writing songs.

"You sure you don't want a ride, Jayce?" TJ called.

"Nah, it's a beautiful California night. The walk will do me good," Jason replied.

"If you say so!" Jared interrupted drunkenly.

"It's just a forty-minute walk. It's fine," Jason said. "I'll see you guys later." Jason shut the door behind himself.

He stood on the porch and breathed in the chill autumn air. It was a clear night, and the moon was full. The walk from their house on Royal Glen to his apartment off Agora Road was a nice one, and he enjoyed walking at night.

Just as he was about to head out, he heard Jared's drunken voice: "I don't know why he still calls you TJ. You're not Tiffany Jackson anymore; you're Tiffany Packer now!"

TJ gave the same response she always did: "You wouldn't want him to call me TP, would you?"

Shaking his head, Jason slowly walked down the front steps. *Maybe I should talk to him about his drinking,* he thought. *Jared never seems jealous or belligerent when he is sober, but he drives everyone away when he is drunk.*

Shaking his head again, he began to sing to himself, *"At*

home drawing pictures, of mountain tops, with him on top, lemon yellow sun, arms raised in a V, the dead lay in pools of maroon below..." Consumed with his rendition of "Jeremy" by Pearl Jam, he walked along. Music was the one thing that had always grounded him. Other than Jared and TJ, he had never really felt a strong connection to his peers, but music—music was his soul. This is where he was himself. If he needed to get out of his head, music was what got him there. He was really getting into the "ooo ooo ooo"s at the end of the song when he heard a rush of footsteps and felt a sharp pain in the back of his head. He saw a bright light, the world spun, and everything went black.

The first thing he noticed was the taste of dirt in his mouth, followed by a ringing in his ears. He was lying on his stomach, and someone was tugging on his shirt.

He looked up to see horses' hooves inches from his face, and he quickly rolled the other way. What the hell was someone doing hitting him with a horse? *Wait, why is it light out? Why am I on a dirt road in what appears to be a Renfair?*

Jason shakily got to his feet and looked around. *What the hell is going on?* he thought. As he dusted himself off, he saw his Levis had been replaced by dirty, torn, roughspun trousers and his Burberry shirt by an equally filthy and shabby tunic.

Someone was tugging him to the edge of the street, and as the ringing in his ears subsided, he could hear a child's excited voice babbling at him. "That was close. You gotta watch out for those merchant caravans. They don't stop for anyone. Are you new here? I've never seen you before. Where are you from? Not a lot of halflings around here. You hungry? You look hungry. Bet you're hungry."

Looking down to see what kid was pestering him, Jason saw only dirty bare feet. Lifting his gaze, he saw a kid who looked to be about ten years old but was slightly taller than himself. *That's a big bitch!* he thought as the line from *Deuce Bigalow* came to mind.

The kid was wearing rags similar to what he had on and was STILL talking. "What's your name? I'm Druston. People call me Dru. Wanna meet Granny? She is kinda crazy, but she is all I have. Come on, I'll take you home. I swiped some bread and apples earlier. Bet there are still some left. Don't mind Granny when you meet her. She looks scary, but she's not."

As his mouth was running a mile a minute, the kid was tugging him toward an alley between what appeared to be an inn and a blacksmith's shop. He planted his feet, resisting the constant pull on his tunic. "Hang on, kid!"

"Dru."

"What?"

"It's Dru. Remember? I just told you that. Are you OK? It didn't look like the horse hit you that hard. Come on. We should get to Cheapside before the guards decide to chase us."

Jason decided he must be dreaming, but not knowing what else to do, he followed the kid—Dru—through the alley, across a street, down another alley, and into an area of town that consisted of poorly constructed, rundown buildings with sparsely thatched roofs. Unlike where he started, the streets were not clean, and the buildings had no signs.

A balding man in his middle years looked up as they passed. "Bringing home stray halflings now, hey Dru?"

"I saw him get run down on High Street. Doesn't seem to have his wits about him. Not sure if he is dazed or an idiot, but he looks like he belongs in this part of town. Leastwise, he doesn't look like he should be a bump on

High Street. He hasn't said more'n a few words since I found him."

"Aye, likely you said enough for both of you. Why don't you let him sit and catch his breath? Maybe try shutting your yap for more than long enough to take a breath. He might talk then."

Dru shrugged, not responding to the man. "Come on. Granny's place is just down this alley." Dru tugged Jason toward a narrow alley between two ramshackle buildings. A few yards down the alley was a tiny house that appeared to be about four feet wide and eight feet tall.

This can't be a dwelling. It must be someone's storage shed, Jason thought, but Dru opened the door and motioned him inside. Jason was shocked as he walked through the door. "Holy Tardis! Where is Tom Baker?" he exclaimed. (He always preferred the older *Doctor Who.*) He was standing in the entranceway to a clean, well-built home that wouldn't have been very out of place back in LA. The decor was medieval chic, not quite Knights of Badassdom level, but close. He didn't see any modern appliances or signs of electricity but wouldn't have been surprised to see Eric and Hung lounging in front of a large-screen TV.

As he stared at the sight before him, he heard a cackle and looked toward the open kitchen area. There, standing behind the butcher block-topped island, was a tall, slender, wrinkled old hag. She had sparse and stringy hair, a long, bent nose, and green skin.

Jason's jaw dropped open, and he stared for a bit before she cackled again and said, "Who be this tender morsel disturbing Meg Mucklebones's rest?"

"They call me Jayce, ma'am," Jason replied.

"And what a fine fat boy you are, Jack!"

Dru interrupted, "Come on, Granny, leave off. You're being creepy again. Besides, his name is Jayce, and he isn't fat. He looks like he hasn't eaten in weeks."

Jayce stared at Meg incredulously. "You know *Legend*?!" he asked.

"Oh, I know many legends," she replied. "Which ones do you want to know about?"

"N-no, I mean the movie... Tom Cruise?"

She just winked at him before Dru interrupted. "I don't know what either one of you is talking about, but you don't need to worry, Jayce. Granny looks scary and talks crazy, but she really is nice." He wandered to the kitchen counter and pulled an apple from a wicker basket. "Here you go. Have a seat and eat this. Then, you can tell us where you came from and what you're doing here."

Jayce perched on a stool and munched on the apple, now more confused than ever. As he finished, Dru handed him a thick slice of buttered bread and asked, "So, where are you from?"

"Well, I live in Westlake but work in LA. I'm a studio musician," he said hesitantly.

"Hmm," Dru replied, "never heard of Ellay, but there are several lakes on the way to the south. Maybe West Lake is one of them?"

Jayce stared at him flatly. "You're kidding, right?"

Before Dru could respond, Meg spoke up. "Why don't you go see if old Master Thatcher needs some help, Dru? I'll get our new friend settled."

"Ok, Granny," he said, sounding disappointed, "sure. But I want to hear all about Ellay and this minstrel job when I get back. Are you any good?" he asked, looking hopeful, but Granny just shooed him out of the house, and he scampered away.

Jayce watched Dru run back down the alley for a moment, and when he turned back, a handsome, slightly plump middle-aged woman stood in Meg's place. She came out from behind the island and walked over to shut the door. When she turned around, she spoke. "I was known as Maddy when I was in the world you came from," she said. "Am I correct in assuming Jayce is short for Jason?"

"That's right," he replied. "What do you mean 'in the world I came from'?"

"Near as I can tell, you have died, and this is the afterlife," she said matter-of-factly.

"What? I was walking home from a game night at my cousin's. We were just starting a new *D&D* campaign. Anyway, I was walking home and... well, I don't know. Next thing I knew, I was here."

"Maybe you got hit by a car or something," she said.

"No," Jayce replied. "I thought I heard something, like someone running... I think someone whacked me on the back of the head. I guess I was a little preoccupied. I was singing as I walked. It evens me out when my brain won't shut up."

"Oh, and that works?" Meg asked.

"Absolutely. I get into the song, and everything else just slips away. It's always been like that."

"Always? It's fun how boys of your tender years perceive time."

"Well, I'm twenty-six, ma'am. I know it's not that old, but tender years?"

Meg shrugged off the comment. "What year was it when you died?" she asked.

"Uhh, well, it's 2024. I guess, if I'm dead, I died in 2024."

"I see," Meg replied. "It was 1985 for me. I was just fifteen years old. What did you do with your twenty-six years?"

"I was born and raised in Westlake Village, California."

"I always wanted to see California," Meg said. "I was from Oklahoma. Did you stay there?"

"Well, no," Jayce told her. "I have a Bachelor's in music

from Berkeley, that's in Boston, and a Master's from the Boston Conservatory. I started college at seventeen and graduated with my MFA at twenty-two."

"So you're very smart or very talented, perhaps both?"

"I guess," Jayce said, embarrassed. "I don't really think like that."

"I was never good in school myself. What did you do when you graduated?" she asked. "I'm always excited to hear about other people's lives back home."

"Let's see... I've been working as a studio musician in LA for two years, but my passion is my band, Knerds of the Round Table. We are a punk band, but we play electric versions of Middle Ages instruments. I play the hurdy-gurdy and sing for the band, but I play lots of instruments. My Master's focused on stringed instruments, though. What else would you like to know?"

"That is enough for now," she said. "I grew up in Oklahoma. And like I said, I was fifteen when I died. I think my father killed me. He used to beat on me and my mom when he was drunk. Fantasy was my escape. I read *The Hobbit,* and I was hooked. I consumed everything fantastic I could after that. The last thing I did was see *Legend* with my friends. When I came home, Mom tried to tell me to run, but Dad came out of the house and threw a beer bottle at me. I remember falling, and that's it. I must have hit my head on the curb or something."

"That's terrible," Jayce said. "I'm so sorry that you had to live that kind of childhood. That also explains the *Legend* bit! It is one of my favorite movies, but honestly, it was never very popular."

Meg shrugged. "We all have our stories, and yeah, people rarely get the reference. I would have tried *Back to the Future* or *Goonies* if you hadn't gotten that."

"Wow, I guess 1985 was a good year for movies!" Jayce quipped. "Those are some well-known classics right there.

Are there many others like us?" Jayce asked. "Sounds like you do this a lot."

"A few," she said. "I don't think this is the normal afterlife. Everyone I have met died young with a tragic story. My theory is that this is a place for us to sort stuff out before we move on."

"I don't have a tragic story," Jayce said. "I've lived a pretty happy life. I'm on the road to making my dreams come true."

Meg gave him a flat stare until the silence became awkward. "If you insist," she said. "If that's true, that makes you the first one I've met. I won't ask for details, but I would bet there is something in your life that you're not being honest with yourself about."

"How big is this world?" he asked, changing the subject. "Maybe you coincidentally just met the people with sad stories."

"The world is very big," she replied. "I traveled for years before coming back here. Every time I met someone from our world, they had first arrived here, just like I did. I had only met a few dozen of us by then, and everyone had different ideas about what was going on, but I started seeing patterns, so I came back here where I could help people as they arrived and maybe piece together some more of the puzzle."

"Ok," Jayce said, "but that doesn't mean it isn't one of many places if the world is as big as you say."

"True," Meg replied, "but nothing I have seen indicates that there is another place people show up."

"Alright," Jayce replied, seeing no point in arguing.

"I came back and dedicated my life to helping young street urchins and newcomers like yourself. It gives me a sense of purpose, and I would rather be settled in one place."

"How did you end up as Meg Mucklebones?" he asked.

"Magic is real in this world, and I arrived as a swamp

witch, much the way you arrived as a halfling. I use the guise of Meg so that people will leave me alone. I don't want anyone to come into my house and discover what I have here. My street kids all know how to keep their mouths shut; we are family. New travelers like yourself have always moved on after getting used to being here. Maybe I've just been lucky so far, but I have faith in the people I help, and it has worked out so far."

"Can I learn magic?" Jayce asked.

"Maybe," she said. "Some do, some don't. I think people should explore the world and discover things on their own. I tried providing all the answers right away, and it was overwhelming for some people, and others got mad at me if I missed something. These days, I provide a safe space and answer direct questions as best I can, but I let people get their own feet under them. I'm here to assure you that this is real, you're not dreaming, and I am here to help if you need me."

"What's with my height?" Jayce asked, looking down at himself.

"This world has many races. You mentioned you play *D&D*? My pastor always said it was evil, but I had a teacher who let us play after school sometimes. This world is kinda like that, with elves and halflings and goblins and such. You are a halfling."

"Huh..." he said. "Why? What or who chose this for me?"

"That is a very good question," Meg told him. "Just like we each find our answers in our past lives on Earth, I believe we are here to search our souls and find those answers for ourselves."

"So you're saying you don't know?" Jayce snarked.

"I know what I believe and what my experiences here have taught me," she said. "Come back when you have had the chance to explore both the lands and your soul. This will give us more common ground to talk about. I don't want to preach; I'd rather have informed discussions."

"So what should I do now?" Jayce asked.

"Have Dru show you around. He is a good boy at heart. He gets into some mischief and has sticky fingers, but he has had to do things in order to survive. He thinks he is taking care of me now, and I let him believe it because it seems to be good for him. The responsibility has helped him grow and see the world differently. I think he will be ready to move on soon. I just have to get him excited about a skill or trade."

"How many people like us have come through since you moved back here?" Jayce asked.

"Well, I don't catch 'em all, I'm sure, but I do my best. Usually, I find one or two a year," Meg replied. "Anyway, get to know the area, figure out how life here works, and ask me if you have questions. For now, I'll show you to your room. You will have plenty of time to explore after you've had some rest."

Chapter Two

The next day, Jayce awoke to Dru shaking him. "Come on, we have to get an early start if we want breakfast," Dru said.

Sitting up groggily, Jayce rubbed his eyes and looked around. "Well, I guess I wasn't dreaming," he said.

The two quietly left the house. As Jayce shut the door, he looked back at the tiny shack, still amazed by what it hid inside. *David Tennant would love this,* he thought to himself.

"Ok, Dru, what's going on?" he asked.

"Gonna get some eggs and bread for Granny to make breakfast," Dru replied.

"Lead the way, Short Round," Jayce said.

"Who are you calling short?" asked Dru. "And I'm not round, either. Better be careful. You're beginning to sound a lot like Granny."

Jayce smiled. "I take that as a compliment," he said.

"That was not a compliment. This area is known as Cheapside. It's where the poor people live. The street I found you on is what we call High Street; it separates Cheapside from the city proper. Both sides of High Street are lined with shops and inns and the like for people passing through. About halfway down the row of shops on the other side of the street is the city gate, which is the only way into Fleet; that's the city's name, by the way. We are going to High Street, and I just need you to make a distraction outside the bakery. Follow me and pretend you don't know me. That'll make it easier. After I leave, wait a little bit, and then meet me at Granny's place, ok?"

"Uhh, sure, but what are you going to do?" Jayce asked.

"Swipe some eggs and bread, of course," Dru said as if it was the most normal thing in the world, and he headed off toward High Street.

Jayce followed Dru, keeping his distance and trying to act like he knew where he was going. They came out onto High Street toward the end of the shops and turned right toward the main cluster of buildings.

Before long, he saw Dru stop outside a shop. There was a table by the door to the shop, which was stacked with freshly baked loaves, meat pies, eggs, and some assorted produce. It looked more like a farm stand than a bakery. Dru looked back, meeting Jayce's eyes for a split second before moving on.

Not sure what to do, Jayce walked up to the other side of the door from the stand, nodded to the attendant, and began to sing Hunger Strike by Temple of the Dog.

Dru don't mind stealing eggs...

When he began singing, the attendant at the table gave him an odd look but shrugged his shoulders and left him alone.

As he kept singing, some of the early morning shoppers began to gather around to listen. Soon, there was a sizable crowd for that time of the morning, and some of the people crowded around the shop stand.

As he was nearing the end of the song, a guard came over and pushed his way through the crowd. "Get back to Cheapside," he said. "We don't need no vagrant beggars disturbing our shops. Move along."

Jayce bowed his head and quickly began to head back the way he had come from. As he headed out, a few people came up and slipped some copper coins into his hands.

"That was amazing," he heard one woman say.

"Can't say as I've heard that song before," said a man.

Before he could talk with any of them, the guard moved

them along and fixed him with a cold stare that made sure he kept going.

After Jayce turned into the next alley to make his way back to Meg's, Dru popped up next to him, holding two hot loaves of bread and sporting bulging pockets that Jayce assumed were full of eggs. "Wow! You really are a minstrel!" he said. "I don't think I've ever heard anyone sing like that before! Where did you learn that song? Did you make it up? Why are you here in rags? You should be in a fancy inn or a castle or something!"

Jayce chugged along on his little halfling legs, struggling to keep up with the taller boy. "I don't think Chris Cornell and Eddie Vedder ever thought someone would use their song that way, but it was all I could think of at the moment. It's not like ASCAP exists here anyway."

"Who is Ascap? Is that who you are running from? You must be running from someone. No one who sings like you lives in Cheapside unless they are trying to hide. Is that why you left Ellay? Are these Eddie and Chris guys going to come looking for you?"

Back at Meg's place, Dru hurriedly unloaded his pockets of eggs and set the two loaves of bread on the counter. He regaled Meg with the tale of Jayce's adventure. He made it sound much more exciting than it actually was. "And you should have heard him, Granny! His voice is amazing! And the song was incredible! Everyone was mesmerized! I could have swiped everything on the table, and no one would have noticed a thing!"

Jayce turned red, feeling a little shame at having helped the urchin commit a crime. "If I had a guitar, I could probably go sing at an inn or something and make us some money," he said. "Do they have guitars here?"

Meg looked contemplatively at Jayce. "No, not that I've ever seen anyway. They do have some stringed instruments, like the lute, the fiddle, and the hurdy-gurdy. There is a luthier in Fleet, but his instruments are very expensive. Not to mention the fact that the guards won't let you into the city looking like Cheapside."

"Hmm, so I need to get a job so I can get some clothes so I can see this luthier," he said. "I worked at a luthier's in Boston to pay my way through college. I'm actually pretty good. I could make a lot of money that way, but I prefer performing."

"Ha, good luck getting a job!" interjected Dru. "I help out old Master Thatcher when I can, but he can't afford to pay me. Says I'll make money when I've properly learned the trade. No one hires people from Cheapside, and you're too old to be an apprentice. Also, there's... umm, well, you're a halfling. People are going to assume you're stealing or something."

Meg smiled at Dru and nodded in agreement. "Fleet is a very small city in the middle of nowhere. People don't see a lot of non-humans here, and the ones that show up like you did don't usually stay long before moving on. I know it's not what you want to hear, but if you want to see the luthier, you should go with Dru to 'obtain' some new clothes."

Dru smiled at this and began to hop up and down in excitement. "Ooh! I know just the places!" he said. "There is a clothier just outside the gate, and next to that is an inn that does laundry for its patrons. They always hang the laundry out to dry in the back. The trick is not to get an entire outfit from one place. Makes you too recognizable. We just need clothes good enough that the guards will let you in."

"I don't know," Jayce said. "Feels pretty shady to me."

Meg shook her head and said, "Don't think of it that way. When you have the funds, you can go back and give the clothier and inn your business; tip them well to repay any harm you may have done."

"I guess," Jayce finally agreed, "but I still don't like it."

"I don't figure I would care much for you if you did," Meg said.

"Hey," said Dru in a hurt voice. "Does that mean you don't like me?"

"No, deary," Meg said quickly. "Your life is completely different; don't go comparing things when one's got nothing to do with the other."

Dru looked down, still sulking, but brightened up quickly. "Let's go get you those clothes," he said. "It's about the time of morning when the clothes should be hanging, and Granny will have breakfast ready by the time we get back." After getting a nod from Meg, Jayce agreed and followed the boy back out the door.

This time, they wound their way through the back alleys to the far side of town and approached High Street from the opposite direction they had before. Crossing the street to the gate side, they walked until they came to the inn that Dru had told him about. Dru led him down an alley and stopped beside a fenced-in yard. Peering through the slats in the fence, Dru nodded.

"All clear. Give me a boost, and I'll meet you at the head of the alley near the street."

Jayce knelt so the boy could climb on his shoulders. From there, Dru grabbed the top of the fence and pulled himself up, and the boy was gone.

Brushing himself off, Jayce looked around the alley. Seeing that no one was there, he made his way back up to the street and sat in the shadows to wait for Dru. After what seemed an eternity but was probably just a few minutes, Dru appeared with a wide grin and a sack in his hands. "Next stop, the clothier. They have a pre-made selection for those what can't afford proper-made clothes."

Looking at Jayce for a minute, Dru suddenly hugged

him and then held his hand at Jayce's waist. "Ok, hold this and wait here," Dru said, thrusting the sack into his hands and running off. Jayce shrugged and sat back down, carefully putting the sack behind his back and leaning on it like a pillow.

Once again, Jayce's nerves made the wait seem forever, but soon, he saw Dru flash past him and continue running down the street. Jayce waited a few minutes more, but Dru didn't come back, so he got up and made his way back to Meg's.

Not having gone to Meg's from this direction before, Jayce got a little turned around and ended up wandering for a bit before he found himself in a familiar location. Still amazed at the sight of the tiny ramshackle little shack with its palatial insides, he shook his head and laughed as he entered the door.

"There you are!" Dru exclaimed. "I was about to go look for you. What took you so long? Did the guards grab you? No, you wouldn't be here if they did. I bet you got lost, then. Did you get lost? It's funny if you did. Cheapside isn't very big."

"Hush, child," Meg said. "Give Jayce what you got for him, and let him change."

Dru lifted a bundle of clothes from the kitchen island and handed it to Jayce. "I think I got it right. Should fit you. I found some clothes in child size, and I thought the shopkeeper saw me, so I ran. Figured you would figure it out when you saw me go by. They should fit, though. Try them on. Not the best clothes, but better than the rags we have in Cheapside. Should be good enough that the guards will let you by...mrff glrp nom..."

Meg shoved some toast in Dru's mouth to shut him up.

Laughing, Jayce took the clothes, added them to the sack he already had, and headed off to his bedroom to change.

When he came back out of the room, Granny took one look at him and began to laugh. "Skittles! You look like Skittles!" she exclaimed.

"I think she is talking about the colors or something. Granny says some strange things. Anyway, sorry about that," said Dru. "Didn't have time to make things match."

"I thought maybe you were trying for a court jester look," laughed Jayce.

He was wearing brown knee-high, heavily worn boots, bright red trousers, and a yellow tunic. He was holding a green cap that looked like something Robin Hood would wear.

"Should be good enough to get you in," said Meg. "The guards aren't really that nosey. As long as you look like you can afford to buy things, they will let you in."

"I also have a few copper coins from busking this morning," Jayce said. "I forgot about that in all of the excitement."

"Hang on to those; they won't get you much, but they help you not look like a vagrant," Meg told him. "Now, sit down and eat with us. I have some things to tell you before you go into Fleet."

Jayce pulled up a stool and filled his plate with scrambled eggs and toast before getting up and grabbing a tankard of water and an apple to have with his breakfast.

As he was finishing up his food, Meg sent Dru off to work with Master Thatcher and turned to Jayce with a serious look on her face.

"Remember yesterday when I said it was good that you have played *D&D*?" she asked.

"Sure," said Jayce, "been playing my whole life. Well, that and other role-playing games. Computer games, too. But you probably don't know about those."

"Sure I do," said Meg. "I used to play *King's Quest* on the computer in the back of my teacher's classroom and *Oregon Trail. Gauntlet,* at the arcade, was my favorite, though."

"Huh, yeah, I guess computers have been around longer than I was thinking," Jayce said. "Anyway, what were you saying about *D&D*?"

"We will get to that," Meg said. "What are your intentions when you see Master Thayer, the luthier?"

"I was going to ask if I could work for him, and then when I've been there a bit, I'll make myself a guitar. It would be fun to play an instrument no one around here knows. That's why I play the hurdy-gurdy in Knerds of the Round Table."

"Well, that should be simple enough if he gives you a job," Meg said. "But if he asks you to do ANYTHING other than work in his shop, you come and see me before heading off to do it."

"Why is that?" Jayce asked, a little confused. "Is he in the medieval mob or something?"

"No, nothing like that. Master Thayer is a good sort of person, and if you tell him Maddy sent you, he will most likely at least give you a chance. No, there are things we haven't talked about yet regarding this world, and I want to make sure you are prepared before it happens to you."

"Why not tell me now, then? And why does he know you as Maddy? Is he like us?"

"No, he is a regular sort from around here. I just have different personas and looks depending on where I go and what I am doing. It's how I seek out and help people like yourself."

"I guess that makes sense," Jayce said doubtfully. "If you have the magic, why not use it? I think it was shortly after your time, but David Bowie once sang, 'Dance, magic dance,' and you remind me of that a little. I feel like you are holding back more than you should, though."

"That may be," Meg replied, "but my experience has

told me to let people discover as much as they can organically. I don't want to color your experience too much."

"Then why help at all?"

"I'm just a person like you, Jayce, and I try to do the best I can with my experiences. I may be wrong; I have been wrong before. But for now, I want you to get to know as many people and have as many experiences as possible before changing your paradigm. Once you know, there is no unknowing."

"Sounds ominous, Meg, but you have been good to me so far. I'll take you at your word for now. I promise I will not run any errands or whatever without checking with you first," Jayce said hesitantly.

Jayce set off to find his first official job in his new life. He went straight through the alleys using the quickest route to High Street and crossed to Gateside before confidently strolling to the city gate.

A moderate number of people were filtering through the gate. As he was about to pass through, a guard stopped him. "Who are you then?" the guard asked. "Haven't seen you before. What's your business in Fleet?"

"I'm going to see Master Thayer," Jayce replied.

"Don't look like you can afford what he's got to sell," the guard said. "You wouldn't be stealing, would ya? You halflings have sticky fingers."

"No, sir! I am an apprentice minstrel, and my Master has sent me to fetch a lute that he has being repaired," Jayce lied.

"Minstrel, ay? Guess that explains the wild get-up. Be off with you then. Just don't go nickin' anything."

"Yes, sir," Jayce replied before pausing and looking back at the guard. "Don't suppose you could tell me how to get there?" he asked. "This is the first time my Master has trusted me with a task, and I have never been in Fleet before."

"Just head straight down the main drag until you come to the market. Ask there, and people will direct you to the shop," the guard said, pushing him along.

Jayce looked around as he walked down the street. Fleet looked like it was pulled straight out of the Middle Ages. The buildings were close together; most were wood, and a few were stone. Thatched roofs were the norm, but some had slate tiles. The streets were narrow. Everyone walked in the center of the street because the sides were filthy, and the stench was not exactly pleasant.

It didn't take long to get to the market. It was a wide-open area in the middle of the city with wooden stalls all around, not unlike a modern farmers' market back home. Merchants called out to entice people to their stalls, children rushed about running errands, and shoppers carried baskets filled with goods from one stall or another.

Most of the coins that Jayce saw were copper like the ones he had, but he saw some silver here and there. He tried to stop at a stall to ask for directions, but the merchant sent him away with an earful about thieving halflings. Eventually, he found a woman willing to talk with him, and she gave him directions to Master Thayer.

Just a block and a half off of Market Street, Master Thayer's shop was a rare brick building with grey slate tiles for a roof and, surprisingly, was the only building he saw with glass in the windows. The rest were just open portals in the wall with shutters that could be shut at night or in inclement weather.

Taking a deep breath, he opened the door and went inside. The shop was very tidy and neatly appointed. There were hooks and pegs on the walls holding all kinds of tools, barrels in the corners with different types of wood in them, and neatly stacked crates that presumably held different pieces and parts. In the center of the shop, there was a display holding two fiddles, a lute, and, to his delight, an instrument that looked like a version of a hurdy-gurdy with a wide body for the drone and a row of keys along the top. It looked like this instrument was meant to be played on a table rather than held on your lap, but seeing it there gave Jayce hope in the level of sophistication available in the instruments here.

A man at the workbench looked up at him. "Can I help you?" he asked.

"Yes, sir," Jayce said. "Are you Master Thayer?"

"If not, I'm in trouble because I'm wearing his clothes," came the reply.

Jayce groaned. *Looks like Dad jokes are universal,* he thought. "Well, sir, I am new in town, and I'm looking for work. I apprenticed as a luthier under Master Carter in Barsoom," he said.

"Hmm, never heard of him or Barsoom, so that won't get you anywhere. Look at the fiddle I've got on the workbench here and tell me what is wrong with it."

Jayce walked over to the workbench and gently picked up the fiddle. He turned it over in his hands and set it back down. "Well, sir, at first glance, it has a worn fingerboard that should be replaced but could still be serviceable if needed. Either way, it is loose and needs to be glued properly. I would repost the bridge as well."

"Looks like you have some knowledge anyway. Why did you leave your last Master?"

"Master Carter's wife caught the eye of the Hekkador of the Therns. There was a lot of trouble going on, and he sent me away to keep me safe. Last I heard, his wife Dejah was in hiding, and the Therns had shut down Master Carter's shop. It was a very ugly business, so my friend Maddy told me I should come to Fleet and said maybe you would be willing to hire me."

"Maddy, ay? She is crafty, that one." Master Thayer laughed.

Jayce couldn't help himself: "She's Crafty" by the Beastie Boys started running through his head. Thayer was still talking.

"Good heart, though, and a right solid head on her shoulders. If Maddy sent ya, that will be enough to give you a shot. I'll not be paying you wages, though; you get a percentage of any repairs you do, and I'll let you make an instrument. If it sells, you get half the profit, and I will let you make another. Sound good?"

"That sounds perfect," Jayce agreed. "When can I start?"

"Right away, boy, right away," Master Thayer said, looking around.

"I don't mean to sound ungrateful, sir," Jayce said, "but can I start tomorrow? Maddy said she had some errands that she wanted me to run after I talked to you today."

"Fine," Thayer told him. "Tell Maddy I said hello and that I expect she will not keep taking you away from your work after this."

Chapter Three

Excited about his new prospects, Jayce hurried home to Meg's place. When he got there, Meg was at her usual place in the kitchen. She was grinding dried herbs with a large mortar and pestle.

"Meg, I got the job!" he said excitedly.

"Good, good, I assumed as much. Before you go off doing things for Thayer, though, we have to get you some starter quests."

"Some what?" Jayce asked, confused.

"This world is more like *D&D* than you know," Meg said. "When people from our world come here, they are called adventurers; they act much like Player Characters, while the residents are like NPCs. This is why I wanted you to have some experience here before you do the starter quests. Many of the people that come here treat the locals poorly because they don't see them as people but rather as tools in a game."

"So... it's like I died and went to an MMO?" Jayce asked.

"Not sure what that is," Meg said

"That's right," said Jayce, "in 1985 terms. So I died and went to a multiplayer arcade game like *Gauntlet*?"

"Pretty much," Meg replied. "If I wasn't here to guide people, they would quickly run into one of the townsfolk who has a quest for them, and that would lead them to more quests and exploring the world. Each quest gives a reward of some kind. Some just give reputation, others give money or items; they all give experience."

"Ok," said Jayce, "this is too much. Where is Ashton Kutcher? I know I'm being punked."

"Again, I don't know what that is, but I assure you this is real," Meg said. "I know it is hard to take in, but you died and went to MMO."

"MMO is not a game; it's a type of game. You know what? It doesn't matter. What do I do now?"

"Follow me," Meg said as she walked to the front door. Jayce followed, still looking around for Ashton Kutcher.

Meg led Jayce to Master Thatcher's place, where Dru was hard at work combing wheat reeds and stacking them to be bundled. "Good day, Thatcher," Meg said.

"Ahh, good day to you, Meg," replied Thatcher. "What can I do for you? Do you need to use Dru for something?"

"Not today. I actually came to introduce you to Jayce here. I was hoping you had a task for him."

"Great timing," beamed Thatcher. "My wheat field should be ready for harvest. Take that scythe right there and get me ten bundles of wheat for Dru to comb."

> *Bloop*
> Master Thatcher has asked you to gather ten bundles of wheat.
> Reward: plus ten reputation with Fleet
> Accept? [yes] or [no]

Like he was wearing some sort of Augmented Reality glasses, the text of the quest hovered before Jayce's eyes. "Uhh, Meg? What the hell is going on? I need some context here. Help, please!" he said.

"Just say or think 'yes' to accept the quest or no to reject it," Meg said. "Formally being offered a quest by regular townsfolk activates your adventurer status. If you were never given a task by someone not from our world, your adventurer status would never activate."

Jayce said, "Yes," and the words disappeared. A small

yellow asterisk appeared in the upper right-hand corner of his vision.

"The asterisk you should be seeing means you have at least one active quest. Think or say 'log' to show the quests, then think or say 'minimize' to shut that window," Meg told him.

Jayce said, "Log," and the quest text appeared before him again, this time with the word [ABANDON] below it. Having played more than a few MMORPGs in his life, Jayce thought, *Minimize,* and the text went away with the asterisk taking its place.

"Now, say or think 'map,' and you will see a map of every place you have been and an arrow pointing toward the nearest quest," Meg instructed.

Jayce thought, *Map,* and just like that, his own personal HUD showed a translucent map overlaying his vision. He could see Cheapside and the parts of Fleet he had been to; the rest was blank. There was a green arrow flashing on the left side of his vision, pointing west.

"Ok, Jayce, go do your first quest and come back," Meg told him. "I will wait for you here."

With that, Jayce followed the arrow out of town. As he reached areas he hadn't been to before, they filled in on the map. He hummed "Travelin' Band" by CCR as he walked. Soon, he came to the wheat field, and suddenly, it occurred to him that he had never harvested wheat before, let alone with a scythe, but he took it out and walked into the field. Strangely, he found that his body sort of just knew what to do. *No weirder than being a halfling, I guess,* he thought, and he went about swinging the scythe, watching the long wheat stalks fall before him. It took most of the afternoon, but eventually, he felt like he had enough wheat, so he started bundling the reeds and tying them with string that just happened to be lying nearby. *Huh, must be plot string,* he thought. When he had ten bundles, he found a hand cart on the edge of the field (*Oh look, a plot cart!* he thought), loaded it up, brought up the map, and headed back to Master Thatcher.

When he got there and offloaded the wheat, he got another notification:

> *BLOOP*
> YOU HAVE COMPLETED THE QUEST: ASSIST THE THATCHER.
> YOU HAVE BEEN AWARDED PLUS TEN REPUTATION WITH FLEET AND THE TITLE "ADVENTURER."
> *DING* CONGRATULATIONS, YOU ARE NOW A LEVEL-ONE ADVENTURER.
> *DING* CONGRATULATIONS, YOU ARE NOW UNBIASED WITH FLEET. COMPLETE MORE QUESTS TO RAISE YOUR REPUTATION.

"Minimize whatever you are seeing and follow me," Meg told Jayce.

"Thank you for the help, Jayce. It was very nice to meet you," Thatcher said.

"It was no problem, sir. I am glad I could help," Jayce replied, still a bit overwhelmed by everything that was going on.

Jayce followed Meg back to the shack like an automaton as he continued to try to wrap his head around everything that was happening.

When they were comfortably seated on stools around the kitchen island, and Jayce had a cup of tea in hand, Meg started explaining. "Now that you have completed your first quest, you are a level-one adventurer. Based on your start as an urchin, you have most likely been assigned the Rogue occupation. Say or think the words 'character sheet' and tell me what you see."

Jayce thought, *Character sheet,* and a character sheet appeared on his HUD. On the top, it said:

> Name: Jayce
> Race: Halfling
> Occupation: Rogue

"Uhh, yeah, it says my name and that I am a Halfling Rogue," he told her.

"Good. Now think or say 'dismiss,'" she said.

Jayce did so, and the character sheet went away.

"Just because Rogue is what you were assigned doesn't mean you have to accept it," she told him. "As long as you don't gain any experience points after your initial quest, you can choose any occupation you want, but once you start adventuring in that occupation, you will be stuck until your next level. Does that make sense?" she asked.

"I suppose," he said. "I mean, I'm familiar with XP and such from games, so it makes as much sense as anything else in this crazy place. I'm still only half convinced I'm not dreaming."

"Your reaction is perfectly normal," Meg soothed. "I assure you, this is happening." She paused and looked him in the eyes. When he didn't respond, she continued, "You can change occupations at the start of each level. This has some benefits and some disadvantages. Just like in games, the higher the level you are, the more powerful you get, but when you change occupations, you stay at the power of whatever your highest-level occupation is."

"So if I decided to be a warrior or something later, I will get the benefits of both?" Jayce asked.

"If you stay a Rogue for the first level and then decide to be a Fighter at the second level, you will only have the power of a first-level character. But, you will have the skills of both a Rogue and a Fighter. Additionally, you will have to get enough experience to advance to the level above your combined level. In other words, if you take three levels in Rogue and one in Fighter, you will have to get the experience necessary to reach the fourth level in order to advance. This can be tough, as you only have the power to fight third-level monsters, so leveling could take longer, but you have more versatility and may be able to fight up a level if you are good."

"Ok, sounds like a mix of TTRPG rules and MMORPG rules so far, but I'm following," Jayce said. "How do you change classes and such?"

Meg smiled. "Sounds like you are going to be a natural at this. You wouldn't believe the difficulty people who have never played role-playing games have in adjusting to this world. To answer your question, just access your character sheet again. But, before you do, let me explain some more things."

"I don't know how much more I'm ready for right now," Jayce said. "I am reminded of a *Far Side* cartoon where the student asks to be excused from class because his brain is full."

Meg nodded, "I get that this is all a bit overwhelming, but let's go over your stats and then see how you feel, ok?"

Jayce sighed. "Alright, drop the knowledge; I'll see if I can pick it up."

"As a level zero, all of your stats were set to eight out of twenty. At level one only, you can reallocate those points by taking some points away from some stats and adding them to others. Be advised, though, that anything below seven starts giving negative effects to any abilities that use those stats. Anything above eight starts adding bonuses. You will also receive bonus stats for your race and occupation. You will not get bonus stats for another occupation if you change after level one."

"Ok, I'm following you," Jayce said hesitantly.

"Good," Meg said. "Additionally, you will be given one stat point every time you level to allocate wherever you want. After level five, you will only gain one stat point at every third level, and you will receive one ability point at every level. I won't overload you with ability points; you will understand what to do with those when the time comes."

"Thanks for that," Jayce sighed.

"Also, you can change your name only at this time, to anything you want, and that's what people will know you as. Now, go ahead and access your character sheet."

Jayce thought, *Character sheet,* and his character sheet once again appeared on his HUD. On the top, it still said:

> NAME: JAYCE
> RACE: HALFLING
> OCCUPATION: ROGUE

Not wanting to change his name, he left that alone. RACE was greyed out, so he assumed he couldn't change that. (*Why couldn't he be a giant or an elf or something? Geesh!*) Moving on, he concentrated on ROGUE, and a drop-down menu appeared, showing:

> ROGUE... FIGHTER... MAGIC USER...

That was it, three choices, but noticing the ellipses next to each occupation, he focused on ROGUE, and it branched out, showing:

> PHYSICAL... MENTAL...

He selected PHYSICAL and saw:

> ASSASSIN, THIEF, BURGLAR.

Not wanting any of those, he minimized that and focused on MENTAL. When it opened up, he saw:

> SHYSTER, BARD.

He tried to select Bard, but it just changed back to Rogue. *Ok,* he thought, *those must be specializations I can pick as I level. I like the thought of being a Bard. That must be why I was sent here as a Rogue.* Just to be sure, he selected Fighter and saw:

Tank... Damage...

He knew he didn't want to be a bullet sponge, so he skipped Tank and selected Damage. He saw:

Ranger... Melee...

He selected Ranger and saw:

Scout, Forester, Archer.

Minimizing that, he selected Melee and saw:

Duelist... Battle Mage...

He selected Duelist and saw:

Blade Master, Dual Wielder, Great Weapons Master.

He minimized that and selected Battle Mage. He saw:

Paladin, Monk, Arcanist.

None of those looked that great to him, and he really just wanted to be a Bard, so he skipped the rest and selected Rogue as his occupation.

On the next section of the page, he saw his stats.

Strength: 8
Agility: 10
Toughness: 8
Stamina: 8
Intelligence: 8

Wisdom: 8
Charisma: 9

Since Meg had said he started at eight, he assumed the higher ones were his race and occupation bonuses. He also noticed that he had one unspent stat point.

Wanting to be a Bard, he figured he would need Charisma, so he put his free point there; not knowing what stats he would need the most, he didn't change any others. So, his starting stats were all eights except Agility and Charisma, which were now both ten.

Moving on, he saw that he had several slots for equipment, which were all empty, and a section for skills, which showed:

Sleight of Hand, Hide in Shadow, and Performance.

At the bottom of the HUD, it read:

Accept character as shown [Yes] [No]

Before finalizing anything, he asked Meg, "Meg? What stats should I choose if I'm going to be a Bard?"

"I figured that was what you would go for," she said. "Agility and Charisma are your primary stats, Intelligence and Stamina being your best secondary stats. You will need Intelligence for your spells when you actually level up to be a Bard, and Stamina is great if you need to perform for longer periods, either on a stage or in a battle. Performing can take a lot out of you."

"You said seven and eight didn't have any bonuses or negative effects, right?" he asked.

"Correct," Meg said.

Looking at the sheet, he took Wisdom and Toughness down to 7, adding those points to Stamina and Intelligence. He could always add a point later, but this was his only chance to take some away, so he wanted to maximize the stats for his occupation.

Satisfied, he selected YES, and the character sheet minimized itself.

"Well," said Meg, "what should I call you?"

"I stayed with Jayce," he replied. "Too confusing to start over with a new name."

"Jayce it is," she said. "Now I have some gifts for you." She handed him a belt with a very small coin purse on it, a short bow, an empty quiver, and a rusty dagger. "This is your starting gear," she told him. "I have upgraded your starter bag to a magical coin purse. This purse can hold any amount of money and up to twenty items. All you have to do is think about putting an item in the purse, and it will disappear from your hand and go into the purse. In order to retrieve it, you just need to think about the item, and it will appear in your hand. The purse also will never weigh any more than it does now, even if you fill it up. I can't give you better weapons until you get more proficient with the ones you have. The more you use them, the more proficiency you will gain and the better the weapons you will be able to use. Oh, and the quiver once belonged to a friend of mine. He left it for me to pass on when he died. He was the only other Bard I've ever met, so I thought it was fitting to give it to you. You can wear it on your back or your belt, and it will adjust to fit correctly. Additionally, whenever you need an arrow, just reach for one, and it will be there."

"Wow!" said Jayce. "That is awesome! Thank you, Meg."

"You're welcome, Jayce. Before you retire for the evening, I want you to go to Mistress Molly at the Pig and Pony Inn. She will give you a quest to go around and meet various folks in Fleet. You will get a small number of coins, some reputation points, and probably some starter gear. Also, talk to anyone you find with a pet; they should also have a quest for you. For some reason, Molly's quest and the pet quest are always common for everyone who comes here. I guess it is the universe's way of helping you get your feet wet, so to speak."

Jayce set off at a jog, excited to see what was in store. Punked or not, he was really starting to have fun! The Pig and Pony was on his map. Even though he hadn't noticed it, it seemed he had passed it on his way to Thayer's. Before he got to the city gate, though, he walked past an old man walking a Jack Russell terrier.

Remembering that Meg told him to talk to someone with a pet, he stopped and turned to the man. His jaw dropped as he got a good look. The man looked almost exactly like the poster of Albert Einstein—the one where he has really wide eyes and wild hair and his tongue sticking out—only this man's hair was even wilder, and he was standing in a cloud of filth like Pig Pen from *Charlie Brown.*

As he stared, the man greeted him. "Well, hello, Joe! Whatta ya know?" he said.

"My name is Jayce, sir; you must have me confused with someone else," Jayce replied.

"Jayce, the ace, all up in my face, walking fast in a race, hitting monsters with a mace," the man replied.

Not sure what to do, Jayce just said, "That's a nice-looking dog you got there, mister. What's his name?"

"Name? Name! He got a name; his name is a name that is Jack is his name. There is no shame having Jack as a name," the old man replied.

"Oh," said Jayce, feeling confused. *I wonder if this guy knows Fezzik from* The Princess Bride *with his penchant for rhymes,* he thought wryly.

A passing man laughed and said, "Don't mind Crazy Chester. He has never been quite right."

Chester laughed. "Right, right, you're bloody well right," he said. "What's that, Jack?" Chester asked the dog. "Oh, you do, huh? Well, ok, if that's what you want." He handed Jayce a bag of treats that suddenly appeared in his hands. "Will you take Jack, my dog? He said he wants to go with you. Won't you feed him when you can?"

Jayce took the treats. "Did you just quote both Supertramp and The Band?" he asked, but Chester was already shuffling away talking to himself. Jayce felt sure Timothy Leary and Gary Gygax had gotten together to play with his mind, but whatever, he was having fun.

Jayce pulled a treat from the bag and fed it to Jack.

> *BLOOP*
> CONGRATULATIONS! YOU HAVE YOUR FIRST PET!
> **WOULD YOU LIKE TO CHANGE ITS NAME?** [YES] [NO]

Jayce selected NO and brought up his character sheet. There was a new tab called PET. He focused on that tab and saw a generic picture of a small dog; it looked kinda like the dog from Monopoly, but beside it was the name JACK. He focused on JACK and saw:

> JACK: LEVEL 1 DOG. 2 BAG SLOTS. [RECALL] [DISMISS] [FEED] [ABANDON]

Wanting to try out his new companion's inventory, Jayce pulled a coin from his inventory and thought about it going into Jack's inventory. Suddenly his hand was empty, and when he checked, Jack had a coin in his inventory. Jayce returned the coin to his inventory and placed the treat bag in Jack's. "Well, that's convenient," he said out loud, much to the surprise of the woman walking past him.

Jayce proceeded to the inn, where Molly sent him to get some supplies from the market; the man from the market sent him to the Lord's manor to drop off some food; the butler in the Lord's manor sent him on another errand after that. This continued until Jayce was thinking, *Why can't these people run their own damn errands?*

By the time he was done with all of the starter quests, it was getting late. He went back to Meg's. As usual, she was behind the island in the kitchen doing something with her herbs.

When he walked in, she smiled. "Well, that took a while. What did you get?" she asked.

He emptied his inventory onto the counter and sorted through it. "Let's see," he said. He counted the coins. "Fifty-one copper coins, along with this outfit." He lifted the clothing, one item at a time. "Basic Rogue leather breaches, basic Rogue leather tunic, basic Rogue leather boots, basic Rogue leather belt, basic Rogue leather gloves, and basic Rogue leather skull cap. Oh, and of course, this guy," he said, recalling the dog. Jack ran up to Meg and nuzzled her leg for attention. "His name is Jack. Please don't eat him."

Meg laughed and petted the dog a bit before looking back at the pile of quest rewards. "This is good," she said. "You have your first armor set. It won't protect you much, but at least it matches."

"I got lots of reputation points, but my character sheet says I'm still just unbiased with Fleet," Jayce told her.

"The points will build as you help more people and complete more quests," Meg said. "The status will change before long."

Chapter Four

Jayce woke up early the next morning and donned his new outfit (except for the silly-looking skull cap; the thing looked like a leather beanie. Jayce didn't think of himself as vain, but he couldn't bring himself to wear the hat).

Summoning Jack for company, he headed to Thayer's. Entering the shop, he saw Thayer sitting at his workbench sipping a cup of tea.

"Good morning, Jayce," the luthier said. "Nice and early, I see. That is a good sign. But before you start, I need you to run an errand for me."

"No problem, sir. What do you need?" Jayce asked.

"I need you to run into Fleet Wood and get some wood from the sawmill there. They should have it ready; you just need to retrieve it. I do all my business with them; they will invoice me later."

> *Bloop*
> Master Thayer has tasked you with visiting Foreman Mackenzie at the sawmill in Fleet Wood and bringing back supplies.
> **Reward:** Reputation with Fleet, 10 copper coins.
> [Abandon]

Jayce minimized the quest log and saw a green arrow on the edge of his vision pointing east. Smiling, he set off and followed the arrow toward Fleet Wood, shaking his head in amusement that he was off to meet—literally—Fleet...

Wood... Mac. He immediately began singing "Go Your Own Way."

Shortly after passing the last shop on High Street, Jayce found himself entering a wooded area.

> *BLOOP*
> NEW AREA UNCOVERED: FLEET WOOD

Well, that's nice, thought Jayce. *At least I'll always know where I am.* Now that he was out of town, Jayce summoned his dagger and placed it on his belt. Then, he summoned his quiver, slung it over his back, and summoned his bow. *Guess I should be ready to protect myself in the woods,* he thought. *I wonder if I can even use these things.* Summoning an arrow, he aimed at a nearby tree and let loose. He missed the tree and hit the one next to it.

> *BLOOP*
> NEW WEAPON PROFICIENCY: BOW
> PROFICIENCY: 1 OUT OF 10

Hmm, typical MMO stuff. I just need to practice, he mused. He shot a few more times at the tree, but his proficiency didn't go up. He started walking down the road again, wondering if he needed something living to shoot at to raise his proficiency.

He saw a rabbit hop from the road into the woods and thought of shooting it but couldn't bring himself to do it. If this were a game, he would just shoot anything that moved until his proficiency went up, but it just didn't feel right here. If this was an afterlife, just with game-like rules, then these were actual living beings. He just couldn't bring himself to kill a poor bunny for no real reason.

He slung his bow over his shoulder and withdrew his knife. He walked up to a tree and stabbed it like it owed him money.

Bloop
New weapon proficiency: Dagger
Proficiency: 1 out of 10

Sheathing the dagger, he moved on down the road.

Soon, he came to a path branching off from the road and a wooden sign that read Fleet Wood Sawmill with an arrow pointing down the path. Jayce turned down the path, double-checking with the arrow on the map just in case the sign was wrong.

Before long, he arrived at the sawmill. It was an open building, almost more of a pavilion, with huge saw blades and other mechanical-looking equipment that seemed decidedly out of place in the medieval environment he had seen so far. There were huge logs strewn about and a handful of men standing around doing nothing. Following the arrow to an official-looking man standing by the saws, he asked, "Are you Mackenzie?"

The man nodded. "What can I do for you?" he asked.

"Master Thayer sent me; said you would have some wood for him."

"Normally I would," the man replied, "but giant termites have infected the mill, and the men won't go in with them in there." Seeing the bow on Jayce's back, the man looked embarrassed as he asked, "Would you kill them for us? I will give Thayer this shipment for free if you do."

Bloop
Supervisor Mackenzie has asked that you kill the giant termites in Fleet Wood Mill.
Reward: Reputation with Fleet, Free wood for Master Thayer.
Accept quest [YES] [NO]

Jayce accepted the quest and moved toward the pavilion containing the mechanical equipment. As he approached, he saw termites that were bigger than Jack the dog. They had fierce-looking pincers on their bulbous heads and shimmering wings on their segmented backs. *Eww, gross!* he thought.

He unslung his bow, summoned an arrow, and took aim at the closest of the termites; he missed. A yellow asterisk appeared at the bottom of his vision, but he didn't have time to worry about it because the offended termite was approaching fast. Jayce had just enough time to get off another shot before switching to his dagger. His second arrow hit the termite, slowing it a bit as it approached. Jayce lashed out in a clumsy swipe with his dagger. The dagger hit the termite, but it still came toward him. Backing up, he tried swiping out with the dagger again, but the termite managed to bite his arm. *Damn! That hurts!* Just managing to keep a hold of the dagger, he plunged it down on the termite's head, and the thing died. *Finally!* Looking at his arm, Jayce saw it wasn't actually damaged; it was just bruised and sore. *Just a flesh wound,* he thought.

Jayce focused on the asterisk at the bottom of his HUD, and notices popped up.

> **Proficiency:** Bow 2 / 10, 3 / 10.
> **Proficiency:** Dagger 2 / 10, 3 / 10.
> Damage received from Termite Bite.
> **Proficiency:** Dagger 4 / 10.
> **Enemy killed:** Giant Termite 1 / 15.

Ok, this is all familiar, he thought. *I'll just pull one at a time and work on my proficiency.*

Picking his bow back up from where he dropped it, he realized that there was a better way to do this. He added his dagger back to his inventory. He then thought about the bow returning to the inventory while the dagger came out at the same time. It worked! Switching between weapons was going to be easy! Aiming, Jayce shot at another termite. This shot was much better, and he had three arrows in it before it got near him.

When he had killed all fifteen termites, he brought up his character sheet and took a look. Everything looked the same, but his armor had a yellow outline. Focusing on his jerkin, it said:

Basic Rogue jerkin. Durability: 96%.

Looks like I am going to have to find a way to repair my equipment, he thought.

Checking his quest log, he saw the quest was ready to turn in, so he went back to Mac.

"I've cleared out the termites, Mac."

"Great job, Jayce. Here is the shipment for Master Thayer," Mac said, pointing to a pile of lumber some workers were placing nearby.

Picking up the wood, he added it to his inventory. Much to his surprise, he found that it only took one slot in his inventory. *That is great!* he thought. He had been afraid he was going to have to find a way to haul it back to town.

"Before you go," Mac said, "there are some bandits been causing trouble down by the crossroad. Best be careful and head right back to town."

"Thanks," Jayce replied and started to head back.

"Just a thought," Mac said, "but if you're feeling pretty good with that bow, you could try taking the bandits down. Lord Fleet has a bounty out for anyone who can stop their marauding. They wear badges to mark them as members of their gang. Turn the badges in to the Magistrate if you want the reward."

Bloop
The Lord of Fleet has offered a bounty on bandit badges. Return 20 bandit badges to the Constable of Fleet.
Reward: Basic iron dagger, 50 copper coins.
Accept quest [Yes] [No]

Jayce accepted the quest and checked his map to see where he should go.

By the time Jayce finished with the bandit quest, his armor was in tatters, his bow had lost much of its spring, and his rusty dagger was broken in half. But he had picked up a rusty short sword, two rusty daggers, a basic short bow, a pair of linen breeches, a pair of leather breeches, and thirty copper coins. Since his inventory wasn't full, he kept everything, thinking he could probably sell or trade what he couldn't use.

It was getting late in the afternoon when he showed up at Master Thayer's shop. "It's about time, boy. I was beginning to think you didn't want the job," Master Thayer grumbled.

"Sorry about that," Jayce replied. "When I got to the mill, they had a termite problem and couldn't get me your shipment. After I helped them with that, I ran into some bandits. Anyway, here is your shipment," he said, handing it over. "It's free because I killed the giant termites."

"You saved me some money then," Thayer said. "Take this silver coin. It is half what I would have paid for the shipment."

"Thank you, sir," Jayce said, sending the coin to his inventory. "May I have the rest of the day off to turn the bandit badges in to the Constable and repair my clothes?"

"Yes, yes, go ahead," Master Thayer told him.

Jayce headed straight for the Constabulary house to claim his reward. Upon knocking at the door, a uniformed guard let him in and led him to an office where he presented the badges and showed them his broken dagger. The Constable opened a safe and brought out his fifty coppers.

He then showed him to the Armory to claim his iron dagger as a replacement for his broken one.

No sooner had he claimed his reward than:

> *DING*
> YOU HAVE REACHED THE SECOND LEVEL.
> YOU HAVE ONE UNSPENT STAT POINT.

Jayce smiled. He had wondered when he was going to level up. Excited to check his character sheet, he hurried back to Meg's.

Dru was sitting at the kitchen island eating. When Jayce walked in, he hopped up and ran over to him. "Back already?" he asked. "Did you lose your job? Did you break something? Crafters hate it when you break their stuff. Maybe Master Thatcher will let you work with me. I hate that work, but at least I'll be able to provide for Meg someday."

"Slow down, Dru," Jayce laughed. "I haven't lost my job; everything is fine. In fact, I've done so well that I have the rest of the day off, and I need to talk to Meg."

Jayce pulled up a stool and told Meg and Dru the story about exterminating the termites and fighting some bandits. He even emptied his inventory to show them the items he picked up and the iron dagger he got from the Constable.

Meg sent Dru off to do Dru things and waited a minute after the door shut. "Well, you look a right mess. Your starter gear is in desperate need of repair. Why don't you go change into your Skittles clothes?"

After changing, Jayce came out with his torn clothes in a bundle. "I need to keep the iron dagger, but the rest is for you, Meg, so that you can pass it on to others like me."

"Thank you," Meg said. "I see your bow is rather useless, as well. What is your proficiency up to?"

"Let me check," he said, looking at his character sheet. "Ten out of twenty."

"Congratulations! When did you level?" she asked.

"Not until I turned in the bandit quest, just before I came home," he replied. "I haven't even had a chance to examine my character sheet yet."

"Nothing exciting happens between first and second level," she told him, "just a stat point to spend. You may be tempted to spend it on Charisma or Intelligence, given your goal of becoming a Bard, but trust me, at this level, you need the Agility. It will help you hit with your bow and dagger and that short sword, if you choose to use it. Anything bigger will require Strength. Agility will also help you avoid getting hit by monsters."

"Ok," he said quickly, allocating that stat point to Agility. He actually felt different when he did; somehow, he felt like he could sense where things were in relation to his body just a little bit better. He took his new iron dagger out and twirled it around his fingers. "Nice," he said, "I can feel the difference."

Meg handed him a new bow. "Yup, eight is average, and twenty is godlike. With every point up, you will notice more and more of a difference. Take this bow; it requires a minimum of ten proficiency to use. It should last you a few levels before you need to replace it."

"Thank you," he said. "I need to run to the tailor to get my armor fixed. I'll be back after that, and we can talk some more. I have a few questions."

"Sounds good," Meg said. "See you later."

"Not much I can do with that," the tailor told him. "Try

over at the Squire's Outfitter. They have a leatherworker there. It's where all the squires and young knight-wannabes get all of their supplies."

Thanking the proprietor for his time, he followed the map to the Squire's Outfitter. Sure enough, there was a leatherworker at a bench in the back, diligently working on a pair of leather breeches.

"Can you repair my gear?" asked Jayce.

The leatherworker took a look. "Been in a few scraps, have ya? Well, I can repair it fine, even reinforce it with thicker leather to provide better protection. Cost ya one silver for the lot, or you can buy a whole new set of properly reinforced padded leather for a silver fifty. The new stuff will be much better than anything I can do with your old items. If you leave your old items for me to use as repair material, I'll even knock twenty copper off. Saves me a lot of work trying to fix this mess."

"Done," Jayce said.

The leatherworker got out a set of leather armor about Jayce's size and had him try it on. "Not a bad fit," he said, making some marks with a piece of chalk. "Leave it here and come back in three days; it will be ready then. Can't do no faster for the price I'm giving you."

Jayce thanked the man and left his old armor set. Thinking a minute before he left, he got the ugly skull cap out of his inventory and tossed it in the pile. "You can take this ugly thing, too," he said. "I'm not going to wear it."

Feeling good, Jayce walked out of the gate and headed back toward Meg's. As he passed the shop where Dru had lifted some of his clothes, Jayce stopped and entered.

"Can I help you?" asked the elderly shopkeeper.

"Yes, ma'am," he said. "I'm afraid my friend stole these clothes so I could get a job. Well, I have that job now and would like to pay for them."

"That is a first," the proprietress said. "Never had a thief come back to pay before."

Jayce took the last of his money out of his pocket and handed it to her. "I'm sorry that we did that," he said, "but I was in a desperate situation."

"That's more'n them clothes are worth," she said, pocketing the money. "Besides, I always keep the stuff I can't sell by the door where the urchins can nick 'em. Come with me." She took him toward the back of the shop and picked him out a nice matching outfit. "This ain't proper tailored stuff, but it's better'n you're wearing. Keep the lot, and you have still overpaid," she said. "I appreciate your honesty, young man. Goes to show not all you halflings are that bad."

> *DING*
> YOUR REPUTATION WITH FLEET IS NOW: ***LIKED***
> MORE QUESTS WILL BE AVAILABLE, AND PEOPLE WILL STOP OVERCHARGING FOR GOODS AND SERVICES.

Jayce smiled as he walked out the door. Everything seemed to be going fine! Time to ask Meg some questions.

Back at Meg's, he had a nice dinner with her and Dru before Meg sent Dru off to bed.

Sitting by the fire with some mulled wine, Meg looked at Jayce. "Have a seat; ask your questions."

"First thing," Jayce said, "I've had the strangest experiences. I met Crazy Chester, who gave me Jack, his dog. Straight out of a song by The Band, if you didn't know, then he quoted a song from Supertramp. The foreman at the mill is Fleetwood Mac. It seems like this world is full of references from our world."

Meg nodded her head. "That is part of why I believe this world is a place for those who need to heal before going on to the next. Each person has some experiences tailored to them; you may even run across inside jokes that have no meaning to anyone but you. I once met a Lycan named Henry, and he was a mild-mannered Janitor, but when I called him Hong Kong Phooey, he didn't get it.

"It took me years to figure it out, but when I came here, most of my experiences were tailored toward self-care and self-love. I met people who wanted to keep me safe and protect me. It took a long time, but I got what I needed in order to learn to love myself and to love living.

"Your experience seems to be fun and full of adventure. You told me you have a Master's degree from a prestigious university, a very good job, and a band you gig with a lot. I don't have all the answers, but maybe you need to learn to relax and lighten up. Or maybe there is more to it than that."

"That all makes sense, I guess, but I told you: I've led a good life. I have nothing to heal from."

Meg shrugged. "We are all here for a reason. You will have to find yours on your own; I can't help you with that," she said. "What else would you like to know?"

"My path to Bard—how long does that take?" he asked.

"How long it takes is up to you," she said, "but at the third level, you will be able to choose a specialty, and at the fifth level, you will get your final occupation. Provided, that is, you don't choose any levels in another class before that. Five levels in Rogue is what it will take to reach the Bard occupation."

"That's not so bad," he said. "It didn't take me long to reach the second level. I can be a Bard in no time."

"Don't be in such a hurry," Meg told him. "Enjoy what you have. As long as you can take care of yourself, and you like the life you're living, there is no need to rush."

"I've never understood taking time to smell the flowers," Jayce said. "I can smell them just fine as I walk by."

Meg smiled and sipped her wine. She let the silence sit for a while before responding. "There is more to stopping and smelling the flowers than just the scent, you know. Maybe think of it like a wine tasting," she said as she swirled her wine around in her glass and tipped it to her nose. "Some things are better when they are experienced rather than merely perceived."

Jayce sat silently sipping his wine for a time. When the glass was empty, he walked it to the kitchen and set it down. "Thanks, Meg," he said. "For everything."

Chapter Five

The next day, Jayce rose early and headed straight for the luthier's shop. When he got there, the door was locked, but Master Thayer opened it quickly when Jayce knocked.

"Good," Master Thayer said. "I like a prompt, early start to the day. I have two lutes and a fiddle in for repair. They are over on the workbench; take a look and make repairs, and I will observe. I need to see where your skills are before I can start to train you."

Jayce just nodded, walked over to the workbench, and got to work. After replacing some pegs and a bridge, he restrung the first lute and looked at Master Thayer, who just nodded for him to continue. The second lute was in much rougher condition, and he decided to remove the soundboard and replace it altogether. He kept looking at Master Thayer as he started the process, but the luthier just watched. Seeing that the man wasn't going to stop him, Jayce went ahead with the replacement. When he had polished and reassembled the lute, he set it aside and picked up the fiddle. He noticed it was the same one from last time. After removing the strings, he got out the thinnest knife in the rack and heated it gently before sliding it between the loose fingerboard and the neck. The remaining glue released easily, and Jayce saw that the fingerboard, although worn, was rather thick, so he placed it in the cradle and looked through the tools until he found just the right scrapers. Looking around, he didn't see a sanding block or sandpaper, but he realized that sandpaper probably didn't exist there. Looking around again, he found a very polished-looking bit of antler and decided that it must be the burnishing tool.

He gently scraped the fingerboard until he was happy with the condition and then rubbed it with the horn until it shone beautifully. Flipping it over, he took a small pebble from the bench and rubbed the back just enough to make sure the old glue was properly removed before rubbing the paste stick along the back and returning it to the neck. He clamped the reglued fingerboard in place. When he was finished, he looked up at Master Thayer and said, "I will let the fingerboard set overnight before I adjust and repost the bridge."

Master Thayer slowly shook his head. "I need to see you make your own instrument. I can't believe your last Master didn't release you to be a journeyman. I'm not sure how much I have to teach you."

Jayce beamed at the praise. "I can work the mechanical portions of the hurdy-gurdy as well. Making and repairing drones is one of my favorite things to do, actually."

Master Thayer nodded. "I will take you at your word for now. Don't get a lot of calls for drone repairs. I do have an order for a new lute. If you feel ready, I would like to have you do the work under my supervision. If you do well, I will allow you to start a project of your own."

Jayce couldn't wait to get started, and before long, he was busy planing and shaping. Master Thayer wouldn't let him use any of the pre-made bits and blanks he had on the racks.

In a matter of days, he had made and dry-fitted all the parts for the lute. Before he could assemble it, however, Master Thayer told him he wanted to see Jayce make some glue and strings. This had Jayce stumped; he had never done anything like that before and told the Master as much.

"At last!" quipped Master Thayer. "I have found something I can teach you! The best glue comes from the hide, bones, and hooves of the Cadarn bison, and the best strings are made from the Maska cat. The whole reason I settled here in Fleet is because both animals can be found in this area. This makes the materials far cheaper than other places."

Jayce had been itching to get out and do some more leveling and thought this might provide the perfect opportunity. "Master, if I hunt these animals, do you know the process of making the glue and strings from fresh kills?"

"Of course I do, boy. Used to get the materials myself when I was younger and poorer. This is an amazing opportunity for you! A master craftsman should not have to rely on anyone for his craft. When I was a journeyman, I even worked at a sawmill for a time in case I ever needed to turn a tree into an instrument."

> *Bloop*
> Master Thayer has given you a quest to make glue and strings from scratch.
> Accept [Yes] [No]

After accepting the quest, Jayce saw that only the first part showed in his log.

> Making the Materials, Part 1:
> Cadarn Bison Hide: 0 / 2
> Cadarn Bison Bones: 0 / 10
> Cadarn Bison Hooves: 0 / 5
> Maska Cat Guts: 0 / 15

Ok, he thought, *simple gather quest. I hope the drop rate is good.*

Before running off to go hunting, Jayce decided to go back to the Outfitter and pick up his gear. Even though it was just a short jog from the shop, Jayce barely made it before they closed. He was shocked by how late it had gotten, but things took much longer without power tools.

As he walked in, the leatherworker looked up from cleaning around his station. "Ah, I was wondering if you would be in today," he said. "Just barely made it, I see. I did a little extra work for you, no charge, my aunt Mae..."

"Aunt May?" Jayce interrupted. "Your name wouldn't happen to be Peter, would it?"

"Er, uh, no. I'm Thorne," the leatherworker said.

"Oh," said Jayce sheepishly. "Never mind. I thought, uh, yeah. What were you saying?"

Thorne continued, "My aunt Mae runs the clothier just outside the gate. Said you were real good to her, and I appreciate that, so I took the hat you left along with your old gear and used the leather to add extra reinforcement around the shins, thighs, chest, shoulders, and upper arms. This set will be a vast improvement over what you had before."

"Well, thank you!" Jayce replied. "Your aunt was very good to me, as well." *Looks like that boost to my rep is paying off already!* he thought.

Jayce took the new gear and inspected it.

> **IMPROVED PADDED LEATHER ARMOR:** THIS PADDED LEATHER ARMOR HAS BEEN REINFORCED FOR EXTRA DEFENSE AND DURABILITY.
> +2 DEFENSE
> **DURABILITY:** 200 / 200.

"Sweet, man! Thanks!" Jayce said before looking up to see Thorne looking at him, perplexed. "I mean, this is really good, thank you," Jayce said after an awkward moment.

The next morning found Jayce once again following the little green arrow on the left side of his map. This time, it was pointing to the southwest of town. It was time to go hunting!

He summoned Jack for company and followed the arrow through Master Thatcher's fields before turning to the south. The fields turned into lightly wooded hills, and his map opened up a new area called Lower Fleet Hills. "Guess they don't put a lot of thought into naming things around here," he said to Jack, who wagged his tail excitedly. "I wonder if there is an Upper Fleet Hills."

The arrow on Jayce's map had disappeared, so he dismissed the map and inspected the area. There didn't seem to be much here. It was a warm sunny day with a light breeze disturbing the long waving grass and rustling the leaves of the few trees in the area. Jack bounced among the grasses, looking like Tigger from *Winnie-the-Pooh,* and Jayce laughed at his antics.

One of the animals he was looking for was some kind of cat, so he supposed they could be hiding in the tall grass, but the other was some kind of bison. Shouldn't he be able to see some grazing the fields?

Equipping his bow and nocking an arrow, Jayce cautiously began to wade through the "waist-high" grass, which was actually tickling his pointy ears as he walked. After a few steps, he knelt to tussle Jack's ears and give him a treat. He sent the dog to try to flush something out of the grass.

It didn't take long before the little guy came bounding back toward Jayce, yipping up a storm. Not far behind the dog, Jayce could see something barreling through the grass, chasing Jack like he was about to be dinner. "Shit, shit, shit!" Jayce said to Jack. "Maybe that wasn't such a good idea."

He pulled his new bow back to a full draw and waited for whatever was following Jack to appear, hoping he would get a shot off before the creature caught up with his traveling companion.

Just as the sinuously waving grass was about to catch up to the bounding dog, Jayce finally saw what he assumed must be a Maska cat. The thing was about two feet tall and four feet long, not including the long tail.

With no time to inspect the thing, Jayce aimed and let loose. The arrow embedded itself deep in the cat's chest below the neck, just to the right of its front left leg. The Maska gave a yowl and tried to bite at the arrow sticking out of its chest. If its heart was where it should be, Jayce felt like he should have hit it, but the beast wasn't dead.

Jack went bounding back and distracted the cat for just long enough for Jayce to aim just behind the front left leg. He had to kill it before Jack got mauled; Jayce got off another shot. Not quite so lucky, the arrow took the cat in its hind leg. Giving up on the arrow in its chest and the yipping dog, the Maska began to stalk toward Jayce. It was bleeding profusely from the wound on its chest and dragging its hind leg behind it. That's when Jayce noticed its hind leg was behind the leg...behind its front leg! *Six-legged cats?!* Jayce didn't have time to ponder the mechanics of that as he quickly drew and shot again, this time taking the cat between the front and middle leg on the right side. At last, the cat fell and stopped moving.

Jayce wasn't sure if it bled out or if he finally hit a vital organ, but he dismissed his bow and drew his dagger as he cautiously approached the downed animal. Its sleek fur was green with brown spots, and its chest heaved laboriously. Suddenly feeling sad for the animal, Jayce approached from behind its head, reached over, and slit its throat.

"Now what?" he said as he knelt to pet Jack, who was panting heavily. "I didn't bother to learn how to skin or butcher animals before I came out here." He didn't need to worry, though. The cat seemed to dissolve before his eyes, leaving a neat stack of items on the ground in its place.

"Holy Houdini, Batman!" Jayce exclaimed. "I really *have* died and gone to an MMO!" Picking up the stack of items one at a time, Jayce found he had one ruined cat pelt, one sharp cat claw, and one Maska catgut. "Aaarrrgghh! Six feet and only one claw? What the hell?"

Fearing that Jack would end up an unwitting sacrifice to a six-legged demon cat, Jayce dismissed the dog and continued his hunt.

Three more cats and only one more gut later, Jayce topped one of the small hills. Looking around, he saw a lone animal in the distance. *It must be one of the Cadarn bison,* he thought. It appeared to be wallowing in a small pond in between two of the larger surrounding hills.

Jayce kept a sharp eye out for more cats as he did his best to be stealthy with his approach.

Bloop

Jayce nearly jumped out of his skin at the sound.

You have learned a new skill.
Stealth: 1 / 20.

Jayce acknowledged the alert and took a minute to get his heart rate back under control. By the time he got close enough to the bison for a good look, his Stealth was at four out of twenty. *Guess it goes up pretty quickly at first,* he thought. *Probably slows down as it approaches my max, though.*

Jayce wondered how in tarnation he was supposed to kill it. Probably eight feet tall at the shoulder and looking like some freak bodybuilder cow, the bison also had large water buffalo-looking horns; only instead of one on each side of its head, there were four. From the top view, it probably looked like a sideways X on the beast's head. It had waded out of the pond and was munching on some grass without a care in the world.

If I looked like that, Jayce thought, *I don't think I would worry about anything either!*

Well, if Master Thayer brought these things down back in the day, Jayce could, too! He summoned an arrow and focused intently on the spot he wanted to hit. He slowly drew the string back to his ear, took in a breath, and held it, willing the arrow to hit the animal in what he hoped was its heart. Just when he couldn't hold his breath any longer, he loosed the arrow.

The arrow looked translucent as it flew, and when it hit the bison, it hit with the impact of a truck. The bison almost fell over as it was knocked several feet to the side.

> *Bloop*
> You have learned a new skill.
> Stealth Shot: Arrow undetectable by target until struck.
> Deals double weapon damage.
> Additionally, deals bleeding damage every second for 5 seconds.
> 3-minute cooldown.
> Can only be used from Stealth.

Jayce stared at the stunned bison as his new skill registered. "This is freaking awesome!" he whooped. Unfortunately for him, his distraction gave the bison time to recover. And it was PISSED! "Fuuuuuuuudge bucket!" Jayce yelled as he turned and ran. "Dwayne 'The Rock' Bison is about to kick my ass!"

Running for his life, Jayce was praying to any god that would listen that he wouldn't run into a Maska cat right now. The worst thing about this world was the lack of health bars. He had no way of knowing how much this monster had left in the tank. Taking a look over his shoulder, he saw that the charging bison had slowed down. It was walking slowly now, staring at him like it wanted his lunch money.

Jayce decided to take advantage of the opportunity and launch some more arrows down range. As fast as he could, Jayce drew arrows and fired them at the bison, barely taking time to aim.

"Come on, Ted Nugent, don't fail me now!" he yelled, wishing he knew the words to even one Ted Nugent song that wasn't "Cat Scratch Fever."

> *Bloop*
> You have learned a new skill.
> Rapid Fire: Shoot two arrows a second for thirty seconds.

"'Wango Tango'!" he yelled. "That's another Ted Nugent song!"

Under the barrage of arrows, the bison went down. Throwing all caution to the wind, Jayce dismissed his bow, summoned his dagger, and did his best WWE flying overhead chop, driving the dagger into the bison's neck as many times as he could before he ran out of breath and lay on top of the dead beast covered in blood and gulping air into his burning lungs.

Jayce stood and dusted himself off while he waited for the animal to disappear.

As soon as the loot appeared, someone jumped from the tall grass and grabbed it.

"What the hell?" Jayce yelled. "I need that loot! It's the whole reason I'm out here!"

"That's what you get for just standing around!" the stranger snarked.

"Who are you, and why are you stealing my loot?" Jayce asked.

"You can call me Fatty," the tall, muscular man responded.

"You can call me Stretch," Jayce quipped. "Can I have the hide, please?"

"Nope," Fatty replied, walking away. "These hides sell really well in Seabeck."

Jayce summoned Jack and set off in the opposite direction from where Fatty had headed. "Guess there are a-holes everywhere," he said to the dog. "Let's put some distance between us before we try again."

By the time his hunt was over, he had killed four bison, untold numbers of cats, and a six-foot, bright yellow snake with wings. The snake had come flying out of nowhere during his hunt but went down pretty easily.

Fatty had followed him most of the day, so Jayce had much less to show for his hunt than he should have. It seemed like the man just popped up out of nowhere whenever there was a corpse to loot.

His armor had held up well and showed a durability of 145 out of 200. He checked his quest log one last time before heading home:

> MAKING THE MATERIALS, PART 1:
> CADARN BISON HIDE: 3 / 2
> CADARN BISON BONES: 15 / 10
> CADARN BISON HOOVES: 6 / 5
> MASKA CAT GUTS: 17/ 15

The trek back to Meg's was uneventful, and Jack's antics made the time fly by. He had just enough time to change back to his regular clothes and drop his armor off with Thorne for repairs before ending up at Master Thayer's to turn in his quest.

Feeling exhausted, he walked in the door of the luthier's shop and unloaded the quest items on the workbench. Thayer came over to inspect the items.

> *BLOOP*
> QUEST UPDATE: USE THE ITEMS GATHERED TO MAKE GLUE FOR MASTER THAYER.
> *DING*
> YOU HAVE REACHED THE THIRD LEVEL, AND YOU HAVE ONE NEW STAT POINT TO ALLOCATE.
> YOU MAY NOW CHOOSE A SPECIALIZATION FOR YOUR PROFESSION.

Jayce dismissed the notices, deciding to deal with them when he got home.

"Good job," Thayer said. "I can't believe you got all of this in one day. Get ready for a long night. Can't leave the fresh hides without preparing them."

Sighing and wishing he had just gone home and come back tomorrow, Jayce said, "Ok, what do I do next?"

Thayer pulled out a long, curved blade with handles at both ends. "This," he said, "is a hide scraper. Follow me."

Jayce followed the luthier out the back door of the shop into a fenced-in yard he had never been to before. There were tall stands with hooks on them, workbenches, and four bricked-in fire pits with metal frames and cauldrons.

Jack settled down on a patch of grass and promptly fell asleep. *Lucky guy,* Jayce thought.

"Watch while I set the first hide, and you will set the rest," Thayer said. Thayer connected the edges of the bison hide to the top of a frame and let the rest dangle while he pulled a bench up and draped the hide over it.

Nodding, Jayce repeated the process with the next bison hide. After being berated by Thayer, saying, "We aren't tanning leather, boy, all the hides will do," he hung and draped the ruined cat hides as well.

Thayer then took the hide scraper and went to the hide he had hung up. Drawing the long, curved knife along the hide deftly, he removed the hair from that section of hide with a single stroke. He then handed the blade to Jayce. "Get to it, boy! Need all the hides scraped, and when the hair is removed, flip it over and make sure any fat or things that aren't skin are removed from there as well."

Jayce placed the blade next to where Thayer had scraped and pulled it down the hide, imitating what he had seen the luthier do. As he pulled, some hair came off, some did not, and then the knife dug into the hide, digging a gouge in it.

"Try again, boy, and hold the knife like so," he said, taking the knife and showing Jayce the correct angle at which to hold the blade before handing it back. "Long and deliberate but quick strokes with an even pressure," he admonished.

Jayce took the knife and concentrated on the angle before taking another scrape along the hide. This time, more hair came off, but he ended up gouging the hide again toward the bottom of his stroke.

"Good start," the luthier told him, "but make sure that angle doesn't change as your arms move down the hide. You will have to change the position of your wrist as your arms move to keep the blade at the correct angle. And you put too much pressure at the bottom of your stroke."

Groaning, Jayce tried again. This time was much better. Far from the nice clean stoke Thayer had made, but noticeably better than his first two.

> *Bloop*
> You have gained a new skill.
> Apprentice Leatherworker: 1 / 250

Oh, sweet, Jayce thought, *more crafting skills.*

Jayce kept scraping late into the night. The first hide looked like a blind man had tried to shave a bear, but each hide after looked better and better. When he was finally done (and his leatherworking had hit 35), he looked around to see Thayer napping in a chair he had brought out from somewhere.

Waking the man, Jayce proudly displayed his work.

"Lucky we aren't trying to make leather," Thayer told him. "Not a one of these is good enough for that, but it will work for our purposes. Take the cauldrons to the barrel over there and scoop some wood ash from the barrel into the cauldrons. About a quarter full will do."

While Jayce did that, the luthier lit the fires. With the ash in the cauldrons and the fires lit, Thayer had Jayce fill the cauldrons a little over halfway with water and set them on the hooks over the fires. He then showed Jayce how the mechanisms that could raise or lower the cauldrons above the flame worked. "Keep the cauldrons full in the flame until they come to a boil," he told Jayce, "then swing them out. Put the bison hides in their own cauldrons, and the cat hides in a third. Swing them back over the flame and bring it to a boil again."

Jayce did as instructed, and the luthier watched, making sure his instructions were followed exactly.

With the hides boiling in the cauldrons, Thayer then had Jayce set the hooves in a fourth cauldron, which he then had him fill with water and set over the final fire. No sooner was that task done than Thayer told him it was time to rinse the hides.

Jayce filled a trough with clean water and lugged the heavy cauldrons over to it. He pulled the hides out one by one, dipping them in the water, wringing them out, and dipping them in again. When the rinse water was dirty, he had to empty the trough and fill it again. After several hours of doing this, Thayer finally declared the hides clean enough. Jayce had to fill the cauldrons three-quarters of the way with water again while Thayer went and got some glue pots. The glue pots were filled halfway with water and set aside. When all of this was done, Jayce had to hang the hides back on the frames to dry.

Thinking he could now take a break, the exhausted wannabe-Bard began to sit down next to Jack.

"What are you doing, boy?" Thayer asked. "It's time to pull the hooves from the water."

Jayce swung the hoof cauldron out of the fire and began to net the hooves from the cauldron. When that was done, he poured the remaining water in the cauldron into a glue pot, thoroughly scrubbed out the cauldron, refilled it with water, and set the glue pot in it, making a double boiler.

Thayer had Jayce watch the glue pot until the liquid inside was nothing more than a thick, gooey paste. He poured the paste onto a piece of waxed parchment until it had dried into a semitransparent rubbery sheet. Next, he took the sheet of hoof glue and placed it in some netting in the corner of the shop to finish drying.

With the sun already on its way back up, Thayer, at long last, sent Jayce home to rest. "Take the rest of the day for yourself, boy. Tomorrow, we will make the hide glue."

Completely exhausted, Jayce stumbled home, with Jack once again bouncing around him excitedly. Jayce barely made it to his room before he fell asleep, thinking to himself he should have taken a bath first. The last thing he saw as his eyes shut was Jack snuggling up to him on the bed and sighing contentedly.

Jayce woke up a few hours later to light streaming in the window, full on his face. Grumbling to himself about wanting to sleep some more, he rolled out of bed, filled the basin, and bathed himself as best he could.

When he walked out into the kitchen, Meg was busy picking apart dried herbs and grinding them with her mortar and pestle. Jack was eating scraps from a bowl at her feet.

"Good morning, lazy bones," she said. "Well, good afternoon, I think, actually."

"How do you stay so clean, Meg?" he asked. "I would kill for a shower."

"What makes you think I don't have one?" she asked.

"Uhh, lack of indoor plumbing, for one," he said.

"I am a powerful swamp witch," she said. "You see my house and think I couldn't figure out a magic shower?"

"May I use it?" he asked.

"Of course not!" she replied. "That is something you have to figure out for yourself. My rooms are warded, so no one other than myself can enter. Wouldn't do to have people see the wonders of a modern world."

Jayce finished munching on a couple of apples in resentful silence. After a while, he looked at Meg and asked, "What is it you're always doing with these herbs? Is it for your witchcraft?"

"Not at all," she said. "I make teas and medicine, occasionally a potion or two. But my magic doesn't require reagents."

"Is that something I can learn?" Jayce asked.

"Oh my, yes!" Meg said excitedly. "Most people think it's boring and don't want to know."

"I'm in a band called Knerds of the Round Table," Jayce said. "I like lots of things that most people think are boring."

Pulling a giant tome off a shelf, Meg walked around the island and opened it to the first page. Inside was an illustration and description of a plant along with its uses. "I have been making this book almost as long as I have been here," Meg told him. "It lists every type of plant I've ever encountered and its properties. Not all of them are useful, and some are poisonous, but if you're going to dabble in alchemy, you must first become well-versed in herbalism."

Jayce flipped through a few pages. "I think I've seen some of these while I was out hunting," he said.

"You have likely seen many of them but didn't pay attention," she replied. "If you want to learn..." she paused while she pulled another big tome from the shelf and walked back to him, "you can start by making a copy of the book." She dropped the heavy book in front of him and opened a drawer, pulling out a quill and a multicolored ink set. "You are an artistic sort. Can you draw?"

"I'm not the best," he said, "but I drew a lot when I was in high school. I wasn't sure if I was going to pursue art or music until I got into Berkeley. Couldn't turn that down."

"Good, good," she said absently. "This will give you something to do when you're not working at the luthier's."

Jayce studied the first page and then began to slowly copy the illustration of the plant into his own book.

> *BLOOP*
> YOU HAVE LEARNED A NEW SKILL.
> APPRENTICE HERBOLOGY: 1 / 250

"Awww, yeah," he said. "'Parsley, Sage, Rosemary, and Thyme'!"

"Hmm?" Meg inquired.

"New skill," Jayce said. "I'm hoping to get a lot of them."

"Ah," Meg said, turning back to her work.

Jayce spent the remainder of the day working on his Herbal.

"I hate thatching," Dru said as he swung the door open and stormed inside. "Stupid reeds always poking my skin. My fingers hurt so bad it hurt to open the door."

Meg smiled patiently at the young boy. "You are lucky Master Thatcher takes the time to teach you," she said. "Both his boys are out as journeymen right now, and like as not, one of them will come back and take over his work. He has no real need for your help."

"I know, I know," Dru said. "I know I'm lucky and shouldn't complain. Lots of kids in my situation wouldn't have a trade to learn at all, but I just wish I had a trade I enjoyed."

The following morning, Jayce got to the shop early and checked on the hides. They were drying nicely, but he had no idea how dry they needed to be. Seeing that Master Thayer wasn't in the shop yet, Jayce busied himself on some repair work that had come in the previous day. Jack curled up under the workbench, and Jayce smiled. "Wish I had you growing up," he told the dog.

"Looks like you have today's work well in hand already," Master Thayer said, startling Jayce from his rapt attention on the citole he was repairing.

"Almost done," he said. "This citole is the last item I know of anyway."

"Well, when you are done with that, you might as well take the rest of the day off. I have nothing to teach you, and the hides aren't quite ready to cut up for glue yet."

"Just need to reburnish this thumbhole. I had to fill in some cracks," Jayce said. "I checked the hoof glue. It seems hard as a rock now."

"Oh, perfect. I almost forgot about that," Master Thayer replied, handing over a stoppered jar. "When you are done there, take the glue down and crumble it into this jar. Then you may have the rest of the day."

It was still morning when Jayce finished his work for the luthier, and he decided to stop by the Outfitter before heading back to work on his Herbal.

Thorne was at his workbench when Jayce walked in. "Oh, hey there!" he said, pointing to Jayce's repaired equipment as he bent down to give Jack a piece of rawhide to chew on. "All done. Didn't take as much work this time."

Jayce handed over the payment and put the items in his

inventory. "Do you need any Cadarn bison or Maska cat hides?" he asked.

"I could always use quality hides, especially from the bison. Makes high-quality, thick leather, and most people aren't willing to take them on. Why? Do you have some?"

"Not right now," Jayce replied before relating his glue-making experience for Master Thayer to the leatherworker. "Wouldn't mind taking the time to get some more, though, and wanted to see if there was a market for it. Or if you would be willing to teach me a bit of leatherworking in exchange for the hides."

"That would be more than fair," Thorne replied. "Best you get a bunch of the cat hides, too, then," he said. "The bison hides are far too valuable to risk you messing them up."

> *BLOOP*
> THORNE HAS OFFERED YOU A QUEST:
> COLLECT HIDES FOR THE LEATHERWORKER.
> BISON HIDES: 0 / 10
> CAT HIDES: 0 / 40
> ANIMAL BRAIN: 0 / 50
> REWARD: REPUTATION WITH FLEET, LEARN LEATHERWORKING.
> ACCEPT [YES] [NO]

"No problem," Jayce replied excitedly, selecting yes. "I can collect herbs for Meg while I'm out there."

Jayce hurried back to Meg with the news.

Walking in the door, he found Meg where she always was. "Are there any herbs you want me to collect?" he asked. "I'm going to go hunting for more hides and would like to work on my herbalism while I'm out."

Meg took down the Herbal Jayce had started. Flipping through the pages, she marked a few with dried examples of the herbs and handed the book to him. "I've marked a few common herbs that are great for tea and a minor restorative," she said. "Get as many as you can, and I'll show you how to use them when you get back."

Jayce went to his room and changed into his armor. He was about to walk back out the door when he remembered that he had leveled when turning in the first part of the glue quest.

"Meg?" he said.

"Hmm?" came the reply.

"I leveled when I turned in my glue quest. Any recommendation on how I spend my point?"

"I recommend at least one more in Agility if you're going out hunting," Meg replied. "Choose your specialization before you go, as well."

Jayce brought up his character sheet, dumped one more point into Agility, and selected the drop-down menu for Rogue. The specializations were no longer greyed out. So, he selected Mental.

> You have chosen to focus on the mental aspects of Rogue. Is this correct? [Yes] [No]

Jayce selected yes and checked his character sheet again.

> Strength: 8
> Agility: 12
> Toughness: 7
> Stamina: 9
> Intelligence: 10
> Wisdom: 8
> Charisma: 11

Jayce was surprised to see the increase in his Intelligence and Charisma stats. "Did choosing my specialization change my stats?" he asked.

"Oh, yeah, it does that," Meg replied. "That's why I told you not to focus too much on the stats for Bard yet. You get boosts when you specialize, but as a Bard, the only boosts you will get for your combat stats are by putting in your points from leveling. You probably want to buff your Toughness in the next couple of levels. Even though you can't see your hit points, Toughness will raise them for you."

"Thanks, Meg," Jayce said as he checked his equipment, called to Jack, and walked out the door.

Chapter Six

Upon reaching the hills, Jayce looked around, excited to see how hunting went this time. Hopefully, no kill-stealers like Fatty would be lurking around. He had maxed out his proficiencies last time, so with leveling, they now all showed twenty out of thirty.

Summoning his bow, he nocked an arrow and entered Stealth. Before long, he came across a pride of cats curled up in some matted-down grass, napping in the heat of the day. He used a Stealth Shot on the big male, and after seeing it go down, he busted out Rapid Fire on the three females. One after another, they dropped as Jayce sang, "let the bodies hit the flooooooooooor!" Drowning Pool most likely never thought about giant green cats when they made that song!

After collecting his loot, Jayce looked around and found some common nettle to pick. Soon after that, he found some mint and some chamomile. He was so focused on picking the herbs that he almost didn't notice the giant snake until he was on top of it. Jack's sudden barking was his only warning.

He fell backward as the snake reared up and prepared to strike. "Damn it!" he yelled as he summoned the short sword. He hadn't fought with it yet but hoped the extra reach would help him not get bitten.

He swung the sword wildly as the snake lunged forward, slicing a line across the snake's face. The snake withdrew and rose again, swaying in the grass like an Indian snake charmer was playing its song.

BLOOP YOUR SKILL IN SHORT SWORDS IS NOW 2 / 30

Ahh, hell, Jayce thought. *This is gonna suck!*

Taking advantage of the snake's pause, Jayce switched to his bow and tried to use Rapid Fire, but before he got more than a couple of shots off, the snake lunged again. Jack bit the snake toward the end of its tail, and Jayce leaped to the side and switched back to the sword. He came up from his combat roll with his sword ready and swung at the snake's neck as it snapped at Jack. This time, it looked like he did a little more damage. When the snake backed off, he tried Rapid Fire again. One of the shots hit the snake in the eye, and it aborted its lunge, giving him thirty seconds to use the ability. The snake went down, and Jayce finished it off with the sword. "I really need to practice with this," he told Jack. "I can't be fighting a snake with a dagger."

The real test came when he found a bison to take on. With his bows at twenty-six out of thirty, he was anxious to see if he could one-shot it using Stealth Shot.

It turned out he couldn't, and the bison was on him way faster than he expected.

Taking a head butt from the bison, Jayce went flying through the air. The pain was excruciating, and his breath did not want to come. The only saving grace was that he got hit by the area in between all the massive horns. He landed awkwardly on his side and rolled to a stop. By the time he was able to breathe, the bison was almost on top of him again. Jack stood by him, growling like the little dog thought it could take on a bison all by itself. Jayce summoned his sword in a panic; he swung it around like a drunk lunatic in a bar fight.

The only good thing that came from his swings was the bison backed off a bit to avoid the clumsy swipes of the sword. This gave Jayce enough time to get his wits about him.

The bison charged again, and Jayce stepped to the side like a matador and stabbed into the side of the monster.

It charged past him and turned to rush again. Jack was running about its legs, yapping up a storm.

Jayce once again called on Rapid Fire, peppering the huge bison with a dozen arrows before he had to dodge again.

As he got to his feet in time to see the bull turning for another charge, all he could think of was the song "Die" by Dope. He was screaming, "Die, mother fucker, die!" when he let loose with another round of Rapid Fire. This time, the bison diverted its charge, but once again, it turned around and prepared to run Jayce down.

Linkin Park ran through his head. "I need a little room to breathe..."

Jayce drew his bowstring back and waited, staring the bison down. The bison stared back for a moment before charging in. Jayce waited until the animal was only a couple yards away before releasing the arrow, striking the rampaging beast in the perfect spot, piercing its heart. The bison stumbled and fell.

> *BLOOP*
> YOU HAVE LEARNED A NEW SKILL.
> **PERFECT AIM**: THIS SKILL TAKES 5 SECONDS TO PERFORM BUT RESULTS IN +5 ACCURACY.

"Nice!" Jayce whooped.

He walked up and finished the bison off with a stroke from his short sword. He really wished he was more than three and a half feet tall. The extra reach would really come in handy with oversized monsters like this one. Not to mention, the "waist-high" grass was as tall as he was.

Jayce checked the loot and saw:

> PERFECT BISON HIDE (RARE)
> BISON BRAIN

Very nice, he thought. *This ought to make Thorne's day*!

Jayce didn't stop hunting until both his and Jack's bags were full of stacks of leather and herbs. He had three perfect bison hides, 40 bison hides, 60 cat pelts, 160 animal brains, many stacks of herbs, and various animal parts. This was sure to take his crafting up a lot.

As he started his way back toward home, he came across the biggest damn bison he had ever seen. He felt good. His stats were once again maxed out, and he hadn't leveled yet, but this thing was MASSIVE; it was easily twelve feet tall, and its bulging muscles were just plain scary.

Taking a chance, he dismissed Jack, entered Stealth, and crept up slowly. When he was as close as he dared get, he drew his bow and readied Stealth Shot. He waited a minute as the beast shifted to munch a different patch of grass. As soon as its head was back down, munching contentedly, he let loose, and without waiting to see where he hit, he immediately followed with a Perfect Aim and then a volley of Rapid Fire.

His first two were just incredible, and the beast looked like it might go down under the Rapid Fire, but it shrugged off the assault and charged in. Jayce switched to his short sword and waited as the bison tore across the grass. At the last second possible, Jayce stepped aside and thrust at the beast's neck, burying the sword deep into its flesh. Unfortunately, the monster's momentum ripped the sword from Jayce's grip.

Switching to his bow again, Jayce immediately let loose with Rapid Fire while the behemoth turned and charged. He kept firing until the last possible moment when he leaped aside and rolled back to his feet. He immediately turned and let another Rapid Fire loose. He was concentrating so hard on how fast he could draw arrows that he began to draw them two at a time.

BLOOP

YOU HAVE LEARNED A NEW SKILL.

> **Rain of Arrows:** This skill allows you to shoot two arrows at a time at the same rate and duration as Rapid Fire. A corresponding drop in accuracy offsets the number of arrows.

With the bull charging him, accuracy wasn't such an issue, and most shots landed just fine. Just as he was about to dive to the side again, the bison fell and skidded to a stop at his feet. He reached down and slit its throat with his dagger.

"Rest well and dream of large women, Fezzik," he said.

> *Bloop*
> **You have killed a rare creature:** Andre the Giant Bull,
> **AREA BOSS** <ELITE>
> *Ding*
> You have reached level four. You have one stat point to spend.

Without hesitating, Jayce put the point into Toughness. If this was a starter area, he didn't want to see what higher-level beasts would do to him.

Summoning Jack, Jayce then checked the loot:

> Extra-thick Bison Hide x2
> Perfect Bison Horns Extra-large x4

Not sure how one monster had two hides, he thought, *but I'll take it!* "I'm glad Fatty wasn't around to steal that from us," he told Jack as the dog sniffed at the hides.

Jayce dropped a stack of cat bones and a stack of ruined cat pelts to make room for the new items in his inventory. Thorne probably didn't want the ruined pelts anyway, and he had plenty of non-ruined ones.

When Jayce got back to the Outfitter shop, Thorne nearly lost his mind. "Whoa!" he exclaimed. "You don't mess about, do you?"

The leatherworker gave Jack his rawhide chew and led Jayce into the cold cellar, where he opened a barrel and directed Jayce to insert the cat pelts into it before sealing it up again. "Just leave the bison pelts with me," he said. "I will take care of them myself."

Grateful that he didn't have to do any scraping tonight, Jayce called to Jack and headed back to Meg's to get cleaned up.

After washing, Jayce returned to the kitchen and unloaded his herbs on the island. "Got my herbalism up to ninety-nine before the skill-ups stopped coming," he said.

"Very good," Meg replied. "When you start bundling and drying the herbs, it should go up some more, and when you get to higher-level areas, picking them will skill you up again."

Meg showed him how to make a drying rack, how to bundle the herbs so they would dry the best, and how to hang them. When he had built his rack, and all of his herbs were hanging to dry, he had reached one hundred forty-nine out of two-fifty.

"Get some rest now, deary, or work on your Herbal for a while, if you like. I will start teaching you alchemy in the evenings when you come back from work."

Jayce chose to get some work done in his Herbal before he turned in for the night. He first made some notes of his own on the pages of the herbs he had picked, noting the lessons he had learned about the best way to harvest each herb. Next, he turned to his first blank page and began copying Meg's work into his Herbal. Surprisingly, adding his own notes got him a few skill-ups. He was very proud of his progress so far.

As Jayce turned in, he checked his stat screen and was surprised to see a new skill.

STORYTELLER
THE ROGUE NOW HAS THE ABILITY TO WEAVE FANTASTICAL STORIES OFF THE CUFF.
MOST PEOPLE WILL BELIEVE LIES THAT THE ROGUE TELLS.

"Well, that's interesting," he told Jack. "I must have gotten that from my specialization. I don't remember getting a notice, though. I should remember to ask Meg about that."

The next morning, Jayce headed straight to the luthier's shop, not wanting to waste a minute of the day. Jack's boundless energy seemed to spill over and put a pep in his step that usually just wasn't there. Jayce almost started skipping as they walked along. Somehow, this dog and this place brought a joy to his heart that he never remembered having before.

To his surprise, Master Thayer was already up and working, completing some repairs.

"Shouldn't I be doing that?" Jayce asked.

"Nope. Last thing you have to do as an apprentice is make the hide glue and finish that lute," Thayer told him. "Honestly, not many Master Luthiers concern themselves with having apprentices make glue anymore. You can buy it readily enough, but I had to teach you something."

Pleased with the Master's praise, Jayce nodded his head and said, "Thank you, Master. I appreciate your approval. Would it be ok if I head over to the Outfitter for a bit? I was going to prepare and tan some hides with Thorne."

"Aye," the luthier said. "He came by and told me of your enormous haul yesterday. I'm not one to stand in the way of a man working to better himself. Those hides are dry enough, and I need to deliver that lute soon, so I'll need you tomorrow."

"Yes, sir," Jayce said, making his way back out the door.

Entering the Outfitter, Jayce didn't see Thorne, and the smith let him know that the leatherworker was down in the cold storage. Jack was sniffing around for his rawhide chew, so Jayce fetched it from the shelf where Thorne kept it and tossed it to the dog. Jack leaped up and snatched the flying hide from the air like a frisbee; his ears flopped as he landed, making Jayce laugh.

As Jayce walked down the steps to the cellar, he saw that Thorne was busy pulling hides from the barrel they had shoved them into last night. "Mornin', Thorne," Jayce said. "I'm ready to start prepping those hides."

Thorne turned around, and Jayce saw that the man must not have slept that night. He had big bags under his eyes and looked completely knackered. "Good man," Thorne said. "Finish pulling these hides from the barrel and bring them to the yard for scraping."

Jayce reached into the barrel where the hides had been soaking in brine through the night. One armload at a time, he lugged them out to the yard and draped what he could, stacking the rest on a table.

Thorne handed him a scraper almost exactly like the one he had used with Thayer. "I understand you know what to do with this?" Thorne asked.

Nodding, Jayce walked over to one of the pelts he had draped, placed the blade on the hide, checked his angle, and pulled the knife along the hide. He felt good about the amount of hair he had taken off and barely cut into the hide at all toward the end of his stroke.

When he looked at Thorne, though, he saw that the man was not pleased. "We aren't making glue here," he said. "You just made sure that hide will have to be cut down significantly before it can be used."

Thorne took the knife from him and said, "Watch. Pay

close attention to my hands and wrist as I draw the blade along the skin." He then proceeded to clean the entire pelt, front and back. While he was doing that, Jayce watched carefully, seeing what the man did differently than he had.

"Man, I thought Master Thayer was good at that," Jayce said, "but you just did twice the work in half the time that even he could do."

Thorne laughed. "Thayer has been doing this far longer than I have, but I do it far more than he does. Here, try again," he said, handing the hide scraper back to Thorne.

Jack gave up on his chew toy and settled down for a nap at Jayce's feet.

This time, Jayce took his time trying to imitate what Thorne had done exactly. He immediately felt the difference, and the results were much better than before.

"You learn quickly," Thorne said. "I'm going to nap on the bench over there. Wake me when you have cleaned ten hides, and I'll inspect them." Thorne went to a bench on the shady part of the yard and stretched out. Jack got up to join him, and Thorne smiled as the little dog snuggled in.

Jayce got busy scraping hides. It still took a whole lot of focus to make sure he got the strokes right; however, it got easier with each hide he did, and the results steadily got better. It was only about two hours before he woke Thorne to check his work.

Thorne carefully inspected each pelt, pointed out areas where Jayce had made mistakes, and described what would cause that mistake. Jayce paid close attention, and when Thorne had him clean one more, he did a job he felt was as worthy as any Thorne had done. It took him five times as long to do, but the work was excellent.

"Nice work," Thorne told him. "I'll have you do the rest on your own in a bit. First, I'm going to show you how tanning works. I know that you have been shown how to clean a hide after it's been scraped, so I'll skip that, but you will need to do it for all of these hides."

Thorne took Jayce back into the shop and showed him one of the hides he had scraped the night before.

"This is one of the bison hides you brought me," Thorne said. "The rest are packed in salt to preserve them until I have the space to cure them." Thorne laid the big hide out, removed a punch from the tool bench, and proceeded to punch holes every few inches all along the hide. They then went back into the yard, and Thorne directed Jayce on how to stretch the hide on the frame. When he was satisfied that Jayce would be able to accomplish this step on his own, they went back down into cold storage, where Thorne opened another barrel and removed a brain. He handed the brain to Jayce and walked him over to the workbench in the corner. He had Jayce cut off about a third of the brain and put the rest back into the barrel. They then placed the brain into a jar with a small amount of water and mashed it with a pestle.

Back in the yard, with Jack running around sniffing everything, Thorne had Jayce rub the paste into the hide on both sides and then cover the whole rack with a sheet of tarpaulin. "We will need to clean and reapply the tanning solution tomorrow and then again the next day. After that, we will leave the paste on for a week. At that point, we will have leather," Thorne said.

Leaving instructions for Jayce to scrape the rest of the hides and stretch and paste nine of them on the remaining racks in the yard, Thorne turned his weary head toward bed, assuring Jayce he would be back in a few hours.

By the time Thorne returned, Jayce had scraped and cleaned all the hides and punched the nine he was going to hang. "Just in time, Thorne," he said as Jack ran to greet the leathersmith. "I was a bit nervous about making the tanning solution on my own."

The two went down to cold storage, where Jayce prepared enough solution for all nine hides before going back up to the yard, where Jack looked put out at having been left behind.

As Jayce stretched and rubbed each hide with solution, Thorne looked on, making corrections where necessary. Once the yard had ten frames covered in tarpaulin, Thorne looked at Jayce appraisingly. “You sure do learn quickly,” he said. “I’ve never seen someone take so easily to tanning before.”

“Thanks,” Jayce replied.

The next week flew by, with Jayce splitting his time between the luthier’s shop and the Outfitter and then working on his Herbal in the evenings. By the time the week drew to a close, he had raised his herbalism and leatherworking both to 200. He had learned to make neatsfoot oil, repaired his own armor, and made some basic items for Thorne to sell at the Outfitter.

He completed the lute he was working on, and Master Thayer had released him to make his own instrument. Jayce decided to make a six-string guitar. Thayer was skeptical but watched Jayce’s progress with interest.

Back at the Outfitter, the hides were finally able to come off the frames. Thorne showed Jayce how to cut the new leather down to make a nice large piece of leather with no holes. He then had him work neatsfoot oil into each piece of leather to make sure it was strong and supple.

Thorne had Jayce pull ten more salted cat hides from the cellar, clean them, and start curing them. “Next week, I’ll let you work a bison hide,” he said. “It’s also time for you to make something larger. How would you like to make your own armor next? I’ll let you use the extra-thick hides you brought back.”

"That would be great!" Jayce told him. Thinking about the timeline, that meant he had a week for these cat hides to cure and another week for the bison hides, which would include the two extra-thick ones he had from Andre the Giant Bull. So, in two weeks, he would be making his own armor! "I think I need a lot of practice before I make that, though," he said.

"Don't you worry," Thorne told him. "I have a few customers who only want lower quality... Oops, I mean lower-priced sets. I'll have you making those."

"That is awesome," Jayce said. "I can't wait to get started."

That night, when he got home, Meg was waiting for him. "Now that your Herbal is finished," she told him, "it is time for you to begin your alchemy training."

"Aaaawwww, yeah!" he said. "Stoodis!"

Jack headed to the pile of blankets Meg had made for him on the floor and promptly settled down for a nap.

That evening was spent learning how to properly steep leaves for tea and what temperature the water should be for different herbal mixtures to make the proper tea.

Meg had given him his first "grimoire," which is what she called a book for taking alchemy notes. He didn't argue that a grimoire should be for spells. He just went ahead and took all the notes he needed in order to make the teas in the future. By the time he was done for the evening, his alchemy was at forty-nine out of two-fifty.

The next two weeks went by in a flash. Jayce made suits of leather armor and learned to make more teas and a basic healing potion. The night before his bison hides were to come down, Jayce finished his guitar and invited Thorne, Thayer, Meg, and Dru to the Pig and Pony, where Molly had permitted him to perform.

Jayce was nervous. He had performed hundreds of times in front of all kinds of crowds, but this was his first time performing in this world. He spent a long time coming up with a setlist.

As he was getting ready to start, Master Thayer settled at the table closest to the stool Jayce would be using. Thorne, Maddy, and Dru sat with him. Jack wandered over and lay down under Maddy's chair. Jayce wondered why Meg didn't come as Meg, but Dru didn't seem bothered, and Maddy is how the other two knew her, so he guessed she knew what she was doing. They all had mugs of beer in front of them, even Dru. *Must not be a drinking age here,* Jayce thought.

He opened with "The Bear and the Maiden Fair" from HBO's *Game of Thrones.* When he was done, the crowd cheered, and Molly smiled from ear to ear. Her sales would be good tonight!

His next song was "Toss a Coin to Your Witcher" from Netflix's *The Witcher* series. He was sure most people didn't understand the song, but they loved it just the same.

He followed that up with Twisted Sister's "We're Not Gonna Take It," but the slowed-down version that Dee Snider had done for childhood cancer. He received a much more somber response at the end of that, so he moved on to the Beatles' "A Hard Day's Night." Once again, the crowd went wild!

At this point, Jayce took a break, and people were fighting over the chance to buy him a beer. Jack came over, and patrons threw him scraps. The dog was in heaven.

After his break, Jayce did his rendition of Flogging Molly's "Drunken Lullabies," followed by Dropkick Murphys' "Barroom Hero." Just as he was finishing that song, a fight broke out in the back of the room. Without missing a beat, Jayce moved into Elton John's "Saturday Night's Alright (For Fighting)."

By the time he finished for the night, he had a handful of copper coins and an even larger pile of silver coins lying around his stool. Given that his first complete set of commissioned armor had only cost him one silver and fifty copper, that was a lot of money.

As he packed away his guitar, Master Thayer approached him, holding a sleeping Jack. As he handed the dog off, he said, "I would like to speak with you first thing tomorrow." He patted Jack on the back and left the inn.

Chapter Seven

Even though he'd had a late night, Jayce woke up even earlier than usual. He sat on the edge of the bed for a few minutes, thinking about his performance the night before. Playing in the common room of an inn was such a different experience from a stage in a club or bar. He reveled in the memories of the night. *Maybe I can start booking more inns,* he thought. The whole concept of the inns here was so different from anything he had ever known. It was sort of like an Irish pub with guest rooms upstairs. The performing area was just a spot cleared of tables near the fireplace.

Shaking his head and rubbing his eyes, he got up and dressed. Jack just looked up and went back to sleep. As he quietly closed his bedroom door, trying not to disturb Meg or Dru, he looked around the kitchen and saw that Maddy was standing there waiting for him.

"Morning, Meg," he said. "Going out as Maddy today?"

"I am coming with you to Master Thayer's shop. We have some business to attend to," she said enigmatically.

After a quick breakfast, he called for Jack, and they set off. He realized this was the first time he had actually done anything with Meg-as-Maddy. It was strange walking with his friend, who looked like a sweet middle-aged lady rather than Meg, the swamp witch.

When they got to the luthier's, they found Thayer waiting at the door. He smiled as he saw them approach. "Come in."

As he walked in the door, Jayce saw that the shop had been rearranged. Everything had been pushed to the walls to make room for a large table. Two men were seated at the table. One was an elderly-looking gentleman with close-cropped grey hair and a grey goatee. He was wearing some sort of formal black robes with purple bars on the sleeves and a black cap with a bright feather sticking out of it. He looked like a professor at a PhD graduation. The other was a younger man who had a large ledger in front of him and a black inkpot and quill. The younger man was wearing a brown robe, more like a monk's robe, complete with a corded belt and tassels hanging down. His head and face were clean-shaven.

"Have a seat," Thayer told him, motioning to the single chair on the opposite side of the table from the professor-looking guy. The monk guy was seated at one short edge of the long table, and Thayer and Maddy took seats on either side of the professor. The lute Jayce had made was sitting in the center of the table.

Having no idea what was going on, Jayce silently took his seat. Jack went under the table and lay back down, looking grateful for the chance to go back to sleep.

"Normally, at this stage," Thayer began, "I would release you to be a journeyman. But the lute you made was more than good enough to be your masterwork."

Maddy then pulled out his guitar and set it in the center of the table. *When did she grab that?* he thought.

"This 'guitar,' as you call it," Thayer continued, "is nothing short of spectacular. It is the work of an advanced Master."

The professor then spoke up. "I am Arrum, Grand Master of the local Crafter's Guild. I am here to witness your promotion to Master Luthier," he said, "among other things."

The monk-looking guy dipped his quill into the ink pot, tapped the edge, and said, "Please spell your full name."

Jayce looked around, stunned. After a pause, he said, "Uhh, it's Jayce, ermm, Jason Howard, spelled J-A-S-O-N H-O-W-A-R-D."

"Thank you," the man said, writing in the book. "Please sign here." He passed the book to Jayce. Neatly written on the bottom line of the ledger, it said: "Jason Howard, Master Luthier." He signed next to it, and the monk guy gave the book to Thayer, who wrote, "Tested by Thayer of Fleet, Master Luthier," and signed his name before passing the book to Arrum, who wrote, "Witnessed and accepted by Arrum Runestar, Guild Master of Fleet." Arrum signed his name and passed the ledger back to the other man. The monk-looking guy, who had yet to give his name, sprinkled some sand on the ink, gently blew it dry, and closed the ledger.

"That being done," Thayer said, "I have some business to discuss."

The monk guy (Jayce really wished someone would introduce him) took out a scroll on fine vellum and handed it to Jayce. Jayce unrolled the scroll and read:

> *Thayer, Master Luthier of Fleet, offers the following business terms for partnership with Jayce, Master Luthier of Fleet.*
>
> *Jayce will work out of Thayer's Luthiery. The crafter shall bear the cost of materials. Profits shall be split 75/25 in favor of the Master who produced the work sold or repairs made.*
>
> *Further, Jayce agrees to teach Thayer how to make a guitar and grants him the right to produce the instrument for sale to the public. In exchange, Thayer shall not charge rent or other fees for Jayce to work in his shop.*

Jayce was flabbergasted. "This is insane!" he said.

Thayer frowned. "Perhaps I could offer you some further compensation for the rights to produce the guitar," he said.

"No!" Jayce answered quickly. "That is not what I mean

at all. Of course, you can make and sell guitars, given how closely you watched me work. I highly doubt I have to teach much, if anything, for you to make the instrument."

Arrum and Thayer looked at each other in surprise, and Maddy just grinned. "As for a partnership," Jayce continued, "I appreciate the offer to work out of your shop and will take you up on that, but what's yours is yours alone. What I make, we will split the profits 50/50 in exchange for you allowing me to use your workshop. Further, I am not sure how much I will be around. I intend to do some more leveling, erm, I mean, do some more hunting and such. I also intend to start playing more inns. I had a lot of fun last night."

Arrum looked at Thayer and spoke. "Are these terms agreeable to you?" he asked.

"More than generous," Thayer replied. "Yes, I accept."

The monk, who Jayce figured was actually a scribe, wrote out the terms and presented them to both Master Luthiers for them to sign. After the document was signed, witnessed, and sealed, the scribe tucked it away in his satchel.

Maddy spoke next as the scribe and Master Thayer rose from the table and left the room.

"I have arranged with Grand Master Arrum to test you for something," she said.

The Grand Master pulled a scrolled sheet of velum seemingly out of nowhere and walked around the table to stand next to Jayce. He unrolled the scroll and placed weights on the top and bottom to hold it open.

Jayce looked at the scroll in confusion. It was covered in evenly spaced runes. They looked sort of like ancient Norse runes, but there were too many of them. He gave Arrum a questioning look.

"Look at these runes," he said. "Study them. Contemplate each one. Take your time; there is no rush."

Jayce began to look over the runes one at a time, studying the shape of each one and trying to sus out any meaning he could. Next, he looked for a pattern in the way the runes were made or laid out. Finally, he went back to looking at each rune individually again, focusing on them, wondering what it was he was supposed to see.

After a long time, and just as he was about to ask the Grand Master what he was supposed to be looking for, one of the runes stood out to him. It seemed to look bolder or brighter—subtly—but he couldn't put his finger on why, yet it caught his attention. Staring at it for a while, Jayce finally spoke. "This one here," he said, pointing.

"What about it?" Arrum replied.

"I am not sure," Jayce replied. "It suddenly just caught my eye. It seems bolder or brighter, or perhaps the others seem faded?"

"That is the rune of heat," the Grand Master told him, taking the scroll away and pulling out a small stone. "I will draw it on this rock," he said, producing a calligraphy brush and some ink. The Grand Master carefully wrote the rune on the rock and placed it before Jayce.

"Place your hand upon the rune," he said. "Bring its shape to your mind. Think of every detail of the rune, every line, every curve, and think about giving the rune heat."

Jayce did as told, placing his hand on the stone. He tried to recall exactly what the rune looked like. He concentrated on trying to form a picture, and when a vision of the rune formed in his mind, he thought about heating the rune. In his mind, it began to turn yellow and glow like it was on fire. Once this image was firmly set, he pushed it down into his chest, through his arm, out of his hand, and into the rock.

"Whoa," he said, pulling his hand away. The rock had become hot to the touch.

BLOOP
YOU HAVE LEARNED A NEW SKILL.
RUNE CRAFTER: 1 / 250

Grand Master Arrum reached out to pick up the stone but found it warm enough that he could not hold it comfortably in his hand. He dropped the stone on the floor in surprise before pulling his sleeve over his hand, picking it up again, and placing it in the fireplace.

"I told you!" Maddy said excitedly. "I knew he could do it!"

The Grand Master made his way back to his seat and just stared at Jayce.

After a very long, uncomfortable silence, Jayce spoke up. "What?" Jayce said. "I just did as you asked."

Arrum cleared his throat. "What you have just done is almost unheard of," he said. "By having a rune stand out to you, you showed you have an affinity for rune crafting. This is rare enough. Besides myself, there is only one other in Fleet with such an affinity. By imbuing the rune with heat, you surpassed the other rune crafter in Fleet. By making it as hot as you did, you surpassed even me in potential."

"Wait, what?" Jayce asked. "You mean you can't make a rock that hot?"

"Oh, I can," Arrum responded. "That hot and more. But I have been a rune crafter since I was younger than you. When I was tested, the rune of cold spoke to me, and I was just barely able to make it perceptibly cooler than it was."

"Oh," was all Jayce could manage to say.

Arrum continued. "Having the ability to make proper runes makes one a rune crafter, but most rune crafters cannot imbue their own runes. They work for a rune master who imbues them after they have been crafted." He looked Jayce in the eye and spoke slowly. "I know of only five other living rune masters in the entire world," he said, "and none with the potential that you showed today."

Arrum gave Maddy the scroll he had shown Jayce, pulled out another, and handed that to her as well. "Master Apothecary Maddy shall retain control of these scrolls," he said before handing Jayce a thick book like the one his Herbal and grimoire were in. "This shall be your Book of Runes," he told Jayce. "Guard it carefully. Maddy will let you study the Scroll of Basic Runes. When one speaks to you, Maddy will look it up on the labeled scroll and tell you what it means. When you successfully imbue an item with that rune, copy it into your Book of Runes. When you have finished all of the basic runes, we shall discuss further runes for you to study. Perhaps you will even discover new runes one day."

"That's a thing?" Jayce asked.

"Yes. Every generation or two, someone discovers a new rune," Arrum said. "There are so few of us that we usually share it right away so the rune is not lost. But there have been those who horde their discoveries."

"Thank you," Jayce said. "This is amazing."

"Thank Maddy," Arrum said. "She is the one who believed you had the potential."

"How did you know?" Jayce asked.

"The way you pick up crafting skills so quickly, the way you lean toward many different artistic disciplines, your potential for bardic magic, and just a feeling I had," she told him. "I actually contacted the Grand Master about you weeks ago but used last night's performance as a way for him to evaluate you."

Jayce turned to Arrum. "I am sorry, sir. There were so many people last night, and I do not recall seeing you.

What about last night made you believe I might have this gift?"

"After all that Maddy told me about you, I suspected she may be right. After watching the way you responded to the crowd, I felt confident in at least giving you a try. It was the way you knew the crowd's feelings and always played the right song to bring the crowd with you on your journey," he said. "Meg told me you completely deviated from your setlist after the first three songs. You were able to read the crowd and affect their mood. To bring them up and back down. You took us all on quite the journey last night, young man, and played not a single song any of us were familiar with. Amazing."

"Thank you, sir," Jayce said, blushing with the praise.

"Come," Maddy said, "we have much work to do." With that, she rose and walked out the door. Jayce called to Jack and followed, still in a state of shock over the whole deal. This had been the most exciting twenty-four hours of his entire life. He hadn't thought anything would top his getting his Master's degree, but all of this was just so much extra.

Jayce and Meg spent the rest of the day oscillating between rune crafting and alchemy.

Jayce stared at the Scroll of Runes for a very long time before his second rune came to him. When one finally stood out, he called Meg over and pointed. The swamp witch looked at the reference scroll and declared it a rune of strength. Jayce immediately inked it onto a sheet of paper and covered it with his hand. He imagined the rune becoming strong. In his mind, the rune grew bolder, thicker, and almost 3D. After a while, the rune took on a rock-like texture. He then pushed that image through his arm, to his hand, and out onto the rune.

When he felt the strength leave him, he looked down at the paper. It looked no different. He ran his hand along the paper. It felt no different. He picked up the paper. It didn't weigh any different. Finally, he attempted to tear the paper. His eyes bulged, his muscles strained, and veins stood out on his arms and face. Try as he might, he could not tear the paper. "Damn," he said, "I need to try that on armor!"

Meg nodded approval and motioned him to join her on her side of the island. "It is time," she said, "for you to learn to make a potion," she told him. "Pull down some peppermint, turmeric, ginger, garlic, holy basil, and ashwagandha."

Jayce pulled down the dried herbs as she instructed. He placed them carefully on the counter. Next, she lit a small fire and placed a cauldron over it. The cauldron looked like something from a witch's Halloween costume and probably held about a quart, he guessed.

Meg directed him to fill the cauldron with water and start it heating up. As the water was heating, she instructed him on how to prepare the herbs properly. Some of them just needed the dried leaves left whole, like cooking with a bay leaf. Others needed to be ground into a powder. One was left in a bunch, reminding him of a fancy cook putting whole sprigs of herbs into a dish.

Once everything was prepared and the water was simmering but not at a boil, she had him stir it counterclockwise and slowly add one ingredient at a time. "While you stir," she said, "think of health and put all of your mind into feeling good and healthy. Imagine what your body feels like at its peak condition and put that into the liquid."

Jayce did as told. He thought about how it felt when he was done jogging or working out, that feeling after you caught your breath but before soreness set in. He thought about the best he had ever felt and pictured himself hearty and hale, strong and full of life. He thought about Kickapoo Joy Juice and *Li'l Abner.* He concentrated on all of this going into the mixture. He stirred and stirred until the mixture had evaporated down to about a third of what it started at.

"Take it off the fire and pour it through this strainer," Meg told him, holding a ring of metal containing some cheesecloth over a small bottle.

He poured until the bottle was full. Meg placed another bottle under the cheesecloth. They made four bottles before the cauldron was empty. Meg gently rested a cork stopper on the top of each bottle. "As the liquid cools, it will thicken up, and the stoppers will set more firmly into the bottles as the air between the liquid and the stopper cools," she told him. "You have just made your first healing potion. If you're going to go adventuring, these will come in handy."

After making the healing potion, Jayce went back to studying the runes. By the end of the day, he had learned heat, strength, cold, sharpness, and defense. He got skill-ups from getting the rune to speak to him, successfully creating the rune, and imbuing the rune, so he ended the day with rune crafting at thirteen out of two-fifty. Those gains didn't feel like much, but he was thrilled with the knowledge he had acquired.

His alchemy had been successful as well. He learned, made, and wrote down the formulas for healing and curing poison and a potion that made you run faster for half an hour at a time.

Chapter Eight

The following morning, Jayce headed to the Outfitter with Jack once again bouncing around him all "T-I-double-Guh–ERRR" style.

"Good morning, Master Luthier!" Thorne greeted him.

"Good morning, Master Leathersmith!" Jayce replied happily. "I see you heard the good news."

"Oh, yes," Thorne told him. "Thayer could not contain himself. And he was over the moon with the terms you gave him for your business."

"Meh," Jayce said. "It was no more than he deserved. He has been very good to me. Now it's time for me to be the apprentice again," he said, walking up to the workbench. "Before I start on my armor, I want you to show me how to tool designs into leather."

"Going for a fancy look, are ya?" Thorne asked.

"Not exactly," Jayce said. "You will see... if I'm successful."

"Oooh! Sounds mysterious," Thorne teased. "Grab a couple pieces of scrap leather and come on over here," he told Jayce as he tossed Jack his chewy.

Already familiar with the scribes and bevels from making cutting marks on leather, he soon learned to use the swivel knife, awls, burnishers, and modeling spoons needed to make basic designs. After a few botched learning attempts, he tooled a rose into one piece and a Celtic Tree of Life into another.

"I'll never stop being amazed at the speed at which you pick things up," Thorne said. "You already work at the level of someone who has been working leather for years. In fact, I want the armor you make to be your journeypiece."

"Wow, really?" Jayce asked. "I didn't think I was that good!"

"You're already better than I was before I set off on my journey," Thorne laughed.

Jayce went to the yard and cut down his two extra-thick hides, along with a few of the regular bison hides and a Maska cat hide.

Back in the shop, he had Thorne remeasure to make sure he got the right fit and set to work making his armor. He very carefully measured, drew, and scribed each piece before cutting. He punched extra-fine holes for sewing. Before assembling it, he very carefully scribed and tooled the runes for strength and defense on the inside of each piece of leather to be used.

"What are those for?" Thorne asked. "And why put them inside where no one can see them?"

"They are runes I have learned," Jayce said. "Grand Master Arrum has been teaching me."

"And you can afford to have him imbue them?" Thorne gasped. "I'm not sure I'll ever have enough money for his services."

"Nope," Jayce smiled. "I'll do it myself."

"You can do that?" Thorne asked skeptically.

"Sure can," Jayce told him. "Haven't tried it on leather yet, but this one here is the rune for strength. It should make the leather harder to damage, and this one is the rune for defense. It should make me harder to hit, or I'll take less damage when I'm hit, but I'm not sure."

"Wow," said Thorne. "That's amazing! I heard the power to imbue runes is the rarest skill in the world."

"That's what Arrum said," Jayce responded. "I'll do some for you if I can get it to work on mine."

"How much do you want for them?" Thorne asked. "I do fairly well, but not buying-runes well."

"Nothing," Jayce assured him. "It's payment for your instruction and a gift for a friend."

"I would be an absolute fool to say no to that," Thorne said.

When Jayce's armor was completely assembled, he placed his hand over a glove and pulled the images of the runes to his mind. He imagined the strength of stone, mountains, and steel. The rune of strength in his mind became bolder and more powerful-looking than he had been able to make it yet. With that image in his mind, he also thought of hummingbirds and master fencers. He thought of a karate master who could block a punch. He thought of anything that was hard to hit or that could defend itself especially well. The rune of defense gained an ethereal, almost ghost-like quality. It looked like if you tried to hit it, you would never connect. Fixing both images firmly in his mind, he pushed them down to his chest, through his arm, and out his palm into the glove. He felt the power leave him, and he slumped down onto a stool.

"Damn," he said, "that was exhausting. It's never drained me like that before." Jack jumped up into his lap and licked his face. Jayce smiled as he petted the dog.

"Did it work?" Thorne asked.

"Sure felt like it did," he said. "Let me finish all of the pieces, and we will test it out."

One piece at a time, with lengthy breaks in between, Jayce imbued the runes on his armor.

Finished, he inspected his new set.

> *BLOOP*
> YOU HAVE CREATED RUNED THICK LEATHER ARMOR.
> **QUALITY:** HIGH
> **DURABILITY:** 1000 / 1000
> **SET BONUS FOR 6 PIECES (GLOVES, BRACERS, JERKIN, EPAULETS, BREECHES, BOOTS):** + 30 DEFENSE.
> MUST BE WORN AS A SET FOR THE BONUS.

"Holy crap, did it work!" Jayce said. "This armor is awesome!"

Thorne inspected the armor next. First, he checked the craftmanship carefully, examining each seam and the finish on each piece. Next, he got out a scribe and scratched at the leather. He got out a dagger and poked at it. "That's some quality craftsmanship, and the strength of the leather is something I've never seen. This stuff should last forever," he said. "Last test: try it on."

Jayce donned the armor, and Thorne checked the fit. "Damn near perfect," he said.

"This is the best journeypiece I have ever seen," Thorne raved. "Get some experience from a few more masters, and you will be making your masterpiece in no time."

Thorne dragged Jayce to the Crafter's Guild Hall.

"Master Thorne," the clerk said, "what can we do for you today?"

"I'm here to register a new journeyman," Thorne told the man.

"And who will we be registering today?" the clerk asked, taking out a quill.

"Master Luthier Jayce Howard will be registered as a journeyman leathersmith," Thorne said proudly.

"Truly?" gaped the clerk.

"Truly," replied Thorne.

The clerk wrote the information down and told the pair to take a seat.

After several minutes ticked by, the clerk came back. "Grand Master Arrum would like to see you," he said.

Thorne looked surprised. "Just to register a journeyman?" he asked. "I've only ever met the Guild Master once, and that was the day I presented my masterpiece."

The clerk smirked. "It's not every day a newly minted Master becomes a journeyman in another trade," he said. "Besides, the Grand Master has other interests in Master Jayce."

The clerk looked skeptically at the bouncing Jack as he led them down a passageway, up a set of stairs, and to a door at the end of a hall. Knocking twice, the clerk entered without waiting for a reply.

"Thank you, Justin, you may go," Grand Master Arrum said.

The same scribe from yesterday was sitting at a small desk beside Arrum's larger one. He opened his ledger and wrote.

"Well, Master Jayce," the old man said, "it seems you are not content with being a Master Luthier and apprentice rune crafter. You are now a journeyman leathersmith? Let me see your journeypiece."

Jayce walked up to the aging Guild Master. "I'm wearing it," he said, twirling to show off his armor.

The Guild Master looked at the armor carefully and raised his eyes in surprise. "You runed it," he said.

"Yes, sir," Jayce told him. "Yesterday, after our meeting, I learned four new runes and three new potions."

"You what?" Arrum yelled.

"I learned four runes and three potions," Jayce repeated.

Arrum buried his head into his hands. "What *are* you?" he asked.

"Umm, a halfling?" Jayce said.

"I know you're a halfling," huffed Arrum. "It's almost unheard of for a person your age to be a master of any craft, let alone a journeyman in another and apprentice in two more."

"Three more. I'm also an apprentice herbalist," Jayce corrected.

"In all my life, I've never seen a person learn five runes

in a single day. How did you find the time to imbue eighteen runes in one day?"

"Well," said Jayce, "the first piece was the hardest, but once I got the hang of envisioning both runes at once, the next piece was easier, and each one after that was a little easier yet. I did the boots last and barely had to take a break between each boot."

All the blood drained from Arrum's face.

"Are you ok, sir?" Jayce asked. "You don't look so good."

"You imbued two runes at once?" Arrum marveled. Then, looking even more shocked, "And you did it eighteen times in one day?"

"Yes, sir," Jayce said. "Is that not normal?"

"Young man," Arrum said, "I have never imbued more than two runes at once in my life, and that drained me enough that I could not imbue again until the next day. For you to do so the day after being apprenticed, and then repeatedly, and still be able to talk to me right now... I would have said that was impossible were the proof not before me."

Arrum looked at the scribe. "Is his entry ready?"

"Yes, sir," the scribe replied, passing the book to the Grand Master.

Arrum turned it around for Jayce and Thorne to sign. "Prepare a journey letter along with his master letter," he told the clerk.

"How soon will you be leaving us?" Arrum asked.

"Uhh, leaving? Umm, well, I don't know, sir," Jayce stammered. "I still have a lot to learn from you and Meg. I still need to help Master Thayer with his first guitar, and I have a few instruments I want to make for myself."

Arrum nodded. "Well, when you are ready," he said, "your letters will be waiting."

"Thank you, sir," Jayce said, seeing the dismissal for what it was.

Thorne whistled as they left the Guild Hall, causing

Jack to bark excitedly. "You are just full of surprises," he said. "One day, I'll be bragging to my grandkids that I knew you."

"Aww, come on," Jayce said. "I put my pants on one leg at a time just like you do." Then after a little while of silence, he said, "Except when I put on *my* pants, I'm Jayce Howard, Master Luthier, journeyman leathersmith, apprentice rune crafter, alchemist, and herbalist. Not to mention, the greatest musician ever born."

Thorne looked at him in shock, but seeing Jayce struggling to keep a straight face, he burst out in laughter, and Jayce joined him.

For the remainder of the week, Jayce split his time between working with Thayer on guitars, runing items for Thorne, and working on his alchemy and rune crafting.

By the time Saturday night rolled back around, he had mastered the three potions Meg had taught him, making them far more powerful than his first attempts. He had learned all twenty of the basic runes: heat, cold, strength, sharpness, defense, anchor, join, push, pull, flexibility, rigidity, mend, break, sunder, split, resilience, expand, contract, float, and hover. He had also helped Thayer make two guitars and made his own twelve-string classical guitar. Everyone just kept marveling at his accomplishments. He felt like he wasn't even really working that hard; he had always learned quickly, and all his professors had always complimented him on his work ethic, but that was just the way he was. He had no idea how to be any different.

Saturday night, though, was what he had been looking forward to the most—his gig at the Pig and Pony.

When Jayce and Jack walked in to set up, he was shocked. The common room was so crowded that he could barely force his way to his spot in front of the fireplace (which, thankfully, was not lit; the body heat was already stifling). Molly had all her staff working, and they were struggling to elbow their way through the crowd. Jack was loving it; he danced among the crowd, getting scraps for his antics.

Molly finally ordered everyone in the place to grab the tables and chairs and bring them to the street. Food was taken off the menu for the night; it was drinks and standing room only.

Jayce opened with the "Bear and the Maiden Fair" again. To his surprise, people joined him in singing the chorus. He had just introduced this song last week and only played it once. *Well, George RR Martin wrote a hit, I guess!* he thought.

He came prepared this time. He busted out some of the songs from *Carmina Burana* in punk rock style. This was what Knerds of the Round Table were known for. The crowd ate it up! By the time he switched to Zepplin, the crowd was so drunk he wasn't sure they could tell the difference, but his acoustic punk version of "Immigrant Song" almost caused a riot.

Not only were people tossing silver coins at his feet, but proprietors from several inns in Fleet proper were begging him to play at their establishments. He made no commitments but was pleased with the offers.

At one point, he saw a group of people mobbing Thayer and placing orders for guitars. Business was going to be good for a while.

When Molly finally pushed the last remaining drunkard out the door, Jayce called her over and pointed at the piles of coins at his feet.

"Help me pick this up, and half is yours," he said.

"I couldn't take your earnings," she said, looking at the money longingly. "I completely sold out of ale tonight, and I was watering it down from the beginning. Luckily, the last few tankards I sold went to people so drunk they didn't notice I had sold them water."

Jayce laughed at that. "I'm glad for you," he told her. "But I have more than I need right now, and I should pay you for giving me a place to play. Where I come from, people pay to come into the venue, and the band gets a percentage of the door fee."

"Now that is a great idea," she said. "Mind if I use that?"

"Not at all!" he laughed. "But you have to tell them not to throw coins at me, then. It would be like paying twice."

"I'll tell them," she said, "but I can't make 'em listen."

"Hey, as long as they have been told, I'm fine with that," he laughed.

Chapter Nine

Sunday morning, Jayce slept in, rolling out of bed around the crack of noon. Jack licked his face as he blearily rubbed his eyes and stretched. "Damn, I needed that rest," he said before washing up and dressing. He donned his armor, thinking it had been way too long since he did some leveling.

As he made his way to the kitchen, Meg set out a plate of fruit, bread, and cheese. "Eat something before you head out," she said, waiting for him to sit down and reach for the plate before she continued. "Going to try and do some leveling today?" she asked as she put out a bowl of scraps for Jack.

"Yeah, I've been loving the crafting, and it's been fun working with everyone, but I really wanna try and hit level five so I can get my final profession," he said.

"Where do you plan on going?" she asked. "This whole area is pretty low-level. Hitting five should be no problem, but it will be a real grind fest if you want to hit six here."

"I was thinking of heading back to Lower Fleet Hills," he said, "unless you know of a better place."

"Best idea would be to check the board in the Mercenaries Guild," she told him. "Don't need to be a member to pick up jobs posted there; they reserve the best jobs for members but put some out for anyone who wants to earn the reward."

"Dang," Jayce replied. "I didn't even know there was a Mercenaries Guild or that they had jobs I could take."

"Sure enough," she said. "Just pull a job off the board

and tell them you want to take it on. When they approve you taking the job, you will get a quest for it. Try looking for multiple quests in the same area to maximize the use of your time. Sometimes, you find quests along the way as well."

"Thanks, Meg," he said. "I don't know where I would be without you."

She laughed and said, "Likely still wearing rags and stealing your meals."

They both laughed, and Jayce finished off the food on his plate before adding some healing and run-speed potions to his inventory.

He was halfway out the door with Jack before Meg called to him. "Take a couple of these just in case," she said, tossing him two cure-poison potions one at a time. Jayce caught them and added them to his inventory.

"Good idea," he said before walking out the door.

Checking his map, Jayce saw that the Mercenaries Hall was just down the street from the Crafters Hall. He made his way there in short order and looked around as he walked in the door. He entered a large room with a reception area in the back. The room was decorated with weapons hung on the walls in between mounted heads of various monsters. It was like an extra creepy version of a hunting lodge.

On the wall next to the reception area was what appeared to be a large corkboard with a bunch of papers pinned to it haphazardly. He walked up and began to read the notices as Jack sat on his feet. He saw several jobs for a place called Upper Fleet Hills. *I guess there really is an Upper Fleet Hills,* he thought, as he pulled the jobs down and went to the reception area.

As the receptionist looked up, he handed the papers to him and said, "I would like to do these jobs, please."

Looking them over, the receptionist frowned. "Ain't

you that minstrel what plays out at the Pig and Pony?" he asked.

"That's me," Jayce replied.

"What experience you got fightin'?" he asked.

"Well, I killed some giant termites at the sawmill. I got the reward for the bandits out there, too. I've also been killing beasts out in Lower Fleet Hills for a while now. Even took that bison people call Andre down," Jayce told the man.

"Is that right?" the receptionist asked. "I'd heard someone finally took down that monster. I suppose you might be good enough to do these jobs then. Upper Hills is full of some pretty badass stuff, though. You sure you want to go there?"

"Sure am," Jayce said confidently.

"Ok then," the receptionist said, taking some notes. "Name?" he asked.

"Jayce Howard," Jayce told him.

The receptionist wrote that down, too, stamped the handbills, and handed them back to Jayce. "Here ya go," he said. "Happy hunting."

> *Bloop*
> You have accepted three new quests.
> Mongo the Half-Giant: A half-giant named Mongo has been terrorizing North Fleet Hills. Bring his head as proof of his demise.
> Reward: Renown with Fleet, 5 silver coins.
> It's a Dead Man's Party: A party of mercenaries were killed taking on jobs in North Fleet Hills, and they were raised from the dead by the Necromancer Danny Elfman. Put the party to rest. Each party member had a medallion that read Oingo Boingo (the name of their group). Bring the medallions back as proof of accomplishment.

Reward: Renown with Fleet, 5 silver coins. Chance to join Mercenaries Guild.

Ending the Threat: The Necromancer Danny Elfman has been killing every party sent against him. He recently raised Oingo Boingo from death, renaming them Boingo and enslaving them to his will. Rid the world of this menace.

Reward: Renown with fleet, 15 silver coins.

Jayce chuckled. *The eighties are still alive and kickin' in this world,* he thought, *but at least it's good eighties.*

Checking his map for the familiar green arrow now pointing to the northeast, Jayce started to head out. Just as he was nearing the gate, he thought about it and turned back to look for the Outfitter shop.

Greeting Thorne as he entered, Jayce asked, "Hey, Thorne. Who do I see about a new sword and dagger, maybe even a bow?"

"Bladesmith is right over there," Thorne said, pointing at the far side of the shop with his chin.

Jayce blushed. "All the times I've been in here," he said, "you would think I'd have looked around."

"No worries," Thorne said before getting back to work on a repair he was doing.

Jayce walked over to the bladesmith. "Hello," he said, pulling out his iron dagger and rusty short sword. "I'd like to get upgraded versions of these, please."

"Don't normally deal with non-humans," the bladesmith said, "but I seen ya working with Thorne, so I suppose you're alright."

Jack growled, and Jayce almost walked out the door after the man's blatant racism, but he really wanted the best he could get before tackling higher-level mobs.

The bladesmith (Jayce made a point of not asking his name) examined Jayce's weapons. "Your dagger ain't bad," he said, as he placed a shiny dagger with what looked like a bone hilt and an S-shaped cross guard on the counter. "This one will be better, though. As for your short sword, anything I have will be better than that."

Jayce picked up the dagger and examined it.

> **BONE-HANDLED DIRK:** STEEL DIRK OF EXCELLENT CRAFTSMANSHIP.
> +5 DAMAGE
> **DURABILITY:** 50 / 50

Jayce set the dirk back on the counter and asked, "What do you have in short swords of this quality or better?"

The bladesmith laid several swords on the counter for Jayce to choose from. His eyes were immediately drawn to a wicked-looking single-edged sword. The hilt was grey, and the blade was black. The back side of the blade was curved closer to the hilt but pitched forward toward the point. The cutting edge was concave near the hilt but widened considerably, starting about a third of the way down the blade, and then became convex to the point. He picked it up and inspected it.

> **NIMBLE FALCATA OF THE ASSASSIN:** ANCIENT FALCATA OF UNKNOWN ORIGIN. MASTER QUALITY CRAFTSMANSHIP.
> +5 DEXTERITY
> +5 STRENGTH
> DOUBLE WEAPON DAMAGE WHEN ATTACKING FROM STEALTH.

"How much is this one?" he asked.

"Should be way out of your price range," the bladesmith said, "but I found it in the basement when we bought this place, and I was the first person to take an interest in it. Very few people around here want a single-edged weapon, and those what do want a cutlass or a falchion. I'll let ya have it for fifty silver. If you leave your weapons in trade, I'll give you the pair for seventy silver."

Damn, Jayce thought, *even with all the money I've been pulling in, that is A LOT.* "I'll give you sixty silver and leave my weapons," Jayce countered, having no real idea of actual value.

"Nope," the bladesmith replied. "Best I could do is sixty-eight. Your short sword is junk. I'm being generous here."

"Sixty-five," Jayce countered back, "and you get an unsellable sword out of your inventory."

The bladesmith winced, knowing he had made a mistake letting that slip. "Fine," he said, "but you're robbing me blind."

After paying the man, Jayce looked around and didn't see any bows, so he went back to Thorne. "Man, your business partner is a real dick," he said.

"Why do you think I never told him that the sword you just bought is easily worth a gold or more?" Thorne replied. "Not many people, even bladesmiths, recognize an enchanted blade when they see one."

"You knew?" Jayce asked, impressed.

"Yeah," he said, "I've always been able to feel enchantments on things. Not rune work, though. I can't clock those as enchanted. But after testing some of the stuff you did for me, I know for certain it works."

"Where can I get a new bow?" Jayce asked.

"Just down the row a bit," Thorne said. "But why don't you save some money and carve a rune or two into yours?"

"I can't believe I didn't think of that," Jayce said.

Jayce's next stop was the luthier's. Thayer was busy making a guitar when he walked in. "You wouldn't believe the demand for these!" he said. "I have people giving a gold extra just to get them on the list!"

"Sweet!" Jayce said. "I just came in to use some carving tools."

"Help yourself, you know that," Thayer said.

Jayce walked over to the tool chest and selected an extra-fine blade. He mapped out the runes for strength, rigidity, and resilience before very carefully carving the runes into his bow. Realizing the day was getting late, Jayce decided to imbue the runes back at Meg's and get an early start in the morning.

When he got home, Dru was there talking up a storm as usual. "Hey, Jayce!" the boy said as he dropped to the ground for a wrestle with Jack. "Back from adventuring already?"

"No," Jayce responded. "I spent longer than expected picking up jobs and shopping. I'm going to head out in the morning." Jayce pulled out his new sword and dagger, letting Dru take a look at them.

"Wooo weee!" Dru said. "You must be rollin' in it to afford things like this!"

Thinking about it, Jayce pulled out five silver coins and handed them to Dru. "I never paid you for all you did for me when I first got here," he told the boy. "It's about time I did so."

Meg snatched four of the five silvers from the boy's hands and pocketed them. "You'll be getting these when you're older," she told the boy, who had suddenly gone from ecstatic to despondent at the rapid gain and loss of such wealth.

After a moment, the boy's smile came back. "A silver is still more'n I've ever had at once," he said.

Jayce pulled out his bow and set it on the counter, showing Meg the runes he had added. She looked and nodded approval.

Jayce placed his hand on the runes and imagined the

bow becoming stiffer and more rigid. He made sure not to imagine it too strong; he still needed to pull it back, after all. He pushed the image down into his chest, through his arm, and out his palm. As soon as he felt the power leave, he began envisioning images of strength and resilience. He spent a long time on these, making the best images he had ever made. When he felt he had done the very best he could, he imbued the runes.

Jayce had to hold onto the kitchen island to keep from falling. He immediately pulled up a stool and sat down, sweat dripping from his brow. Jack whined at his feet in concern. He took several minutes to recover and still felt exhausted when he looked up.

Meg slid a cup of tea over to him. "Try this restorative," she said. Jayce sipped on the tea for a while, not even noticing that Dru had gone silent and was staring at him in awe.

Half an hour or so later, Jayce was beginning to feel himself again. He picked up the bow and strung it. He could feel the new draw strength as he strung the bow. Suddenly, he was very glad he hadn't put more into it. When it was strung, he inspected the bow, seeing durability at 1000 / 1000. He pulled the string back to his cheek, and his arm shook with strain when he tried to hold it. Yup, this bow would last him a very long time. Accepting a second cup of tea, Jayce went off to bed, hearing Dru whisper as he walked away.

"I didn't know he was magic," the boy said.

Chapter Ten

Jayce had been traveling for about an hour when his map finally told him he was in Upper Fleet Hills. The land had steadily been getting higher, and ahead of him, he saw some very large hills or perhaps small mountains. The road up here looked like it had once been well-maintained but had fallen into disrepair. Jack was busy sniffing everything they passed and often fell behind before running back up to walk beside him.

He kept following the road until he came to what had obviously been a wealthy hamlet. The abandoned buildings still looked serviceable and well-constructed despite years of vacancy.

Jayce looked through a few buildings, and seeing nothing of note, he decided to keep going. At the edge of town, he looked down the road and saw a huge man walking toward him.

The half-giant was carrying a club that looked like it must weigh a hundred pounds. It was resting on his shoulder like the giant was an enormous Babe Ruth posing for a picture.

"I guess we found Mongo," Jayce said to Jack before dismissing him for his safety.

The monster saw Jayce in the street and stopped. It slowly brought its club down from its shoulder as it stared at him with a low growl coming from its throat.

"Candygram for Mongo," Jayce said, wishing he had a box of explosives.

Mongo had obviously never seen *Blazing Saddles* and

was not amused. The huge man started lumbering toward Jayce, who summoned his bow and let off a Perfect Aim before following up with Rapid Fire.

After a slight stumble, Mongo charged, swinging his club like a baseball bat straight at Jayce's head. Jayce tried to step aside but took a glancing blow to his right bicep. The force of the hit sent him spinning away and dropped him to his knees. Thankful for his new runed armor, he got back to his feet and ran toward the nearest building. The pain in his arm was intense, but he didn't think anything was broken.

Jayce ran into the two-story building and up the stairs before exiting through a window onto the roof of the front porch. Mongo had started to follow him toward the building but stopped when he saw Jayce come out on the roof.

"Little man, come down!" the monster said. "Mongo hungry!" Jayce let off another Perfect Aim in response, followed by Rain of Arrows. The roof he was standing on was only shoulder-high to Mongo, and the giant brought his club down in an overhead strike, attempting to squash Jayce like a bug. Jayce jumped to the side, and the club smashed through the roof like it was made of paper. As Mongo brought his club up for another strike, Jayce had just enough time to get one more Perfect Aim off and jump toward the roof of the short one-story building next to him.

He barely made the jump and rolled forward to keep from falling. Jayce got to his feet and spun around to make more shots. Mongo was just standing there, not moving. The giant's enormous head slowly turned toward Jayce, and he saw there was an arrow sticking out of its eye.

"Mongo MAD!" the monster roared.

Mongo has become enraged

Jayce took off running as the half-giant started swinging

his club around. Randomly smashing anything in its way, the giant rampaged down the street in his direction.

Weaving his way through buildings, Jayce tried desperately to lose the creature as it relentlessly smashed its way toward him.

Running out of breath, Jayce ran around a building and saw the next building over. It had a front porch with enough room under it for him to crawl in. Rolling under the porch just in the nick of time, Jayce entered Stealth and watched as Mongo came around the corner. The terrifying behemoth swung its club at the building Jayce had just been standing next to.

Mongo looked around, confused. "Where little man go?" Mongo roared, seemingly coming out of his enraged state.

Jayce waited until Mongo started walking in the direction Jayce had been running. With the half-giant's back to him, Jayce stealthed his way toward him and struck out with his falcata, hamstringing the beast.

Mongo went down to one knee, roaring in pain as Jayce swung again, drawing a line of blood down Mongo's back.

He was fearing what the beast would do next. Jayce backed off to a safe distance and used Rapid Fire, trying to put as many arrows as possible into the half-giant before it took his head off.

Mongo went down to all fours under the barrage of arrows but stubbornly refused to die.

Jayce ran and jumped with all his might, landing on Mongo's back like a bull rider at a rodeo. Before Mongo could adjust to the new situation, Jayce began plunging his dirk into its back repeatedly until it finally gave up the ghost and collapsed.

Too tired to move, Jayce was surprised to find himself falling a few feet into a pile of loot as Mongo disappeared.

Seeing nothing more than Mongo's head, a pile of coins, and some shiny baubles that had obviously been looted from wealthy homes, Jayce sent it all to his inventory and got to his feet. Leaning on his knees, Jayce took some deep breaths, summoned Jack, and readied himself to continue.

Jayce followed the road further up into the hills. After several miles and several hundred feet of elevation, Jayce spotted a hexagonal building with a tall tower rising from its center.

"Well, that looks like a Necromancer's keep if I ever saw one," he said to Jack.

Entering Stealth, Jayce slowly worked his way toward the keep. Jack seemed to sense the tension and remained quiet. The structure was situated on the edge of a cliff overlooking a verdant valley. Jayce stood behind an outcropping of rocks and studied the entrance. There were no windows at all until the top of the tower. The lower hexagonal part was dark stone with some moss and vines creeping up the walls. The entrance was a pair of iron-bound double doors.

Jayce considered attempting to scale the tower and enter through the windows but decided not to take the chance. He continued observing the entrance for a long time but finally decided he had no other options. He would have to just walk through the front door. The question was whether he should try to slowly open it and sneak in or just swing it open and rush in. *Sneaking in would be best,* he thought, *but if anything were near the door, it would just give them time to attack me before I knew they were there.* After some consideration, he made his decision.

"Sorry, Jack, gotta leave you for a while," he said. "Stay boy, stay."

Taking a deep breath, Jayce threw both the doors

open and summoned his falcata. Two animated skeletons turned to face him.

Without taking time to look around, Jayce rushed the nearest skeleton, swinging his falcata at the undead monster's neck. Taken by surprise, the monster did not have time to react and crumbled to dust as its head went flying across the room.

Jayce received a notification but left it minimized.

The other skeletal warrior was swinging a sword of his own toward Jayce's stomach. Parrying the blow, Jayce's riposte nicked the skeleton's ribs but didn't seem to do any real damage. It swung again, this time coming toward Jayce's face. Ducking low, Jayce swung wildly at the skeleton's arm and saw the sword go flying with the hand and arm from the elbow down still attached.

Spinning around as he rose, Jayce swept his sword in a wide arc, hitting the skeleton on its opposite arm near the shoulder.

Watching the skeletal arm drop to the floor as the creature attempted to kick him, Jayce laughed out loud. "It's just a flesh wound," he said in his best John Cleese imitation. Reaching out, Jayce calmly separated the skull from the body of the skeleton with a final blow of his sword.

Looking around the room, Jayce saw that the lower portion was a wide-open hexagon surrounding the base of the tower. It was sparsely decorated with some shabby furniture but there was nothing, and no one, around.

Hoping that the noise hadn't alerted anyone to his presence, Jayce took a moment to check his notifications.

QUEST UPDATE

IT'S A DEAD MAN'S PARTY: A PARTY OF MERCENARIES WERE KILLED TAKING ON JOBS IN NORTH FLEET HILLS, AND THEY WERE RAISED FROM THE DEAD BY THE NECROMANCER DANNY ELFMAN. PUT THE PARTY TO REST. EACH PARTY MEMBER HAD A

Medallion that read Oingo Boingo (the name of their group). Bring the medallions back as proof of accomplishment.

Richard Gibbs 1/1
Kerry Hatch 1/1
Johnny Hernandez 0/1
Leon Schneiderman 0/1
Sam Phipps 0/1
Dale Turner 0/1

Two down, four to go, Jayce thought. *At least they weren't all standing by the door. That would have sucked.*

After retrieving the two medallions that dropped, he walked around the base of the tower twice, looking for anything of interest. Finding nothing, he went to the open doorway that led to stairs heading up into the tower.

Jayce climbed the stairs in Stealth mode. They ended at a doorway on the second floor. The door was partly open, and Jayce peered inside. There were two more skeletons just walking aimlessly about the room. Taking careful aim, Jayce let loose with Stealth Shot, taking one of the skeletons in the back of the head, causing it to fall to pieces on the floor. The other skeleton looked around and spotted him. Drawing a bow of its own, it fired at the gap in the door.

Jayce ducked behind the door and heard a thump as the arrow hit the door opposite his head. Switching to his falcata, Jayce dove through the door and rolled to his feet. He came up next to the creature swinging at its left femur as he rose.

There was a cracking sound as the bone fractured but didn't break. Jayce parried a blow from the skeleton as it swung its bow at his head. Jayce's parry snapped the creature's bow in half, and he swung at its fractured leg again, chopping all the way through.

The undead monster fell to the ground and began to

crawl toward him. Jayce stabbed down with his sword, pushing cleanly through the skull. At once, it turned into a pile of bones. Jayce collected the fallen medallions. His quest update showed that this had been Sam and Dale.

On the next floor, Jayce took down Johnny and Leon without too much trouble, but just as he gathered their medallions, he heard a voice ring through the tower.

> *"LET'S HAVE A PARTY. THERE'S A FULL MOON IN THE SKY.*
> *IT'S THE HOUR OF THE WOLF, AND YOU'RE GONNA DIE."*

"You got the lyrics wrong," Jayce yelled back, looking around. Nothing was there. Jayce went to the stairs and looked up. The stairs wound up the wall of the tower for several stories before ending at an opening in what Jayce assumed was the top floor of the tower. There was a sickly emerald light emanating from the opening.

Jayce tried to enter Stealth but found he was unable. *Guess it doesn't work if he already knows I'm here,* he thought. Having no other options, Jayce walked up the stairs, keeping his eye on the opening as best he could.

Reaching the opening, Jayce poked his head up to see what was there. He immediately had to duck again as a green burst of energy came shooting at his face. *Shit!* he thought. *How am I going to get up there?*

Mustering up his courage, he went down a few steps before running back up as fast as he could and leaping through the opening.

Blast after blast followed him as he hit the ground running.

Jayce quickly started to zigzag toward the source of the energy blasts. Just as he was juking back to the right, a blast caught him full in the chest, throwing him back against the wall and leaving a blackened patch on his armor. Pain ran through his body like an electrical shock. "I zigged when I should have zagged," he moaned.

Before him stood a skeletal mage with green fire surrounding its head and hands and the head of a staff it was holding.

"You must be Danny," he said, beginning to hum the theme of Tim Burton's *The Nightmare Before Christmas.*

Once again rushing the mage, Jayce swung his falcata at its staff, hoping it was the source of the creature's power. He made contact, and the sword wedged itself in the staff, sending shocks down his arm. "Uuuuhhh!" he yelled as he yanked his sword free and dodged another bolt of energy flying from the Necromancer's free hand.

"Damn it, Danny, that hurt!" he cursed as he swung at the skeleton's head.

Danny batted the sword aside and swept his staff at Jayce. Jayce bent backward, *Matrix*-style.

"Man, I'm cool," he said as he stood up straight. Swinging his sword downward in an overhead strike, Jayce put all of his strength into the blow.

Danny moved, and Jayce's sword was embedded into Danny's clavicle and scapula. The skeleton twisted and wrenched the falcata from Jayce's grasp.

In a desperate gamble, Jayce tackled Danny in a [sportsball reference here] analogy. The pair tumbled across the ground, with the skeleton trying to bite at Jayce.

Now what? Jayce thought. *The problem with grabbing the bull by its horns is that you can't let go.*

The skeleton straddled Jayce, but Jayce had a hold of both its wrists. The monster was leaning as far forward as it could and trying to bite Jayce's face. They struggled in this stalemate for what seemed an eternity until Jayce managed to put Danny's hands together and swing them to the side. Maintaining his hold on the wrists, Jayce stood up and began to swing Danny by the arms in a circle, lifting the undead mage from the ground and letting him fly toward the wall. As he let go, Jayce summoned his bow and let loose with Rain of Arrows.

Looking like a porcupine, Danny got back up and started rapidly tossing energy bolts at Jayce, forcing him to dodge as fast as he could.

Jayce took an energy bolt to the thigh and fell sideways. Catching himself as he fell, Jayce summoned a health potion from his inventory, bit the cork, and spit it aside. He ran around the outside of the room as he chugged the potion and threw the empty vial at Danny. As soon as the skeleton ran out of energy bolts, Jayce stopped and got a Perfect Aim off before following up with another Rain of Arrows.

Danny flew backward as the Perfect Aim hit him in the forehead. As it hit the wall, the skeleton sprouted even more arrows, one of them catching it in the head right next to the Aimed Shot, shattering its skull. The Necromancer, named after the coolest movie scorewriter ever, turned to dust.

Looking around the room, Jayce saw nothing save the Necromancer's staff and a chest against the wall. He picked up the staff and inspected it.

> Necromancer's Staff of Cosplay: *This staff looks really cool.*

"What the...? I got ROBBED!" Jayce yelled. "Worst boss loot EVER!"

Continuing to grumble to himself, Jayce walked over to the chest and used the staff to push it open.

The chest opened as Jayce stared at it for a moment. "Not a Mimic," he said, walking up to peer inside.

Inside the chest was a box. "What is this? Amazon?" he said. "Who else puts a box in a box?"

Jayce reached down to grab the box when it bit him. That's right—the box *was* a Mimic.

Jayce stood up, and the Mimic, which Jayce named Bitey McBiterton, held on. He shook his arm, trying to dislodge Bitey, but the Mimic was tenacious. Finally, he just started bashing the Mimic into the wall.

The Mimic turned to dust, and a box dropped to the ground. “Aww, come on!” Jayce yelled.

Poking the box with his sword first to make sure it wasn’t another Mimic, Jayce bent down and picked it up. Thoroughly tired of boxes at this point, he passed it into his inventory without opening it.

Back outside, Jayce wrestled with Jack before checking his quest log to make sure all of his quests were complete. “And that’s it for today,” he said as he started back home. “No way I’ll make it back before dark. Maybe I’ll sleep in one of the houses in Mongo’s village.”

It was already dark when Jayce got to the village, so he let himself into the first intact house he found. Feeling bushed from the day, Jayce pulled a ration from his pack, shared it with Jack, and leaned against the wall. Jack curled up on his lap as they fell asleep.

Jayce had been poking around the town for close to an hour when he came across a broach in the shape of a holly branch with emeralds and rubies forming the leaves and berries while the branch was made of gold.

> *BLOOP*
> THE ANCIENT BROOCH: THIS BROOCH APPEARS TO BE VERY OLD AND VERY VALUABLE. FIND THE OWNER AND RETURN THE BROOCH.
> REWARD: UNKNOWN

“Woo!” Jayce said to Jack. “A pickup quest!” After searching for another hour and finding nothing, Jayce decided to head home. Just outside of town, something he could only describe as Smeagol from *Lord of the Rings* tackled him to the ground.

Summoning his dagger, Jayce stabbed blindly at Gollum or whatever was on top of him while Jack barked and growled. The thing eventually went limp and turned to dust.

"Aw, maaaaaaan!" Jayce said, spitting dust from his mouth. "That's gross!"

> *Ding* You have reached level five. You may now choose your final occupation.

"Wooooo hooooo!" Jayce whooped, jumping and punching the air. *That seems awfully quick,* he thought. *Wonder if I get XP from crafting?*

Jayce quickly brought up his character sheet, popped his stat point into Toughness, and focused on the Occupation menu, selecting Rogue, then Mental. He almost couldn't contain himself as he chose Bard.

> *Congratulations! You are now a Bard. You have new skills available and one ability point to spend.

First, Jayce checked his skills and saw:

> *Summon Magic Instrument*
> Instantly summon one magic instrument of the Bard's devising. All spells are doubly effective while the instrument is being played. Lasts five minutes.
> Cooldown: 23 hours 55 minutes.

Shelving the implications of that for now, Jayce looked at his abilities menu. His options were Charm Person, Heal, Inspire Person, and Melody of Mockery.

> *Charm Person:*
> This ability gives you the chance to charm an individual.

If you are successful, they will follow one command from the Bard.
They will not harm themselves or others.
Failure results in the person not speaking to or dealing with the Bard for one to five days.
Heal:
Heal one person of the Bard's choice for a minor amount of health.
Cooldown: 1 minute
Inspire Person:
The Bard can inspire one person (no self-cast), making them twice as likely to succeed in their task.
Cooldown: 1 Hour
Melody of Mockery:
The Bard can roast one target, dealing mental damage.
Cooldown: 5 Seconds

Charm Person was good, but Jayce didn't feel he had any immediate need for it. Heal was always useful, but he also had potions. Inspire Person wasn't any good since he was soloing at the moment. Melody of Mockery—now there was a skill he could use! "More damage equals more survival," he said, selecting that skill.

Just as he was about to close out the menu, he thought to check his stats, and he saw that his Intelligence and Charisma had each gone up by two.

Chapter Eleven

Having no further issues on the way back, Jayce went straight to the Mercenaries Guild.

The same receptionist was behind the counter. "That was fast," he said. "Either you're a badass, or you gave up."

Jayce didn't reply. Instead, he dumped Mongo's head on the desk along with the Oingo Boingo medallions. "You didn't specify proof of Danny's death," he said, "but I've got this," and he summoned the cosplay staff.

The receptionist nodded, accepting the staff. "I'll be right back," he said.

After a while, the receptionist returned with the staff and a coin pouch containing twenty-five silver coins. Right behind him was a swarthy man with a mustache. The man looked an awful lot like Danny Trejo, which is to say intimidating as heck.

"Jayce," the man said, "minstrel, dog father, and tough guy. Who woulda thought?"

"Bard," Jayce corrected.

"There's a difference?" the man asked.

"Don't worry about it," Jayce replied.

"I'm Gerault, the Grand Master of the Mercenaries Guild. I am offering you the chance to join our organization."

"I'm not sure I want to be a mercenary," Jayce replied. "What does it entail?"

"It's very simple," Gerault said. "You pay your buy-in and get your choice at some of the best jobs, which we reserve for members. The guild takes fifteen percent of all rewards. In turn, you can stay in one of our chambers long-term or sleep in the common room for short-term stays. You get to use the guild's crafting spaces and can take advantage of special pricing on new gear and repairs. If the local guild hires out for a battle, you are encouraged but not required to join them. The rewards for battling with us are great, though."

"Well, in that case, I would love to join," Jayce said.

"The buy-in is one gold," Gerault replied, "and we give you a writ of membership, so you never have to pay a buy-in at associated guilds, which is pretty much all of them. Well, on this continent, anyway."

Jayce thought for a moment and brought out the baubles he had found. "Are these worth anything?" he asked.

"Hmm," the Guild Master said, inspecting the pieces. "These and the twenty-five silver we just gave you will do."

"Thank you, sir," Jayce said.

The Guild Master gave Jayce a look. "Gerault. You can call me that, or, now that you're a member, you can call me brother. We don't 'sir' each other around here."

"Got it, brother," Jayce said. "I will tell Molly that guild members get in free when I perform."

"I like it," Gerault told him. "I'm sure the other brothers will, as well."

Jayce's next stop was at the Outfitter shop, where he changed his armor while Jack went to town on his latest rawhide chewy. Turning the armor over to Thorne, he said, "I'm not sure I've the skill to repair this on my own now that it's been runed. The stuff is really tough, but I took a bit of a beating yesterday."

"You want me to help you with it or just repair it myself?" Thorne asked.

"That's a good thought," Jayce said. "Let's set it aside and work on it together when I get the chance to come back."

"Sounds good to me," Thorne said.

"Oh, hey, I almost forgot," Jayce said. "You have any idea who this belongs to? Found it up in Upper Fleet Hills at a house in an abandoned hamlet."

"That would be Fleetwood Hills," Thorne said. "Was where all the rich people lived before Mongo and Danny moved in. Can't say as I recognize it, but if you head to the Lord's manor, someone there may know more."

"Thanks, man," Jayce said. "See you later."

Jayce left and went to see Thayer before heading home for the evening.

When he got there, Thayer was sitting down and having a drink. As soon as he saw Jayce, he got up and offered him a cup of spiced wine.

"Thanks," Jayce said, accepting the cup and pulling up a chair. Jack curled up between them and promptly started with the cutest little doggy snores.

They sat in companionable silence for a bit when Thayer looked at Jayce. "It's been a long time since I had an apprentice," he said. "Working with you reminded me how much I like it. Don't suppose you know anyone who would like to learn?"

"Ya know," Jayce replied thoughtfully, "I just might. Little scamp named Druston out in Cheapside. You would have to keep an eye on him to make sure your tools don't go missing at first, but if he ends up liking it, I think he would be a great apprentice."

"You talk to him," Thayer said. "If he works hard, I'll train him. But if he tries to steal from me, I WILL call the guards. If he wants to learn, bring him on by."

"I'll do that," Jayce said. The pair of them lapsed back into silence, just enjoying the company.

By the time Jayce stumbled home with Jack, he and

Thayer had had several cups of wine each, and Jayce spent some time teaching Thayer some of his songs on the guitar. Being a Master Luthier and proficient at several stringed instruments, Thayer picked up the guitar fast.

When Jayce spoke to Dru the next day, the boy was literally dancing in the street.

"Of course, I want to!" he said. "If I can roll in the money like you, I'll be able to take care of Granny and others in Cheapside!"

"You will need to work very hard, do everything you are told, be respectful, and most importantly, never steal from your Master," Jayce admonished. "If you cause trouble, it will reflect on me and Granny, too."

"I'll be good," Dru promised. "No more stealing from now on."

Jayce handed Dru another silver coin. "I'll give more to Granny for you, as well," he said. "I don't know if Thayer will have a room he wants you to stay in or not. Most apprentices work for room and board and only get one day off a week. When you get so you can do some repairs on your own, Thayer will have the option of giving you a percentage of the cost, but he isn't obligated to. You will also need to learn to play the instruments," Jayce told him. "You don't have to be great at it, but good enough to be able to know the quality of your work."

"Really?" Dru asked. "If I get good, could I play at the Pig and Pony with you?"

"I don't know how much longer I will be here," Jayce said, "but when I am around, absolutely."

When they told Meg the news, she was grinning from ear to ear. "I'm so proud of both of you boys," she said.

"I missed you when I got up," Jayce said. "I leveled up! I'm a Bard now!"

"Well, good for you," Meg told him. "I've seen people get there quicker, but never with so many more accomplishments."

Meg motioned to a stool. "Have a seat," she said, "I have something I need to talk to you two about."

Jayce and Dru both sat as instructed. Meg remained standing and waited until they were both seated and Jack had settled down before continuing.

"I'm taking in a new child," Meg said as she stood aside to reveal a shy little girl. The girl reminded Jayce of Newt from the movie *Aliens.* He almost called Meg Sigourney Weaver before he realized that was probably after her time.

"This is Emily. She lost her family last night," Meg said. "I don't have enough rooms for all of you, so Dru is going to have to move in with you until this apprenticeship works out," she told him.

"That actually isn't a problem," Jayce said. "Now that I've joined the Mercenaries Guild, I can stay in a room there."

"Good," said Dru. "I like having my own bed."

"This is awesome!" Jayce said. "I'm so happy that you can be here for Emily! I'll pack my stuff right away." Pausing, he knelt down a respectful distance from the girl. "Do you want to come help me, Emily?" he asked. "It'll get you into your room faster."

The little girl just shook her head and looked at her shoes. She clung to Meg's dress like it was Linus's safety blanket.

"That's fine," Jayce told her. "I'll get my stuff out so you can move in."

Jayce went to his—Emily's—room and gathered all of his stuff. He didn't have much, and his pouch had twenty slots, so that wasn't a problem. When he came back out, he stopped next to Meg. "Still ok if I come round and work on herbalism and alchemy?" he asked.

"You'd better," Meg told him while hugging him. "I expect social visits, too."

"As long as I'm in Fleet, I'll always do that," Jayce said. "Just don't want to disturb you if you need time with the little one."

"She will be fine; just needs to know we are here for her," Meg said. "All we can do is let them know we love them and hope they figure things out. Look at Dru; he was much the same when he came to me. He was only on the streets a few months before I got him."

"Well, I'm sad to go," he said. "It wasn't this hard leaving my parent's home when I went to college. But I'm also extremely happy for Emily." He looked down to see the girl kneeling and petting Jack. "She couldn't have found herself in a better place."

Meg gave him another hug. "Thank you," she said. "It has been a pleasure having you here, and I look forward to daily visits."

"You got it," Jayce said before giving Dru a quick hug, calling Jack, and heading back into town.

Jayce moved into the Mercenaries Guild Hall. There were only a few residents at this time, so he had his pick of rooms. After emptying his inventory into the provided armoire, chest, and desk, Jayce left the room, locking the door. *Haven't had to do **that** in a long time,* he thought.

At the front desk, Jayce asked the now familiar receptionist if he knew anything about the brooch he had found but only received the same answer he had gotten from Thorne. "Off to the manor it is, then," he said to Jack as they walked out the door.

As he approached the Lord's manor, a pair of guards stopped him.

"What's your business here, halfling?" one guard sneered.

"I need to speak with Lord Fleet or a member of the gentry," Jayce replied.

"What business could the likes of you have with people like that, then?" the guard asked.

"That is a matter between them and me," Jayce said, not trusting the man.

"Go on, get out of here," the guard snarled. Jack snarled and barked at the man, who moved to kick the dog. Jayce slipped between them, eyeing the guard. Just as he was about to turn away, Grand Master Arrum strode up behind him. "Master Jayce," he said. "Is this man giving you a hard time?"

The guard snapped to attention. "Good morning, Grand Master," the man said. "I didn't know he was with you, sir. Lord Fleet is in his study, sir."

"Come along, Master Jayce," the Grand Master said, not even acknowledging the guard's existence.

Jayce followed him into the manor; Jack gave the guard a final sniff as he trotted by. When they were out of earshot, Arrum turned to Jayce. "Never understood that attitude," he said. "What do you need with Lord Fleet?"

Jayce showed the brooch to Arrum and explained how he had gotten it. "The very influential Holly family used to live up there," Arrum said. "That could belong to one of them. Come along. We will ask Lord Fleet; he may know for certain."

When they came to the study, Arrum knocked twice and entered. The Lord looked up. "Ahh, Grand Master Arrum," he said, "what a pleasure! And who is this?"

"Frederick, may I present Master Luthier Jayce? Jayce also happens to be *my* apprentice."

"Oh, yes, I have heard of you. You play at that public house outside the gate, don't you?"

"Thatsa me!" Jayce responded like Mario.

Both of the other men looked at him strangely, and Jayce cleared his throat. "Uhh, yes, sir. That's me."

"Such a pleasure to meet you, young man. I should like to hear this music that has made such a splash as of late."

"Come on down to the Pig and Pony Saturday evening, sir," Jayce said. "I'll be there."

"Uh, hmm, well yes, uh, what is it I can do for you, Master Jayce?"

Jayce took out the brooch and handed it to Lord Fleet, explaining how he had found it. "Yes, yes, I have seen this on the breast of Matron Holly. It's a family heirloom, I believe. She will be most pleased to get it back." Lord Fleet paused. "What is it you were doing out there?" he asked. "It is a most dangerous place these days."

"I took on a job to get rid of Mongo," Jayce said.

"Oh my, and you were successful?"

"Yes, sir," Jayce said.

"The Hollys will be most pleased about that. Now, if only we could deal with that Necromancer."

"Oh, I took care of that, too," Jayce said, stretching.

"Really?"

"It's no big deal," Jayce replied. "Just killed a bunch of living skeletons and the powerful mage that raised them, all in a day's work."

"I do say!" Lord Fleet responded, not getting the humble brag. "That is most remarkable! I believe we all owe you a debt for that. Hang on to the brooch. I shall drag Matron Holly to the, erm, Pig and Pony. I should like to see *her* in a place like *that* and see her reaction when *you* present the brooch. Now, if you will excuse us, the Grand Master and I have business to attend to."

Thinking about it as he left, Jayce smacked himself on the forehead. "I better tell Molly about this. I don't think she would be too happy for the Lord to show up as a surprise," he said, shaking his head.

After Molly had gotten over her shock, she frantically set into motion planning for the big event.

Now very excited for Saturday, Jayce spent the rest of the week crafting and practicing "Malagueña" and some other classical songs on his 12-string, along with one of his favorite songs to play, "Ocean" by John Butler. By the end of the week, he had reached 250 / 250 with herbalism, rune crafting, and alchemy.

Jayce spent Saturday morning practicing in his room in the Guild Hall; Jack was an adorable audience when he wasn't sleeping.

Jayce nearly jumped out of his skin when he stepped out of his room to cheering. The hall was crowded with what seemed like the entire guild. "You're gonna show them hoity-toity types what a working man can do!" Gerault said, slapping him on the back.

"Thank you all," Jayce laughed. "I didn't know I had an audience."

"If you ever came out of your room right after practicing, you would see that you usually do," came the response. "We are all excited for tonight."

"I guess word really got around, huh?" Jayce said.

"Wait until you see what they got going outside the Pony!" one of the mercenaries shouted.

Uh oh, Jayce thought. *What is happening now?*

Chapter Twelve

Walking out the gate, Jayce saw that the front of the Pig and Pony had been completely remodeled, and a stage and pavilion were being erected in the street. There were people he recognized from the Crafter's Guild swarming all around, along with a crowd of Cheapside folk working on the front of the Pig and Pony and the structure in the street.

Feeling overwhelmed, Jayce hurried to Meg's. "What the heck is going on?" he asked her. "This isn't for my performance tonight, is it?"

Jack immediately ran over to Emily and rolled on the ground in front of the girl.

"Oh, Jayce, you have no idea what you've done, do you?" Meg asked. "You invited the Lord of Fleet to come to the Pig and Pony, and he ACCEPTED," she continued. "The inn may be close to the gate on High Street, but the gentry still consider it Cheapside. With the Lord announcing he would attend, most of the courtiers will be there as well. I can't recall the region's elite EVER deigning to pay attention to Cheapside before. You're a bit of a hero. More money has poured into Cheapside this week than in the last year combined."

"I had no idea," Jayce said.

"That's what we love about you, Jayce," she said. "You always choose to do the right thing with no motivation other than it is the right thing to do."

"Guess I was just raised that way," Jayce said. "Spike Lee said, 'Do the right thing.'"

Meg kept Jayce at her place the rest of the afternoon. Emily sat on the floor with Jack while Jayce played his music. Then Emily stood up next to Jack; she watched Jayce for a bit and started bending her knees and bobbing to the music. Jayce completely lost track of time; he was surprised when Dru came in.

Little Emily looked at Dru, let go of Jack, and climbed up onto Jayce's lap. Jayce looked at Meg, who raised her eyebrows. Emily didn't say anything; she just sat there hugging Jayce. After barely even coming out from behind Meg's skirts all week, Jayce never expected this from her.

"Everything is ready," Dru said, grinning.

"What's ready?" Jayce asked.

"You'll see," came Dru's smirking reply.

Meg scooped up Emily. "Let's go," she said, and they all walked out the door.

As they got to High Street, a crowd had already formed.

"Still got an hour or two before I'm supposed to go on," Jayce said. "What gives?"

"Wait and see," Meg told him.

"Who are you, Neil Gaiman?" Jayce asked.

"Who?" Meg responded.

"Guess he wasn't that big yet in 1985," Jayce said. "He is my favorite comic book writer and author. He says, 'Wait and see' a lot."

"Got it," Meg said, leading him through the crowd. When they got to the pavilion Jayce had seen under construction, he could see it was roped off. Grand Master Arrum and Master Thayer were there to greet him.

"Let's get you all set up," Thayer said, taking him to the stage. Jayce walked on the stage and played from a few places while crafters listened from around the area.

Finally, they picked a spot and marked it with tape before taking his stool off the stage and replacing it with a podium.

An upright bass for Thayer and a set of nakers and a tabor for Thorne to play sat at the back of the stage. These were for a surprise that the three had been practicing for the crowd. Jayce was beginning to understand why Arrum had insisted on imbuing the rune for Amplify into all of the instruments.

After setting up, Jayce was led back into the Pig and Pony—through an opening where the wall had been! The entire front wall of the inn had been replaced by sliding wall panels that had been slid out of the way, leaving the common room of the inn open to the street.

"Holy cow!" Jayce said. "This is amazing, Molly!"

"Gonna be quite the crowd," Molly said. "Lord Fleet paid for everything," she beamed. Just then, trumpets sounded, announcing the arrival of the Lord.

"I had no idea it would be such a production," Jayce said. "I figured he would just show up for a few minutes at some point and then leave."

"Come on," Molly said. The ever-growing crowd parted, making a path so Jayce could walk to the pavilion. Inside the pavilion, chairs had been set up, and several of the most influential people in the region were seated there. They all stood and greeted him as he approached. Molly led him to a seat in the front row before disappearing back into the crowd.

A short tune from a trumpet played as a herald walked up to the podium.

"What is going on?" Jayce said, perplexed.

Loudly and clearly, the herald intoned, "Lords and Ladies, Lord Fleet would like to welcome you to today's ceremony and celebration."

The crowd clapped as the herald stepped aside, and Lord Frederick Fleet stepped behind the podium.

The herald announced, "Grand Master Arrum of the

Crafter's Guild; Grand Master Gerault of the Mercenaries Guild; Master Thayer, the luthier; Master Thorne, the leathersmith; and Master Maddy, the apothecary."

Each person stepped out onto the stage one at a time as their name was called. When they were all set, the herald looked at him and called, "Master Jayce, the luthier." The whole crowd erupted into cheers, including the gentry in the pavilion.

Jayce stood and walked onto the stage in a haze. He suddenly felt awkward; he always felt more comfortable in front of a crowd than in one, but this was different. *What the hell are they going to do?* he wondered. His social anxiety, normally reserved for individuals and small groups, suddenly had him paralyzed.

The other masters were standing in a half circle around Lord Fleet, and they motioned Jayce to stand before them. He hesitantly did as he was told.

Grand Master Arrum handed a fancy letter case to Lord Fleet, and he withdrew a paper from the top of a small stack.

The herald spoke: "Apprentice Jason Howard has successfully completed a journeywork of exceptional craftsmanship and is hereby released by his Master, Thorne, Master Leathersmith of Fleet, to begin his journey."

Lord Fleet handed the letter to Jayce.

"Apprentice Jason Howard has successfully completed a journeywork of exceptional craftsmanship and is hereby released by his Master, Maddy, Master Apothecary of Fleet, to his journey."

Fleet handed Jayce another letter.

"Apprentice Jason Howard has successfully completed an apprentice-level study in herbalism and is hereby released to journey by his Master, Maddy, Master Herbalist of Fleet, until such time that he can present an original discourse on herbalism or contribute new knowledge to the field of study."

Lord Fleet handed Jayce yet another letter.

"Journeyman Jason Howard has successfully created a masterwork and has been recommended for Master Luthier by Master Luthier Thayer of Fleet. He is hereby promoted to Master Luthier by Grand Master Arrum of Fleet."

Lord Fleet handed the letter to Jayce.

"The Mercenaries Guild has accepted Jason Howard as a member and has been awarded honors for exceptional services."

Lord Fleet handed Jayce *that* letter.

"For combating brigands and banditry, slaying giants, monsters, and an evil sorcerer that plagued the part of Fleet known as—" the herald hesitated, glancing at Lord Fleet to confirm the name change. When Lord Fleet nodded, he continued, "Hollywood Hills, Lord Fleet would like to present the key to the city to Jason Howard of Fleet."

A clerk approached and handed a box to Lord Fleet, who opened the box and displayed it to the crowd. It held a large ornate golden key set with diamonds and had the word FLEET engraved on it.

"Finally, Matron Holly would like to present Master Jayce with a personal token for restoring her family's ancient brooch."

The old lady handed Jayce what looked like an exact copy of the brooch he had in his inventory. He pulled the ancient brooch out and handed it to Matron Holly, who hugged it to her chest and thanked him.

Bloop

You have completed the quest: The Ancient Brooch.

Reward: Renown with Fleet, A brooch worth 10 gold pieces.

You are adored by Fleet.

You have been awarded the key to the city of Fleet worth 10 gold pieces.

DING
YOU ARE NOW AT THE SIXTH LEVEL.
YOU HAVE ONE ABILITY POINT TO SPEND.

Jayce almost missed Grand Master Arrum, who motioned for him to speak just when he got the notifications. *Crafting and Reputation have to grant experience,* he thought. *I haven't done anything.*

Jayce turned toward the cheering crowd, which quickly quieted down. "I'm speechless," he said. "I had no idea this was happening. I'll think of something to say when I come up to play." The crowd erupted into cheers again. Jayce and the others cleared the stage while workers removed the podium and set up Jayce's stool, Thayer's upright bass, and Thorne's drums.

When the workers had cleared the stage, the crowd began to chant, "Jayce! Jayce! Jayce! Jayce!"

Jayce walked back onto the stage, feeling like a rock star. In front of his stool had been placed what looked like a microphone stand with a wooden dowel on it where a microphone would be. Jayce laughed as he noticed the rune for amplification on the dowel. He was going to have to learn that rune!

Jack ran around the stage, twirling on his hind legs and bouncing about. The crowd laughed and cheered.

Jayce grabbed the "microphone" and looked out at the crowd. "Good evening, Fleet!" he yelled. "Lords and Ladies," he said into the microphone, "masters, journeymen, apprentices, my brothers at the Mercenaries Guild, and all citizens of Fleet, especially my fellow denizens of Cheapside!"

The crowd erupted. Jayce just stood there basking in

the feeling he was getting from the crowd. He was used to crowds and cheer, but that always felt like a part of the job. Here, in this place, it felt warm and inviting. He loved it!

When they at last settled down, Jayce said, "It's too early to get rowdy."

"Awwwwwwwww!" came the response from the crowd.

"Don't worry," he said, "we'll get there. We got aaaall night!"

The crowd erupted again.

Jayce sat on his stool, summoned his twelve-string, and immediately started with "Malagueña." The crowd quieted down as his fingers flew across the strings. The silence deepened as he continued his classical guitar set. When he was almost done with his classical set, he said, "This last piece is by a very famous man where I'm from, John Butler. This is his song 'Ocean.'" He played "Ocean" with every bit of nuance and feeling he could muster. As the song went on, the crowd listened in silence as if ensorcelled by the melody.

When he finished, he sat silently a moment before putting up his twelve-string. The crowd was completely still, having been enraptured by the song.

When Jayce stood, the crowd cheered loud enough that Jayce wished he had earplugs. "I'm frickin' Metallica!" he said quietly as he exited the stage for a break.

After a short break, the crowd was again chanting; this time, it was "Rowdy! Rowdy! Rowdy!"

Jayce grabbed Thorne and Thayer. "Come on!" he said. "Stoodis!"

The trio walked on the stage to whistles, cheers, and applause.

Never having performed in front of a crowd before, Thayer and Thorne looked at him and mouthed the word "crazy" at him.

Jayce grabbed the mic and settled the crowd down. "I have a very special song I want to play for you," he said.

"This is another one from John Butler, originally performed by the John Butler Trio. We are going to try and do it justice. This is 'Wade in the Water.'"

The crowd waited in silence during the opening notes of the song, but as soon as the drums kicked in, they went wild. Even amplified, Jayce was surprised that the crowd could hear them over its own roar.

When the song was done, Jayce looked at the crowd. "My good friends: Master Thayer on the bass and Master Thorne on the drums!" he said. "I'm Jason Howard, and we are just happy to be here."

The crowd erupted again.

Waving for them to settle down, Jayce said, "They don't know this yet, but I'm inviting Thayer and Thorne to join me on any songs they would like to."

This brought another deafening roar from the crowd. Jayce made "Dio fingers" and yelled, "METAAAAAAAL!"

The crowd had no idea what he was talking about, but they screamed anyway.

Before he could call out a song to the others, the crowd started to sing the chorus to "The Bear and the Maiden Fair."

Jayce took the hint and said, "Ok, ok! I get it. You all know this song, but we are going to do the version from a band called The Hold Steady." He turned his head and said in his best Marty McFly, "Alright guys, this is a blues riff in B; watch me for the changes, and try and keep up, ok?" before blasting into the punk rock version of the song.

Hours later, Jayce closed out the longest set he had ever played. Thorne and Thayer had hung in and played with him on many of the songs.

It was a good night.

Chapter Thirteen

Jack licked Jayce's face, waking him up. Still lying in bed, Jayce brought up his character sheet. Looking it over, he couldn't see anything new other than the one ability point he had available. He checked his abilities and saw that Melody of Mockery had been replaced by Folie à Deux. Looking it over, it seemed to be Melody of Mockery, but it could affect *two* enemies. Before choosing this upgrade, he looked back over the others. He was still soloing, but what if he met more people to adventure with? It might be nice to have a healing or inspiration spell at his fingertips.

In the end, he went with Charm Person, but not because he thought he needed it; oh no, he had a more devious purpose in mind. He grinned as he got up. He was so excited that he laughed out loud as he left the Guild Hall and headed to Meg's.

After a quick breakfast and playing a song or two for Emily, Jayce left Jack there and headed to Thayer's.

In the shop, Jayce could see Dru cleaning and sharpening tools under Thayer's watchful eye. He stood there a moment, watching the boy with a smirk.

When Dru finally noticed him, he stopped what he was doing and began to babble. "Jayce!" he said. "Last night was amazing! I'm going to learn to play like that. I want to sing, too. I learned all of the words to some of your songs. Can I use them?"

While the boy continued with his barrage, Jayce calmly brought out his guitar and, smirking, began his rendition of Tones and I's song, "Dance Monkey." Dru stopped talking, looking at Jayce quizzically and listening to the sound of the unusual song. Soon, Jayce added Charm Person to his song. Dru began to dance.

"Dance for me, dance for me, dance for me, oh-oh-oh..."

Dru looked panicked; he couldn't stop dancing. Jayce looked at Thayer and smiled as Dru danced his little heart out.

After a couple of minutes, Jayce stopped, and Dru plunked to the ground. "Not funny," he said.

Thayer and Jayce burst into laughter. "Worth it," Jayce said.

Thayer waved Jayce over to the workbench. "How would you like to make a delivery for me?" he asked. "Got some customers that live out near Seabeck-on-Taff. Made some repairs for 'em. They will come get their instruments eventually, but I figured you were going to move on soon anyway. Might as well save them some time."

"I can do that," Jayce said. "Arrum said he wanted to show me my next steps in rune crafting before I left. I'll swing by here when he is done with me."

"Great. Can't leave without saying goodbye to us anyway," he said, motioning to Dru. "You were right about him being a scamp, but he is a right hard worker and driven to boot."

At the Crafter's Hall, Arrum brought Jayce to an open room filled with small desks. There was a stool, a quill, and an inkpot at each desk.

"This is where scribes train, or sometimes even work if they are hired to copy something lengthy," Arrum said. "It is perfect for our next lesson. I gave you your journey paper a smidge early just to make it a part of the ceremony, but before you go, you have something else to learn."

"Looking forward to it," said Jayce. "Is that amplification rune one of the things I get to learn next?"

"That rune is usually learned when a student is more advanced, but I can at least give you a copy of the rune to study on your journey. Maybe it will come to you," Arrum said. "What I need to teach you is called combination crafting."

"Wait," Jayce said, "I have some questions about the basic runes. Is that ok?"

"Of course," Arrum replied, "always best to be solid on the basics."

"First," Jayce started...

Arrum had two identical wooden disks hovering above the desk at the same height. He pushed them both at the same time, and one of them kept moving at the same height after it left the desk, while the other dropped down to hover at the same height above the floor as it had been above the desk.

Arrum next stood on the lower disk; it settled to the floor, then sprang back up to the same height when he stepped off. Last, he climbed onto the one that had stayed hovering at the original height, and it didn't drop at all.

Still sitting on the floating disk, Arrum asked, "Did that answer the question?"

Jayce laughed. "Yes, it did, and you didn't have to speak a word."

"Ok, then, no more questions unless they are ones you cannot find the answer to after experimenting yourself."

"I think the difference between using push and hover was my last question anyway," Jayce said, "and you have definitely shown me how to better learn the uses of runes. I hadn't thought about just making things and playing with them to see what they do."

"Experimenting, not playing," Arrum said. "Now, down to business. Have a seat."

Jayce sat at one of the small desks. Grand Master Arrum sat across from him, picked up the quill, and drew the rune for resilience on a clean piece of paper. He then drew lines coming out of it and connected some, creating a new rune altogether. He turned the page back to Jayce. "What do you see?" he asked.

"Well, the resilience rune," he said, "sort of." Looking at it more closely, he realized it was an optical illusion. "When I look at it differently, I see the rune for contract, instead."

"Good," said Arrum. "I knew you would catch on fast." Arrum placed his hand on the rune, and almost immediately, there was a flash of power. He lifted his hand again. "Touch the rune," he instructed Jayce.

Jayce placed a finger on the rune, and the paper began to shrink. When he took his finger off, the paper returned to its original state.

"Whoa!" Jayce breathed. "That's amazing!"

"I want you to sit here until you can duplicate that and come up with a combination of your own. Come see me in my office when you have succeeded."

As Arrum strode out of the room, Jayce studied the combination rune, trying to figure out how it was done. Even though he had seen Arrum make it, he still couldn't figure out exactly how to reproduce it, let alone imbue it.

After several hours, something finally clicked, and Jayce picked up the quill, deftly reproducing the original. "Bam!" he said, waving his hands in front of him.

Now, to imbue it. In his mind, he pictured exactly what the original had done when touched. He focused on the way it contracted as he touched it and sprung back when released. It took several minutes of concentrating, but eventually, he felt the image settle into his mind, repeating like a GIF.

When it was ready, Jayce imbued the page and touched the rune. The paper performed perfectly. *Hell yeah!* he thought.

Jayce then spent several hours staring at his basic runes, trying to think of a way to combine some. Getting nowhere, he at last gave up and headed back to his room for the night.

As Jayce closed the door to his room, he was hit by inspiration. *How do I make that work, though?* he thought.

Very late into the night, Jayce took his door off the hinges and brought it to the crafting room in the Guild Hall. It being the wee hours of the morning, there was no one else about. Jayce laid the door down and carefully glued a piece of burlap to cover the entire back of the door. He then turned the door over and began carving. First, he carved "hover" into the upper left-hand corner, and then immediately below that, he carved the new combination he had thought of—Shatter and Mend. Jayce then imbued the door. Jayce laughed as he set the door waist-high on its side and let it hover. He then pushed it with one finger, guiding it back to his room.

Once at the room, Jayce reattached the door to the hinges and shut it. *Damn it!* he thought. *I didn't account for that.* Looking up, Jayce could not reach the carvings now located on the top left-hand side of the door. He went back into his room, got the stool he had used to attach the top hinge, and shut the door from the outside again. He touched the rune, and the door shattered into pieces with a sound that would accompany the violent act of shattering a thick wooden door.

People came running out of their rooms. Guild Master Gerault showed up in his underclothes with his sword bared. "What the hell is going on?" he roared.

Jayce turned crimson. "Sorry about that," he said. Where the door should have been was a drooping burlap cloth with splintered wood attached to it. The only part of the door that remained in place was the bit he had written the runes on. It still hovered where he had left it.

"What happened to your door?" Gerault demanded.

"Uh," Jayce said, reaching up from his place on the stool to touch the shatter and mend rune, which caused the door to reassemble itself. "It's just fine, see?"

Gerault walked up to inspect the rune. When he reached out and touched it, the door exploded and draped from the hinges again. Everyone assembled jumped back, startled. Gerault touched the rune again and reassembled the door.

"Very clever," he said, "but now the door cannot be locked."

"Oh, yeah, didn't think of that," Jayce pondered. "Be right back," he said, running off. He returned a few moments later with a carving knife and scratched a line through the runes, turning it back into a regular door. "I'll pay you for the damage to the door," he said.

"Don't worry about it," Gerault said. "It's fine now, and the artwork will remind us of you when you're gone. You can literally say you left your mark on the place."

Jayce laughed. "Sorry to disturb everyone's sleep. I didn't realize it would be so loud." The rest of the crowd grumbled to themselves as they returned to their rooms to get what little sleep they could before the day started.

Jayce spent the next few days working with Arrum on combinations. He also received a copy of the rune of amplification to study. The days flew past.

It was Thursday, and he was getting ready to move on.

All of his friends made him promise to do one last Saturday night gig at the Pig and Pony.

The stage and pavilion had long since been removed, but the changes to the inn were permanent. Molly once again pushed back her new collapsible wall; Jayce's going away party was going to be HUGE.

Not only did his usual fans show up, but the entire Crafters and Mercenary Guilds were there, along with a few of the Lords and Ladies he recognized from the ceremony the previous week. Jack even had his own fan section that cheered when the dog came prancing in.

He must have played "The Bear and the Maiden Fair" three or four times throughout the night, as it was a popular request, and people loved to sing along. Thorne and Thayer joined him later in the night, and they rocked Cheapside almost until sunrise.

When he arose late in the afternoon that day, Jayce decided he would run some errands and then leave the following morning when he could get an early start.

When Jayce got to the Crafter's Hall, the receptionist told him that Grand Master Arrum had had to leave for an undisclosed amount of time but that a gift had been left for him.

The man handed Jayce a backpack he had taken from behind his desk. Jayce looked at it for a moment; it looked like a plain, if not well-built, leather backpack. Looking inside, Jayce was surprised to see it wasn't empty. It felt empty, but inside were several pots of ink and a ream of paper. The top paper in the ream had a note written on it.

Jayce,

I'm sorry I didn't get to say goodbye, but I'm sure our paths will cross again. Keep working with the basic runes and practicing developing combinations. Next time you find yourself in town, come back to me and demonstrate what you have learned.

When you have progressed enough, I will give you a book of master runes to work with.

This pack can hold up to twenty-five items or stacks of items. It will only hold crafting material, though; all else will be rejected.

-Arrum

Testing this out, Jayce attempted to send the sword from his inventory to the crafting bag. Nothing happened. He then summoned his sword and tried to place it in the crafting bag. It wouldn't go.

Well, at least I'll have a large crafting inventory, he thought.

Thanking the receptionist, Jayce went to the crafter's shop in the Hall. There, he picked up an entire leatherworking set, a basic woodworking set, and the tools he figured he would need for instrument repairs on the road. He also got several empty vials and several bags of stoppers. He could reuse the vials, but stoppers often broke when they were removed.

Feeling like the party the previous night had been an adequate goodbye for most, he only made one more stop before heading toward Seabeck.

When he entered the door, little Emily ran up to him and jumped into his arms. He gave her a big hug and set her down. "I'm going to miss you, little one," he said, "but I'll come visit sometimes. I promise." He set her down to play with Jack.

Jayce gave Meg a big hug and thanked her for all she had done for him.

"Pish posh," she said, "it was nothing. Now, don't you be leaving without taking some potions and food." She opened a cupboard and brought out ten healing and ten running potions, two cure-poison potions, and twenty restorative potions. She also pulled out a week's worth of bread and dried rations.

"Thank you," Jayce said, knowing he would lose any argument he put up about taking the items.

"You know that I have many guises, right?" Meg asked Jayce.

"Sure," Jayce replied. "I've only met Meg and Maddy, but I sorta assumed you had more."

"When I first settled down here, I met a young girl named Fiona. She had just appeared in this place. She was very scared and lost. She ran from Meg, and Maddy wasn't any more successful, so I took on the appearance I sometimes used of a traveling merchant named Themiscura."

"Ok," Jayce said, wondering where this was going.

"I found her running down the road away from Fleet and offered her a ride. She wouldn't get in the driver's seat with me but climbed into the back of the wagon. I took her to the very swamp where I perfected my magic. It is off the path, and there is not much there. It already had a reputation as haunted from the time I spent there. I thought it would be the perfect place for her to heal for a while."

"Ok," Jayce said, again not knowing what else to say.

"It's not exactly on the way to Seabeck, but it's not that far out of the way in the big scheme of things. I have been stopping by to deliver goods and check on her as Themiscura several times a year. I would appreciate it if you could stop by and see if she is ready to accept someone else."

"Of course," Jayce replied, "how should I find her?"

"Just ask anyone in or around Seabeck where the ogre swamp is. I'm sure they will be able to tell you," Meg told him.

"I'll do it," Jayce assured her.

"Last thing you gotta do is name that sword," Meg said.

"What?" Jayce asked. "Why?"

"Because every famous sword has a name," she said. "You cannot name it Sting or Excalibur, though. Too many of those in this world already."

"I bet," Jayce laughed, giving the name serious thought. "What do you think, Emily?" he said after a while before laying his sword on the table for the girl to look at.

Emily stared at the sword very seriously. "It's called Dyrnllwyd," she said. "It means Grey Hilt."

Meg looked at the girl in surprise and then back to Jayce. "I believe that may actually be the sword's ancient name," she said. "Emily has shown a penchant for magic, but we have yet to nail down exactly what she can do. This is a new insight I shall have to explore."

Jayce turned toward the door, and Jack jumped up to join him.

"Jack?" said Emily quietly, and Jayce stopped with the dog. Emily immediately ran to Jack, hugging him and petting him. Jack, in turn, bathed Emily's face before rolling over to get his belly rubbed again.

Seeing the two together, Jayce made a decision. "I don't want to separate them, Meg," he said. "I think she needs him more than I do."

Meg nodded. "If you choose to give away a pet, just ask the new owner if they want the pet."

"Emily?" Jayce said, kneeling. "Would you like Jack to stay with you while I'm gone?"

The girl vigorously nodded her head, and Jayce got a prompt.

TRANSFER OWNERSHIP OF JACK TO EMILY? [YES] [NO]

Jayce selected yes and tousled her hair as he stood. He took a few steps toward the door as he watched the pair at play. Looking up, he made eye contact with Meg across the room; she was already fetching down some dried herbs for tea, tincture, or some other concoction.

She smiled and nodded her head in approval. He smiled back as he slowly opened the door. As he took one last look, capturing the scene in his memory—Emily playing with Jack on the floor, Meg watching, eyes full of love—a thought struck him as he went to the door. *This is the childhood I wish I had had.* He quietly closed the door.

Chapter Fourteen

It didn't take Jayce long to miss Jack. The dog was no good in a fight, and the two bag slots were barely enough for the dog to carry his own food and water, but the pooch had been good company while traveling.

Checking his quest log, Jayce reread his one remaining quest.

> SPECIAL DELIVERY: DELIVER A LUTE TO SIR JOHN ROYCE OUTSIDE THE PORT CITY OF SEABECK-ON-TAFF.
> REWARDS: REPUTATION WITH SEABECK-ON-TAFF
> UNKNOWN

A quick check with his map showed Jayce that his destination was to the south. "Well, one step at a time, I guess," Jayce said as he hitched up his pack and resumed walking.

Meg had told him that Seabeck was a good week's walk to the south and that it was a fairly large port city. Rather than just follow his quest directions, Meg had also told him to follow High Street west until it turned south, where it became Seabeck-on-Taff Highway. She insisted that taking the road would save lots of time, bypassing lower-level areas that would cost him time but not provide much experience.

He hadn't been on Seabeck Highway long when he saw a small group of men on the side of the road ahead of him.

As he approached the men, they spread across the road. "Looks like we got another one what's tryna use our road," said one of them as he spat at Jayce's feet.

Jayce stopped and looked up at the men. *Sure hard to be intimidating when you're three-foot-six,* he thought.

The men stared back at him for what seemed an eternity, but it was probably mere seconds before they finally realized Jayce was not going to say anything. "This here road is under our protection," the spitting man growled. "You want to use it, you're going to have to pay."

"Really?" Jayce said. "What are you protecting the road from?" he asked.

"What?" asked the apparent spokesperson.

"You said you're protecting the road. What from?" Jayce asked again. "I'm not sure what sorts of thing would threaten a road."

"No. We protect the travelers *on* the road, you twit," the man said. "You pay us for safe passage."

"Oh," responded Jayce. "In that case, no thanks. I can take care of myself. I appreciate the offer, though." Jayce stepped around the flummoxed man and started down the road.

"Wait right there!" came another voice.

Jayce turned around to see one of the other men draw his sword and step forward. Taking this as a signal, all the men drew their swords.

"I see," said Jayce, "not really an offer then?"

"Think of it as a tax," the new speaker said.

Jayce counted out loud. "Let's see, you make two, and those guys are three and four. Guy standing in the back brings it to five. That's hardly fair, don't you think?"

"Fair enough," the original speaker said, "for us."

Without waiting for more banter, Jayce lashed out with Dyrnllwyd, taking the first man in the throat before shoving the newly made corpse into the oncoming men.

As the next leading man struggled with the body, Jayce stepped around him, swinging again, this time slicing an ear off one of the bandits. "To the pain!" Jayce said in his best Dread Pirate Roberts voice.

Weaving his way through the bandits, Jayce blocked swing after swing. As he finally broke free, he spun around with both Dyrnllwyd and his dagger at the ready.

This time, two men struck out at once: Van Gogh and the second speaker. Jayce fainted toward Van Gogh, and the man over-responded, giving Jayce the chance to duck under his sword and come in low at the second speaker. His sword cut a fine line along the man's gut, causing him to step back and hold his hand to his stomach in an attempt to keep his intestines inside his body.

"Three left," Jayce said to Van Gogh and the two unharmed bandits. "Still think it's fair?"

Seeing Jayce barely scratched from the skirmish so far and two of the bandits dead, Van Gogh turned tail and fled.

"Coward!" called one of the two remaining men as they attacked Jayce together.

Unfortunately for them, one of the men tripped and swung his sword into his partner.

"Oh shit," Jayce said, "musta rolled a one," as he took advantage of the two men's entanglement, finishing the now-wounded one off and taking a swipe at Jack the Tripper's unprotected hamstring.

"Looks like I got another one what's tryna use my road!" Jayce said in imitation. "How much is my protection worth?"

Jack Tripper balanced on his left leg; his right was no longer able to support his weight. "I ain't got nuthin," he said. "James over there keeps the loot," indicating the first man to die with his chin.

"Well, I don't like being mugged," Jayce said, "so I can't just let you go."

The three dead men disappeared, leaving three piles of loot. "Oh my! And it looks like he wasn't the only one with loot after all!"

One-legged Jack just stood there bleeding.

"Strip," Jayce said. "Take it all off."

"What?" said the man.

"You heard me," Jayce told him. "Strip or die."

As the man stripped, Jayce gathered the other loot drops and put them in his inventory. He then took the clothes that One Leg had removed and cut them into strips, leaving them behind but taking everything else the man had dropped. "Bandage yourself up with the cloths and find something else to do with your life," Jayce told the man. "You're not very good at banditry."

Jayce put several miles between himself and the scene of the attack before he began to think about finding a place to stop for the night. Thorne had told him that the road between Fleet and Seabeck-on-Taff was pretty well traveled and had travelers' way-stops at intervals. So, Jayce decided to keep going until he found one. It was well after dark when he saw lights ahead.

As he drew closer, he could see that it was two lanterns: one outside of a small stable and one outside the door to a large inn. Jayce could hear the sounds of people drinking and carousing from a good way off. "Seems like a good place to stop," he said.

The sign hanging on the door proclaimed this place to be "The Traveler's Rest." "I could use some of that," Jayce said as he opened the door and walked in.

The large dining room was crowded, and Jayce had to struggle to push his way to the bar. Once there, Jayce had to convince a patron to allow him to use their stool. Once he was standing on the stool, a barmaid finally looked at him. "What'll it be, small fry?" she asked as she passed a tray of overflowing mugs to a serving wench.

"Need a place to sleep for the night," Jayce told her, "and some food."

"You sure you can afford that?" she asked. "Last hairy doorstop we had in here ditched without paying."

"I can pay," Jayce replied. "I can also provide entertainment if you would like."

"Don't need none," the barmaid said. "This is the last stop before Fleet; we are always crowded. It'll be two silver for the room and another for the food, which you can eat in your room."

"That's rather steep," Jayce said.

"It's the best you're gonna get from me, shin-licker," the barmaid responded. "Don't need your kind robbing us blind."

Sighing, Jayce took three silver from his inventory and passed them to the barmaid, who, in turn, gave him a bowl of stew, some bread, and a key. "Third floor, all the way at the end of the hall," she said.

Adding the food to his inventory so he wouldn't spill it, Jayce went up to the third floor. When he came to the door at the very end of the hall, he unlocked it and looked inside. It was a storage closet. There were a few extra mattresses piled on the floor and several changes of bedding on the shelves. Jayce sat on the pile of mattresses and ate his stew before shrugging out of his clothes, pulling some sheets down on top of him, and falling asleep.

Jayce found that rising early and traveling late put him at an inn every night. Turns out they were spaced for a human on a wagon to be able to travel eight to ten hours a day. Also, it turned out that as intolerant as the people of Fleet were, the people out here in the countryside were far worse. Every traveler he neared clutched their purse close and gave him dirty looks. Innkeepers continued to give him closets to sleep in, and prices were insane. Still, he was making steady progress toward Seabeck-on-Taff. On the fifth day of travel, the signs on the road changed from Seabeck-on-Taff Highway to Fleet Highway, and he came to a crossroads. Stopping, he checked his map and saw that the arrow pointed in the direction of the new road but a bit further south of where the new road looked like it was headed.

So, Jayce thought, *go down this road hoping it turns south, or stay on the main road hoping there is a side road further down?*

After spending several minutes deliberating, Jayce finally decided to see where the new road led. Several hours down the road, he came across a fort or a small walled settlement—he wasn't sure which.

"That'll be far enough, lad," a voice called out from the wall.

"I'm no lad," Jayce responded, "just the size of one."

"What's your business with the Free Company?" the man called back.

"I'm looking for Sir John Royce," Jayce said. "I heard he lives near here someplace. I have a delivery for him from Master Thayer of Fleet."

"Sir John, ay?" the guard asked while he swung the gate open. "This ain't the place you're looking for, but the Marshal is good friends with Sir John. Come on in."

Jayce walked into the compound as a second man went running off into the keep. "Wait right here," the guard said. "Marshal Harley will be out soon."

The wait wasn't long before a lean, dangerous-looking man came out of the keep and strolled over. The man had short(ish) black curly hair and a thick beard with a touch of grey in the center. "I am Harley, Marshal of the Free Company," the man said, looking down at Jayce.

"Hi, Marshal," Jayce responded. "I am Master Luthier

Jayce. I was recently in Fleet, and Thayer bade me to deliver a lute to Sir John Royce. Do you know where I may find him?"

"Sir John is my friend," the Marshal said. "If you have a delivery for him, you can rest here, and I will take you to him on the morrow."

"As long as I don't have to sleep in a closet," Jayce replied.

The Marshal looked at him for a moment before smirking. "No, none of that. We of the Free Company are not so small-minded, pardon the pun."

Jayce laughed. "I'll take the pun over the mistreatment any day," he said.

"Come into the common room," Harley told him, "and break out that lute if you can play it."

"Oh, I'll do you better than that," Jayce replied, summoning his guitar.

Chapter Fifteen

W*here am I?* Jayce thought as he rubbed his bleary eyes. Looking around, he could see that he was in a small room, but a room nonetheless. It felt nice after all of the closets. Sitting up in bed, he let memories of the night before rush in. It felt good that people wanted to hear him play again. All the rejection at the way-stops was beginning to bruise his ego.

It turns out the Free Company was a semi-retired group of mercenaries. When he discovered this, he presented his membership papers for the Mercenaries Guild, and the already welcoming group became instant friends.

Jayce walked out into the compound yard and saw men milling about the fire. There was a pot with some kind of porridge being served, so Jayce grabbed a bowl and spoon and got in line.

As he sat down on a log by the fire to eat his breakfast, he was joined by Marshal Harley and a couple of other members of the Free Company.

"Where did you get that guitar?" Harley asked. "I've never seen one before."

"I made it," Jayce responded. "Taught Thayer to make them, too. They are becoming very popular in Fleet."

"Thought you was a mercenary?" said one of the other men. "How'd you know to make that instrument and teach a Master Luthier no less?"

Jayce struggled to remember the man's name... *Jayden,* he thought. "Oh, I am a Master Luthier, as well. Also dabble in herbalism, alchemy, leathersmithing, and rune crafting."

Jayden's mouth dropped open. "You're having me on," he said. "You're way too young for any of that."

"No, really!" Jayce said, taking out all of his apprentice, journey, and master paperwork.

Another man walked up to the fire. "So, there is no way you're any good in a fight, then?" he challenged.

"Nope, I can hold my own there, too," Jayce said.

"Prove it then," the newcomer said, walking over to the weapon rack and selecting two practice swords.

"Cool it, Sam," Harley commanded.

"No, no, it's alright," said Jayce, standing up and stretching. "I could use some exercise anyway."

Sam tossed one of the swords to Jayce. Jayce took a few swings and asked, "You got a shorter one? This sword is taller than I am."

Harley walked over to the weapon rack and sorted through the exercise weapons for a bit before spinning around and tossing a heavy wooden short sword over to Jayce.

Jayce dropped the larger sword and plucked the short sword out of the air. "The reach is right, but this thing is more like a club than a sword. No worries though, it'll do."

"You sure you want to do this?" Harley asked. "You have nothing to prove here."

In response, Jayce walked up to Sam and assumed a defensive stance. Men soon gathered around, and Harley spoke up again. "This is a friendly match. If you make contact with your opponent, back off and let them recover. First to three hits wins."

Jayce kept his eyes on Sam. The man said nothing, and for a few seconds, no one moved. Suddenly, Sam lunged forward with a thrust toward Jayce's face. As Jayce stepped aside and parried, Sam took one more step and spun, swinging his sword wide and slashing neck high for Jayce.

Ducking under the swing, Jayce poked his wooden sword into Sam's chest and scurried back.

Sam reset with a look of shock on his face. "Lucky hit," he spat. "Let's see you do it again!" This time, Sam rushed in, feinting low before bringing his sword up at the last second to skewer the halfling.

Jayce easily batted the sword aside and slapped Sam on the shoulder with the flat of his wooden blade.

Sam did not back off to reset. Instead, he rushed in, swinging with a two-handed blow that looked like it would have knocked Jayce senseless had it connected. Despite the surprise attack, Jayce danced backward, parrying once again, and caught Sam on the chin with his riposte.

Sam charged at him, but Harley intercepted the man, pushing him back. "You challenged, and you lost, Sam," Harley yelled into the enraged man's face. "Take laps around the perimeter until you are ready to come back and shake Jayce's hand."

Sam threw his practice blade on the ground and took off running as instructed.

"He isn't really a bad sort," Harley said. "He is used to being the talented, tough guy. Don't think he liked you coming in taking his place."

"I don't plan on taking anyone's place," Jayce responded. "I don't think I'll even be staying that long after I make my delivery."

"Don't worry about it," Harley said. "He will cool down, and you are welcome to stay as long as you wish."

"So, what does a semi-retired mercenary troop do?" Jayce asked.

"Custom carriages," came the response.

"What?" Jayce asked.

Harley led Jayce to a corner of the practice yard where a carriage sat torn apart. "This is a carriage we are just starting for Duke Steven of Seabeck. We strip down what they provide and make custom changes." Motioning to a man hard at work on the carriage's chassis, Harley continued, "Jonesy over here does most of the chassis and exterior bodywork. Sam, who you just met, does custom features on the interior, such as hidden compartments, arrow slits, anything you can dream of, really. He is really good at making mechanical additions to the interior. I do the interior finish work, upholstery, and such."

Well, that's not a crafting skill you see in video games, Jayce thought to himself.

"We also have a bowyer, a fletcher, a bladesmith, an armorsmith, and a general blacksmith. We keep pretty busy just manufacturing these days, but we still keep in shape and hire out when the situation calls for it."

"I'd like to stay a bit and learn from you guys if it's ok," Jayce said. "Sounds like there are lots of skills I could learn here."

"Well, I've sent a messenger for Sir John. He should be along sometime today. Let's wait to talk until he gets here."

Jayce was in the practice yard sparring with Sam again when Sir John showed up. Sam had calmed down and offered his apologies, asking Jayce if he would spar with him some more. They spent hours sparring, and Jayce was able to learn a lot. Until this point, he had relied on skill-ups and natural talent to survive; Sam taught him actual forms and techniques.

"Take a break, gents," Marshal Harley called out, interrupting their latest bout.

Jayce placed his practice sword in the weapons rack and picked up a towel. Wiping the sweat from his face and hands, he walked over to the Marshal.

"Jayce, this is Sir John," Harley said. "John, this is the man we have been talking about."

"I hear you have a delivery for me," John said.

"Yes, sir, one moment," replied Jayce as he fetched his bag and summoned the lute from Thayer. "Here ya go," he said, handing the instrument off.

Sir John turned the lute over in his hands, strummed it a few times, adjusted the string tension, and strummed again. "Beautiful," he said. "Master Thayer always does the best work." Looking at Jayce for a moment before continuing, John said, "I'm told you are a Master Luthier yourself, among a surprising number of other things."

"True," Jayce replied. "I have a love of learning and a habit of picking up new trades."

"I also understand you have a guitar," Sir John said.

Jayce looked up in surprise. John just said that he knew what a guitar was. "Sure do; a few of them, actually. Made them myself."

"Do you know 'Free Bird'?" John asked, winking.

Jayce summoned his six-string and began.

"If I leave here tomorrow"

John joined in at *"For I must be traveling on now.."*

By the time they finished the song, the entire Free Company was gathered around.

Jayce laughed while John shouted, "Play some Skynyrd, man!"

"There's one in every crowd," came Jayce's standard response.

Putting his guitar away, Jayce gave John a serious look. "I guess we should talk sometime."

"I think so," John replied.

Jayce sat back and sipped the IPA that John had brewed. "Mmm, now that's a taste I've missed," he said.

"I was here a few years before I started experimenting

with home brewing," John replied. "I was only twenty-two when I died. I was working at a brew pub in Colorado at the time, so I understood the basics behind brewing, but it has taken me a long time to get it right on my own."

"So, you agree with Meg then? We are dead, and this is some kind of purgatory?" Jayce inquired.

"She was the first person I met when I got here, and I haven't seen anything to dispute her theory. I was at home playing *Dark Age of Camelot* and got a real bad headache, so I logged off and stood up to go get some aspirin. My eyesight got blurry, I felt dizzy, the left side of my body went numb, and I woke up here," John replied.

"What about the 'everyone died a tragic death' part?" Jayce asked. "Other than dying way too young, it sounds like things weren't that bad for you."

"I made some mistakes in my youth," John sighed. "Went to juvy, got out, made more mistakes, and did six months in the county lock up. The gig at the brewpub was my first legit job, and I was just starting to get my life in order."

"Wow, ok, so I guess I'm the only one with no tragic backstory," Jayce responded.

"I have an additional theory," John told him. "Everyone from our world that I've met here was some kind of fantasy nerd, really into Tolkien or *D&D* or computer games. I kinda think that maybe this is one of many purgatories, and this one is designed for us nerds to feel at home and work through our shit before we move on. Or maybe this is one of many afterlives and not a purgatory at all, just an afterlife for messed up fantasy nerds."

"Makes sense, I guess; I still don't feel like I fit the tragic backstory requirement," Jayce mused. "But it seems we are all just guessing here. When did you die, by the way?"

"It was the fall of 2002," John said. "A Sunday, I believe."

They both sat back in silence and sipped their IPAs. Jayce had left the Free Company's keep and accompanied

Lord John back to his home. It turned out Lord John lived a pretty humble life for someone who called themselves a Lord. He had a very large estate, but most of it was untouched woodland. His home was a modest place with a kitchen, living room, dining room, two bedrooms, and two and a half bathrooms. It did have indoor plumbing with hot and cold water, and both full baths had modern-feeling showers. Behind the house was a small brewery, a stable, and a workshop. He had a rather impressive garden where he grew his grains and hops but no castle or gaggle of servants or other accoutrements of nobility.

After a while, John cleared his throat and spoke, "Well, you told me of your life back home and a bit of your experience here. What level have you reached?" he asked.

"Only level six," Jayce responded. "You?"

"Twenty-one," John said. "Stopped worrying about it after level eighteen and focused on living my best life. Could be much higher by now if I wanted, I suppose. Six, hmm? So, you are a proper Bard, then? Not just a Rogue with an instrument?"

"Yeah, felt like the natural choice given my background," Jayce said.

"Definitely not a common choice. Most are knights like myself or mages of some sort. I've met a few priests and rogues, but you're the first Bard I've known. We need to get you acting like a Bard, though."

"What do you mean?" Jayce asked. "Am I not 'turtley enough for the turtle club'?"

John laughed. "That was one of the last movies I saw before I died," he said. "What I mean is you fight like a primary DPS. As a Bard, you should play a support role, as well as a secondary DPS and secondary healer. I haven't met any bards in person, but I've heard stories about one. Meg knew him, I believe. Every party wanted him along. You will be capable of buffing, debuffing, inspiring, damaging, and healing with your words and music. You should focus on developing those attributes along with your archery and melee skills."

"Yeah, I get that," Jayce said, "but up until now, I've only been soloing. I guess I've just been playing as a Rogue with no real use for my other abilities."

"Oh, you would be surprised how much you can use on your own as well as in a party," John told him. "I have a carriage at Harley's place that we haven't finished because I want to make the outside fireproof and bulletproof—well, arrowproof and boltproof anyway. To do that, we need to acquire the hide of a cave drake, possibly multiple cave drakes. If you want, I can gather my party. There is a cavern system a few days from here that has a bunch living in it. It's well above your level, but we could carry you, train you to work with a party, and probably power-level you a bit. What do you say?"

"Now that sounds like a good time!" Jayce gushed. "How long will it take before we can get started?"

Chapter Sixteen

John sent messages to his party members requesting they gather in one week. While they waited, John and Jayce went back to the Free Company to stock up on supplies and get Jayce some more sword training. At first, Jayce had assumed that the Marshal was part of John's party, but it turned out that all of the adventuring party members were from back home. When he asked John about it, John had laughed. "Two things," John said. "First, it is much easier if everyone in the party is from Earth. We can discuss levels and abilities and reference back home without freaking out the locals. The second thing is that you seem to be operating under a misconception. The Marshal's last name is Harley, not his first name."

"Oh," said Jayce. "With all the strange references from our world that I keep running into, I just assumed his last name was Davidson or something crazy like that."

"Well... it's not much better, really," John laughed. "If you ever watched reruns of seventies television, anyway. His name is Marshal William Harley."

It took Jayce a few seconds to put it together. "*Land of the Lost*?" he asked.

"Yeah, that's what it makes me think of anyway," came the reply.

"Le sigh," Jayce said, "this place is full of groaners."

"That it is my friend, that it is."

With the Marshal and his men taking turns drilling Jayce, his swordsmanship and archery vastly improved in the week they had for training. It wasn't a lot of time, but much like his ability to pick up crafting skills in this world, everyone was confounded by his rapid progress with weapons. Even John was perplexed by how quickly Jayce seemed to learn and develop muscle memory.

The night before everyone was supposed to arrive, they headed back to John's manor. "Most of us learn rather quickly," John said as they walked toward home. "But I've never seen anyone learn as quickly or as thoroughly as you do. Were you some kind of genius back home?"

"No, not really," Jayce said. "I always had a knack for music and learned new instruments rapidly. I guess I was considered a virtuoso, but it's not like I was great at everything. No, learning and doing at the rate I am is new to me, as well. Even though art and music came easy to me, it still took a whole lot of work to get good. Things here don't take anywhere near the effort they did back home."

"Huh," John replied. "You're just an anomaly all the way around, I guess. Congratulations, Buffy, you are the chosen one."

Jayce laughed. "So does that make you Willow? Zander? Cordelia?"

"Considering how much longer I've been here than you and that I'm training you, I'll take Giles."

"That works, I guess."

They arrived back at John's manor to smoke rising from the chimney. "Looks like at least one of our party has already arrived," John said.

As they walked through the door, they were greeted with the most amazing smell Jayce had ever smelled. Whatever was cooking was enough to make Jayce drool. Looking up from the stove, a huge man with pale green skin, pointy Elvin ears, and small tusks where his lower canine teeth should have been smiled and roared in greeting, "Johnny boy! It's been way too long, my friend! What adventures do you have for us now?"

"Kull! Good to see you! More importantly, it's good to smell your cooking again!" John said with a genuine smile that seemed to take up his entire face. "Jayce, this is Kull, the best camp cook and toughest Tank you will ever meet."

"Hello, Jayce," Kull said.

Jayce gave him a respectful nod.

John looked around and smiled at a slender woman with a slightly elongated, sorta snake-like face and said, "This is Peri, short for Pericardium. She is our healer."

The woman smiled at Jayce as he took in her large, leathery wings and tail. She spoke in a lilting Irish accent and an ever-so-slightly sibilant voice, "I am a dragonkin shaman. I specialize in healing, both physical and mental, if you need someone to talk to."

"Thank you," Jayce stumbled, wondering if he looked as overwhelmed as he felt at the sight of these adventurers.

Waving his hand in the direction of a tall, slender man in black robes, John said, "This is our sorcerer; he prefers to introduce himself."

The man seemed to smile behind his long, greying beard and mustache. "There are some who call me... Tim."

Jayce groaned but played along. "Greetings, Tim the Enchanter."

Tim smiled and, whooping with joy, rushed at Jayce with his hand held up for a high five. Jayce smiled and slapped the man's hand.

Shaking his head, John introduced Jayce. "Guys, this is Jayce. He is only level six, so we will have to power-level him a bit, but my intention is to go hunting for drake hides in the Howling Caverns. I need the material for some crafting, and Jayce needs to learn to use his bardic powers. He has only ever soloed so far and needs to learn how to be a proper support class."

Jayce blushed slightly and waved at the adventurers. "Hello," he mumbled.

The group sat around the kitchen table and ate the food that Kull had prepared. It was every bit as delicious as it smelled. Jayce couldn't place what the food was, yet he kept his curiosity to himself. Having seen a few episodes of *Delicious in Dungeon,* he decided it was best to just enjoy the meal.

"Has anyone seen Morri?" John asked. No sooner did he make his query than there was a knock at the door. "She always did have a flair for the dramatic," John said as he rose to answer the door. "Probably would have poofed right into the room if I didn't have wards on the place."

John opened the door, and a stunningly beautiful red-haired woman stepped in. She was wearing black leather armor with shimmering black scales sewn into it, giving a slight oil-slick look to her appearance. A wide crown of some sort of black metal held her flowing red locks back from her face. It had a nose guard jutting down in the center and a row of three-inch spikes sticking out around the circumference. A large black crow on her shoulder gave a squawk in greeting.

"Jayce," John said, "this is Morrigan, our battle mage. Morri, this is Jayce, our Bard."

"Pleased to meet you," Morri said in a surprising southern drawl.

Once everyone had eaten their fill, they gathered around the fireplace in super-comfortable, overstuffed chairs that had somehow appeared for their use. "Ok, Jayce," John said, "it's time to fill everyone in on what you can do."

"Nothing like putting a guy on the spot," Jayce laughed. "Ok, let's see... Well, my primary weapon is the bow, but I'm pretty good with my sword." As he spoke, he lay his falcata on the table. "I can also handle myself with daggers. So far, I guess I've only fought as a Rogue. With my bow, I've got Stealth Shot, Rapid Fire, Rain of Arrows, and Perfect Aim as special abilities. Umm, what else? Uhh, I can make potions of healing, run speed, and cure poison. I am a rune crafter. For my bardic abilities, I have Charm Person and Melody of Mockery. I've never used Melody of Mockery and only used Charm Person once; it was a practical joke on a young friend of mine—made him dance."

Morri was looking at his sword. "This blade is very old," she said. "Does it have a name?"

"Well, yeah, at least I think so," Jayce said. "I've been told it's called Dyrnllwyd. But that is a mouthful, so I've just been calling it 'sword.'"

Morri laughed. "Oh, darlin'," she said, sounding like a Southern Belle. "Just because it came with a name doesn't mean you can't give it another one. There is indeed power in a name, but you can call it Bob the Dyrnllwyd and refer to it as Bob. The official name will retain its power, and you can call it something you can pronounce."

"Hmm," said Jayce. "I could call it Joe Momma. It would be funny to say I swung Joe Momma at the dragon."

No one laughed.

"A swing and a miss," Jayce said. "I guess it reminds me of a shadow a regular sword might make. How about Shadow?"

"That sounds like a good name for that sword," Morri pronounced with a nod. "Every powerful sword should have a proper name. Shadow Dyrnllwyd, or Shadow Grey Hilt. I like it."

"I do, too," Jayce said, smiling. "But why are so many people concerned about me naming my sword?"

"Well, bless his heart," Morri said to John, "he really is fresh off the boat, isn't he?"

"Yes, he is," John replied. "But I've not seen anyone who picks up skills and talents faster than Jayce here. I've a feeling he will be more powerful than the rest of us in no time."

"Still haven't answered the question," Jayce said flatly.

It was Peri who spoke up next: her sibilant, lilting Irish accent lending a note of authority to her voice. "Names have power in this world, even more so with powerful objects like yours. Start thinking of your sword by its name; give it a personality. So far, you have likely unlocked the most basic of its abilities, probably some stat increases, but if you bond with it like it is your friend, you will unlock more of its power. You have a very powerful relic of ancient times in your hands. I've seen very few like it. It actually kind of blows my mind that you have such a sword. Most people never see a relic of such power."

"Thank you," Jayce said, turning a glare at John. "Finally, someone with straight answers in this place."

Over the next few days, Kull prepared rations for the trip while the others took turns sparring with Jayce and helping him think of Shadow as more than just a short sword. His already growing prowess with the blade increased immensely, and on the third day, he got a surprise.

> *BLOOP*
> **YOU HAVE FORMED A NEW BOND WITH SHADOW, AND A NEW SKILL IS UNLOCKED:** SHADOW STRIKE
> STEP THROUGH THE SHADOWS AND STRIKE AN ENEMY. THIS STRIKE CANNOT BE DODGED OR BLOCKED.
> WEAPON DAMAGE X2
> THIS ABILITY MAY ALSO BE USED TO STEP INTO A SHADOW IN STEALTH. IF THE WIELDER DOES NOT MOVE, THEY CANNOT BE DETECTED BY ANY NON-MAGICAL MEANS.

Jayce stopped in the middle of the sparring session and stared at his sword. Morri was just barely able to stop her swing in time, barely missing his face. "What the hell are you doin', darlin'?" she asked. "I almost killed you there!"

"S-sorry," Jake said. "It's just that I got a new skill from Shadow."

"Well, if you let that distract you in a real fight, you'll be dead for sure. What did you learn?"

The others gathered around to hear the answer. "Very nice," John said. "Give it a try. The step, not the strike."

Jayce held Shadow in front of himself and imagined stepping into the shadows by the corner of the building. Suddenly, his perspective changed. It was very disorienting, and he stumbled for a moment.

Peri looked at him. "Dead on," she said. "Now, if you can practice not falling over when you do it, you'll be right hard to find."

After a few more attempts, Jayce grew accustomed to the disorienting nature of the move, and even though the group knew where he had stepped, they could not see him until he took a step forward.

"Remarkable," John said, just as a familiar sound rang in Jayce's head.

> *DING*
> YOU HAVE REACHED LEVEL SEVEN.
> YOU HAVE ONE ABILITY POINT TO SPEND.

"Woah!" he exclaimed. "I just leveled!"

"I was hoping you would level before we left," John said. "What abilities do you have available to choose from?"

"First, explain how leveling works," Jayce said. "It doesn't seem to have any consistent rules."

Kull answered this question. "It is rather complex, and no one knows the exact mechanics, but from what we can tell, there are a few ways to make progress. First is grinding; just killing things or practicing with your weapons and skills makes some progress toward the next level. The more difficult the fights are for you, the more progress you make. The second is learning a new skill. This can be crafting, weapons, magic, or anything that you had to work at to learn. The more work it takes to learn the new skill, the more progress you make. Third is quests. Completing quests can be an immense boost. Once again, the more difficult the quest, the faster the leveling. Finally, milestones. This one seems to be the most powerful but also the rarest. Suppose you accomplish a feat that significantly alters the world around you or of such heroic difficulty that it warrants fame. In that case, you can level on the spot, even if you just leveled immediately before accomplishing the milestone."

"Damn," Jayce said. "No wonder I couldn't figure out how it works. That's a lot."

"Now, what abilities do you have available to choose from?" John repeated.

"Oh, right," Jayce said. "Charm People is there, but greyed out; Heal Person, Inspire Person, and Folie à Deux, but it's also greyed out."

"The two that are greyed are likely upgrades. Charm People is the upgrade to Charm Person, and Folie à Deux must be the upgrade to Melody of Mockery. Those will take two points to choose. Upgrades to those will take four points, then eight, etc."

"That makes sense, I guess," Jayce said. "So, should I pick one of the ones available or hold on and upgrade something next level?"

"That is entirely up to you," John said. "Given our group makeup, Charm People and Heal are probably the lowest priority. Peri is a full-blown healer, and Morri has some healing abilities. Tim can use mind control if we need to charm someone. Inspire Person sounds like it could be a great help in battle. It likely provides a bonus to hit or damage or some such thing. I have no idea what Folie à Deux means, but deux makes me think it just has your Melody of Mockery affect two targets rather than just one."

"What do you guys think?" Jayce asked the rest of the group.

"I think Inspire Person would be the most useful ability you could get for now," Peri answered.

"Aye, that one sounds good to me as well," Tim said.

Taking a moment to select Inspire Person from his menu and close it out, Jayce smiled.

> *BLOOP*
> YOU HAVE LEARNED THE ABILITY: INSPIRE PERSON
> A PERSON OF THE BARD'S CHOOSING GAINS AN ADVANTAGE TOWARD COMPLETING ANY TASK. THE BARD CHOOSES THE PERSON AND SINGS THEM AN INSPIRING VERSE THAT INCREASES THE TARGET'S ABILITY TO ACCOMPLISH THE TASK.

"Right," Jayce said. "Who wants to be inspired? Someone try to jump onto the roof of John's house."

"Tim, why don't you give it a go?" John said. "You are probably the least athletic of us all."

"Hey!" Tim said. "I resemble that remark."

Jayce had an idea and decided to use his Summon Magic Instrument skill, which he had never used before; he wanted to see if he could summon an electric guitar.

He concentrated for a second, and a perfect copy of Chuck Berry's cherry red 1958 Gibson ES-355TD appeared in his hands. With a smile, he began to play and sing Johnny B. Goode.

Tim let out an excited shout and ran at the manor house. As he approached the house, he jumped as hard as he could, shouting, "Go go! Go, Timmy, go!"

To everyone's amazement, Tim flew through the air like Michael Jordan, landing high up on the roof.

"Damn!" shouted John. He turned to Jayce. "Will it work like that every time?"

"Well," Jayce hedged, "not really. I can only summon a magical instrument once every twenty-four hours, and it doubles the effect of anything I do with it."

"Still," John said, "he really flew! Probably couldn't have made it without the extra boost from the guitar. Nice one, by the way."

"Wasn't sure I could summon an electric or that it would work without electricity, but I guess a magical instrument can be anything."

"I think we are finally ready to head out. Everyone accept the quest that Will gave me, and we will start first thing in the morning."

Bloop
Sir John would like to share a quest with you.
Not on the Upholstery: Gather 20 pristine cave drake hides for Marshal William Harley.
Reward: Renown with the city of Seabeck and the Mercenaries Guild. 1 gold for every regular cave drake hide delivered and 5 gold for every pristine drake hide beyond 20.

Chapter Seventeen

The first two days were extremely uneventful. They traveled through pretty tame lands, mostly consisting of forests and small fields. They talked while they traveled, and Jayce sang traveling songs that seemed to speed them on their way just a little faster than they went without his songs.

On the third day, the forest began to grow swampy, and John called for a halt. "We are close to Fiona's swamp," he said. "Would you rather skirt around, which will add a day or two to our journey, or cut through and hope she doesn't get a whiff of us?"

"Fiona?" Jayce asked. "The ogre?"

"Ogre of the Swamp," Kull confirmed. "She doesn't like people intruding in her swamp. She isn't a bad sort, really, just likes to be left alone."

"I think we are fine to cut through," Morri said. "She doesn't tend to bother those who don't bother her; more likes to yell at us than attack, really."

"I'm supposed to check on her," Jayce said, surprising the group.

"Well, this is a story I'd like to hear," John said.

"Remember Meg in Fleet?" Jayce asked.

"Sure," they all replied.

"She is the first one most of us meet," Peri said.

"Well, she sometimes travels in the guise of a merchant named Themiscura..."

"Like the mythical home of the Amazons?" Morri interrupted.

"Exactly," Jayce responded before continuing. "She tried to help Fiona when Fiona first arrived but couldn't gain her trust. So, she took on the guise of Themiscura and offered Fiona a ride out of Fleet, which brought her to this swamp, I guess. Meg told me she stops by on occasion to bring her things and check on her."

"That sounds like Meg, alright," quipped Morri.

"Anyway," Jayce continued, "Meg asked me to check on her if I was in the area. I had kinda forgotten, actually, with everything going on."

"Not sure she will allow that," Morri replied. "She is famous for not wanting company."

"I agree with Morri," Tim replied. "So long as we keep ourselves to ourselves and don't linger, she probably won't mind."

"That's true enough," Peri said. "I healed her once when I was passing, though, when she was sick; she knows me. That one has been through more'n I can guess, but she is kindhearted for all her gruffness."

"It's decided then," John said. "We will camp here tonight and head through the swamp tomorrow."

"But what about checking on her?" Jayce said. "I promised Meg."

"If she makes herself known to us, you can talk to her," John told him. "Probably save us a lot of grief if you do. But if she doesn't want to be bothered, we can always try on the way back."

"That sounds reasonable, I guess," Jayce said. "As long as I can fulfill my promise to Meg, I'm good with that."

"If we don't dally and Jayce sings us some good traveling songs, we should be through in less than a full day's march," John told them.

Sure enough, "Travelin' Band" by CCR, "On the Road Again" by Willie Nelson, "Life Is a Highway" by Tom Cochrane, "Road Trippin'" by the Red Hot Chili Peppers, Frank Sinatra's "It's Nice To Go Traveling," "I've Been Everywhere" by Johnny Cash, and "I'm Gonna Be (500 Miles)" by the Proclaimers had them covering ground at an insane pace. The more Jayce concentrated on the songs hurrying them along, the faster they went. After a few hours, his throat went dry, and his voice began to crack. He gave singing a rest but still strummed his guitar, choosing Metallica's version of Bob Seger's "Turn the Page" to kick off his instrumental set. As the sun began to set, the land was firming up, and John declared that they were exiting Fiona's swamp.

"Someone has been following us," Peri declared as she turned to face the deeper parts of the swamp. "Thank you for allowing our passage, Fiona," she said. "If you would like, you can come out and request a song. I'm sure Jayce would love to play something for you."

After a few moments, a stocky green woman came out of the swamp, looking like a live-action version of Fiona from *Shrek*. "Do you know 'I Am a Rock' by Simon and Garfunkel?" she asked.

"Of course," Jayce replied as he began to play.

When the song was done, Fiona gave a sad smile and disappeared back into the swamp. "You guys can travel through any time you want," she said as she disappeared. "Just sing me something nice when you do."

"I had no idea she was there," John said, flabbergasted.

"Oh yes," said Peri. "She has been following us for hours. If I weren't already attuned to her energy, I would not have noticed; she was very careful to be stealthy. Usually, she tries to scare people into leaving her swamp without them seeing her. Showing herself and screaming is her next step. She only resorts to violence if people refuse to leave;

even then, it's just enough to speed them on the way. She really is a rather gentle soul despite her reputation."

"Guess that makes her one of us," Kull said.

"Well, it's good to know she doesn't mind us passing through," John said. "We can camp here for now. One more day of magical speed, and we should reach the Howling Caverns."

"I want to try and talk with her on the way back," Jayce said. "Tell her Themiscura says hi and such."

"I think we can do that," John said. "She seemed to enjoy your singing well enough."

The Howling Caverns were aptly named. A wind blew through the mouth of the cave that was the entrance to the dungeon, a sound that reminded Jayce of an Aztec death whistle: sometimes a low moan but as the wind picked up, becoming the full-blown scream the whistles were famous for.

"Well, that's not horrifying at all," Jayce said as they approached.

"You think that's scary?" John asked. "Wait until you fight your first cave drake."

"Have you ever been in a dungeon before, Jayce?" Kull asked.

"No," Jayce replied. "Is it different from just fighting beasts and finishing quests?"

"Oh yes," Kull said. "Every dungeon is different, but what you need to know is that things 'respawn' after time. In other words, if you spend too long in the dungeon, then things you killed early on will be there again when you go back."

"Wow, this really is an MMORPG," Jayce responded.

"Very much so," Kull said. "Additionally, when you

clear a dungeon and leave, it resets, and you can go back in. This works up to three times a day. This particular dungeon is a few levels above you. We cleared at level fifteen, and that wasn't easy at all."

"What level are you all now?" Jayce asked.

"I am, as you know, level twenty-one," John said. "I am the highest level among us. Peri is twenty, and both Morri and Kull are nineteen."

"Should be pretty easy for you then," Jayce said. "Should I just sit in the back and soak up the experience?"

"Not at all," John said. "In fact, at first, it will be just you and Peri going in. The first several fights will be difficult for you but not impossible. Peri will not interfere except to heal you as needed. If we all went in, it would do you no good. You need to gain a few levels before we all fight together, or you won't benefit at all. Basically, we want you to be at a level where you can legit fight the monsters and survive for at least a short time. When you are there, we will do the whole thing together. There are three sub-bosses that drop pristine hides, and the final boss drops two if you're good enough at skinning. That means we will have to complete the dungeon at least four times to get the hides I need for my carriage."

"Sounds good," Jayce said, drawing Shadow and looking at Peri. "Shall we?" he asked.

Peri motioned for Jayce to go ahead. As he entered the mouth of the cave, all the noise stopped. It was like they had entered a different world. Looking behind himself, he saw Peri appear as if out of nowhere. Looking through the mouth of the cave, Jayce saw only a bright light.

He turned back again and began to walk cautiously into the gloom of the caverns. Despite not having a light, it remained illuminated enough that he could see—not well, but good enough to keep moving. After a short while, he heard the sound of feet scuffling ahead. He stopped and summoned his bow. Nocking an arrow, he prepared a

Stealth Shot and crept forward. Soon, he saw three grey creatures that resembled Gollum from *Lord of the Rings.*

"Goblins," Peri whispered in his ear, "servants of the drakes. Take them out."

Jayce fired a Stealth Shot at the first goblin he saw and followed up with Rapid Fire. There wasn't enough space in the dungeon for Rain of Arrows. The first one went down under the barrage of arrows, and the second was severely wounded. Jayce drew Shadow and charged.

"Melody of Mockery!" Peri shouted to him.

Feeling stupid and momentarily unable to think of anything good, Jayce just sang at them as he swung Shadow: "Nanny nanny boo boo, you guys stiiiiink!"

The already wounded goblin stumbled as he was mocked, and Jayce took off his head with Shadow. The final goblin growled and looked around, confused.

With a little more confidence, Jayce yelled, "Yeah, you! You're ugly, and your mother dresses you funny!" The goblin looked like someone had just punched him right in the face. Jayce stepped forward and swung again, this time trying to disembowel the horrid little thing. "Your mother was a hamster, and your father smelt of elderberries!" he shouted.

His swing was true, and a look of shock came across the goblin's face as he looked down at his guts spilling from his stomach.

"Well done," Peri laughed. "Not sure about your choice of Mockery, but it worked."

"That seemed rather easy," Jayce said. "I thought this was supposed to be hard for me."

"Those are just some random wandering goblins," Peri told him. "The first room is just ahead. Be ready."

Jayce collected the few coins left behind when the monsters disappeared and walked on. He quickly found the tunnel opening up a bit. He entered Stealth, drew his bow, and crept forward again. As the tunnel opened into a large cavern, he could see what looked like a dragon with no wings curled up in the center of the room. Several goblins were waiting along the edges of the room to serve the drake should it need anything.

Jayce went back to Peri and asked, "Should I kill the goblins first or focus on the drake?"

"Take out the minions first," she told him. "Unlike the bosses, no more will come. When we fight a boss, it's best to take the boss down first because more minions will replace the ones we kill as long as the boss lives."

"Right," he said, readying a Stealth Shot. As he came to the entrance of the cavern again, he aimed at the closest goblin and removed him with one shot. Stealth being blown, he focused an Aimed Shot at the second and let loose with Rain of Arrows, hoping there was enough room in this cavern that the ability would work.

As the last of the arrows found its mark, Jayce used Shadow Step to get behind the farthest of the goblins and swing with all his might, severing the head from its shoulders. The remaining goblins turned in his new direction and rushed while the drake unfurled itself and stretched. A goblin swung a rusty sword toward Jayce's face, and he blocked it and struck back with a riposte. While he did so, however, another of the smelly little monsters caught him in the shoulder with its rusty blade. Luckily, his armor took the bulk of the damage, and the rusty sword broke as Jayce returned the swing with one of his own. This gave yet another little guy a chance to jab at him with its spear, which luckily missed and threw the monster off balance. "Missed me, missed me, now ya gotta kiss me!" Jayce yelled at it. The goblin tripped and fell in front of Jayce, who quickly finished it off. By this time, the drake was ready to enter the fight. It took a deep breath, and Jayce Shadow Stepped behind it. *Thank goodness for that ability,* he thought as he watched the space he was in moments before fill up with green gas. The goblins remaining there began to cough, then boils formed on their skin, and finally, their skin began to melt off their bones.

Jayce quickly dismissed Shadow and summoned his bow, aiming Rapid Fire as best he could at the drake's head. Arrow after arrow found its mark, but the creature bellowed and swung toward him, swiping with a giant claw. The drake's taloned appendage was as big as Jayce and sent him flying toward the opposite wall. As he flew through the air, he yelled, "You hit like a girl!" and then he smacked into the wall and slid to the ground. Shakily, getting to his feet, he spun around with Shadow at the ready. The drake took in a deep breath, and Jayce once again Shadow Stepped. This time, he stepped to the side of the drake and swung with all his strength while shouting, "Real dragons have wings, stupid face!"

Shadow dug deep into the belly of the beast, making it roar in pain. This time, it turned away from him and swung its enormous tail. Jayce had just enough time to try and jump. Unfortunately, his little halfling legs didn't propel him high enough to clear the tail, and it connected with his lower legs, spinning him through the air. The good news was the connection wasn't enough to send him into the wall again. The bad news was the air was knocked out of his lungs when he landed on his back. Before he could recover, the drake placed the point of a claw at his throat and slowly applied pressure, making it hard to talk.

"Your... feet... stink!" he gasped, and the drake reeled just enough for Jayce to roll out from under its claw and rush to his feet. One more Shadow Step took him away from the already swinging claw, and he again buried Shadow in the beast's side, yelling, "Can't catch me! I'm the gingerbread...oomph!"

He was cut off as the tail swung and caught him in the stomach. As the creature's tail brushed him aside, Jayce chopped away at it hoping he could cut it off, giving the creature one less thing to attack with. He made it about halfway through when the drake pulled its tail out of the way and spun around with its breath at the ready. This time, Jayce dove forward, landing between its two front legs and stabbing upward with all of his strength. The drake roared again and stumbled as Jayce pulled Shadow out and plunged it back in over and over again.

At last, the beast succumbed to the attack and fell right onto Jayce. Unable to breathe and unable to move the huge lizard off of him, Jayce began to panic. Just as he thought he was going to die beneath the thing, Peri found him and hauled him out from underneath.

"Probably a good idea not to kill it while it's on top of you," she told him.

"Thanks for all the help," he responded.

"You didn't need any," she said, "at least not until you had it die on top of you. Now hurry and skin it before it disappears."

Jayce complied, skinning the beast and getting one drake hide for his effort. In the places where the bodies of the goblins had been, there were laying a few copper coins; he scooped those up, too.

Peri took in his bruised, battered, and bloody appearance and stepped up to him. She clapped her hands together and rubbed them, Mister Miyagi-style. She held them up to his face and slowly moved them around his body without touching him. When she was done, a single bead of sweat dropped from the end of her nose.

Jayce was about to make a snarky comment when he realized he felt completely refreshed. No cuts, no bruises. He wasn't even tired.

"Wowsers!" he said. "That's a neat trick!"

"Thank you," she replied. "Shall we continue?"

Two days of delving into the dungeon, up to the first boss, and then exiting for a reset saw Jayce reach level eleven. He had thirty-some-odd drake skins and hundreds more copper coins. At level eight, he had placed a point into Toughness, bringing that to nine, and at eleven, he placed one in Charisma, raising that to thirteen. At level nine, he used two ability points to raise Inspire Person to Inspire Party. Level ten got him Heal, and at eleven, he banked the point for later.

When the third day dawned, John told him it was time for the whole party to go in. "Now it's time for you to turn to your support role," John said. "I need you in the back of the party with Tim and Peri. Kull is our Tank, while Morri and I will be melee damage. Tim will use Ranged Magic, and Peri will Heal. You use your support skills and your bow."

"Got it," Jayce said.

The first bits that Jayce had already been through were rather boring. The rest of the team took things down very quickly, and all he really did was lob a few arrows and sling a few insults.

John stopped the party just outside the first boss's chamber. "Kull, you will Tank the big guy; kite him around clockwise as slowly as you can. Morri, keep the minions busy. Everyone else, focus on the mage. When he is down, switch to the boss. Remember, don't stand in the fire. Ready?"

"Ready," the others said in unison, and Jayce looked around a little before shrugging his shoulders and saying, "Ready."

With that, Kull led them into the room. He produced two long, sharp teardrop shields, but the strap was on the rounded end, and the grip was closer to the pointy end. He wielded them like weapons. Near the door was a drake easily twice the size of the drakes that they had been fighting. In the center of the room was what looked like some sort of dragonkin in flowing purple wizard's robes, complete with little moons and stars all over it. It held a tome in its hands and looked up, startled at their approach.

Kull batted the drake in the face with one of his shield things, drawing its attention. "Hulk smash!" he yelled. As the drake turned toward him, he took a step back, and the drake spat a pool of viscous liquid at his feet. As soon as the fluid hit the ground, it lit on fire, leaving a pool of fire at Kull's feet. Kull took another step back and slapped the beast in the face again.

While that was happening, John rushed the mage, and Morri moved off to the side where goblins were coming out of a side entrance. They all moved with such practiced skill and teamwork that, for a moment, Jayce just stood there and watched. A ball of fire flew past him and hit the mage, bringing Jayce out of his stupor.

The mage shrugged off the blast and reached for John with lightning crackling around its hand. Jayce used Perfect Aim and took a shot at the mage. The arrow slowed as it approached and just barely penetrated the mage's cloak before hanging there like a pin. "Bet you can even read that book, dum dum face!" Jayce shouted as he nocked another arrow.

A second miniature fireball hit the mage, this time causing it to step back a bit before it attacked John again. This time, the lightning on its hand gave John a jolt, and he went to his knees for a moment before rising again and swinging his sword at the mage's midriff. Jayce's second arrow took the mage in the shoulder as Jayce yelled, "Suck it, Shawn!" Another little fireball from Tim struck the mage in the chest, and John plunged his sword into its throat.

"On to the big guy!" he yelled.

Jayce turned his attention to the drake that was following Kull around the room. They had almost made their way back to where Jayce was standing, and there were little pools of fire every few feet behind them. The first of which was just starting to sputter out. Jayce followed Peri and Tim to the center of the room, out of the path of the drake and its pools of fire. Tim sent what looked like a giant icicle flying at it while Kull continued to batter it with his shields. Peri finished sending some heals off to John, who joined Kull in front of the wingless dragon. Jayce sent several Perfect Aims into the side of the beast as rapidly as he could. Before long, the drake dropped to the floor and breathed no more. Peri topped Morri's health off and sent another Heal at Kull, who had several burns and gashes.

"Finish them off!" John yelled, and everyone tore into the goblins, taking them down in no time.

Jayce skinned the large beast while John looted the goblins and the mage.

"First pristine hide of the quest," Jayce said, holding it up before sending it to his backpack.

John pocketed the silver that dropped from the goblins and held up a wand that had dropped from the mage. "Minor Wand of Shadow," he said. "Anyone want it?" No one replied. "For sale then," he said, sending it to his special satchel.

After a brief rest, they continued with more random drakes and goblins until they reached the second boss. "Kull, take fire; I'll take ice. Morri, take warriors. Everyone else, take the warriors first, followed by ice, then fire. Any questions?" No one spoke. "Ready?"

"Ready," they all said in unison. Jayce was proud of himself for being quick enough to join in this time.

Once again, Kull and his two stabby shields led the way, followed by John, then Morri. When Jayce made his way into the room, Kull had a drake's attention at the back of the room. He would smack with his shields before putting them together and hiding behind them while fire blew out of the creature's mouth.

John had another similarly sized drake facing away

from the rest of them as well. This one was breathing frozen air toward John, who danced around and used his buckler to avoid direct hits.

Morri was in the midst of some more of the dragonkin-looking things that she had told him were, in fact, drakelings. This time, there was no mage, but the six of them all wore armor and carried two-handed swords. Morri swung her sword in a wide arc in front of several of them. As it passed by, it seemed to draw energy or life force of some kind from them, and she seemed to get just a little bit bigger. Jayce sent Perfect Aim after Perfect Aim into the warriors while Tim again used his mini fireballs that he called Fire Blasts. Peri kept her eyes roaming around the group, healing anyone who needed it.

When the drakelings were all down, John shouted, "Ice!" Everyone but Kull joined him in attacking the ice drake. Tim continued to use fire. Morri used her sword with various effects, from life stealing to lightning to a magical poison. Jayce just continued to send Perfect Aim after Perfect Aim into the monster. It took a while, but it went down.

"Fire!" yelled John.

Everyone turned to fire, and Kull switched from a completely defensive stance to a balanced stance and began to attack, taunt, and defend. Other than Tim switching to ice bolts, the fight went just like the ice fight had, and, in time, the fire drake dropped as well.

Jayce skinned the two drakes, and John looted the warriors. "Just some silver and a few weapons; everyone here has better," he said.

"Two more pristine hides," Jayce called.

"Just the final boss to go," John told him. "It's a bit of a slog to get there, though. You might level before we get to him and almost definitely will when we are done if you don't before."

Two hours later, after killing drakes and goblins, Jayce hit level twelve and decided to bank the skill point for later use. An hour after that, the group gathered outside of the final boss's cavern.

"This isn't a simple tank and spank," John said. "Kull, you Tank for the first stage. When he gets to half health, he will summon his mate and become invulnerable. At that point, I will kite him away from the group while Kull tanks the mate. When she goes down, phase three starts. Everyone kill goblins as fast as you can; this is a timed phase, and they keep pouring in the whole time. We need to have the goblins finished off before the final phase. The boss comes out of his invulnerable stage and drops insane AOE damage. You're going to take damage, so just focus on taking him down as fast as you can. His damage builds on itself, and we need to get him down before it exceeds Peri's ability to heal it. Phase four is a DPS race; dump everything you have into it. Ready?"

"Ready!" they all called.

Phase one went very smoothly: a basic tank and spank, and no one took any real damage. Suddenly, they were all frozen in place, and Jayce started to freak out until he noticed no one else seemed concerned. The largest drake yet popped into the middle of the room. She was a very pale blue and somehow alluring, like a Disney cartoon.

As soon as he could move, John poked the first drake as hard as he could with his sword, and it turned to swipe at him. Backing off, John led it away from the group.

While that happened, Kull was swinging both stabby shields in circles like an enraged child, leaving thin lines of blood on the hide of the beast. It looked down like it was amused and swatted him aside.

Morri stepped up and wielded lightning from her

sword while Tim poured lightning from his hands into the enormous lizard.

Jayce went back to Perfect Aim after Perfect Aim, all the while singing "Fuck You" by Lilly Allen. This wasn't a Melody of Mockery but an Inspire Party song, and it worked. Everyone dealt as much damage as they could while focusing on staying safe so the healer could conserve her magic for the final stage.

Now and then, the big drake would drop a circle of ice on the ground that had to be avoided, and of course, the first drake continued to swipe out randomly as it chased John around the room.

When the mate looked like she was about to die, Kull yelled, "Take cover!" Everyone crouched behind one of the large boulders strewn about the cavern as she exploded, sending shards of ice everywhere. As soon as the ice shards stopped, a flood of goblins came pouring into the room.

"One minute!" yelled John.

Everyone turned to fight the pathetic creatures. Individually, they were not a problem, but hundreds of them continued to pile into the room. Kull swung wildly, taking down three or four with each swing of a stabby shield.

I need to know what those things are called, Jayce thought.

"Thirty seconds!" John called while everyone continued to mow down goblins. The little hits were starting to add up, and Peri was back to healing.

"Ten seconds! Get down!" Jayce was swinging away with Shadow while standing next to Morri. No one stood near Kull, whose crazy stabby shields made the bodies pile up around him. Tim was using a lightning attack that daisy-chained from one victim to the next.

"Switch!" yelled John as he stopped backing up and took the fight to the boss.

Jayce summoned his electric guitar and began to belt out Queen's "We Are the Champions." A pulse came off the drake, and Jayce felt his life force begin to leave him.

Death energy emanated from the boss! Peri held a staff aloft in both hands, and a wave of healing energy pulsed out of her, effectively erasing what the boss had just done.

"Use it all, guys; this is it!" John called.

Jayce continued belting out Queen while everyone used the most powerful attacks they had. Another pulse of death magic, another wave of healing. This time, Jayce knew he was not completely healed. Then, another pulse of death and another wave of healing.

Jayce was growing weak and switched to "Another One Bites the Dust."

Another pulse and another wave.

Jayce felt like he was about to die. Peri sent an extra Heal his way, giving him a little more strength, and he continued his song.

Another pulse. Another wave.

Jayce knew he wouldn't survive another pulse, so he poured his soul into the song. He wasn't paying any attention to the rest of the party, just wishing every bit of inspiration he had to his friends.

John poked him in the ribs. "You can stop now. It is dead."

Jayce un-summoned the electric guitar and looked around. The party was staring at him. He blushed. They all laughed a bit.

"Really got into that one, ay?" Peri said.

"Hey, I guess... I didn't think I would last another pulse of that death magic, so I really wanted you guys to kill it."

"I had a few more heals for ya, don't worry," Peri told him. "Now, skin the beast."

John walked over to a chest that had appeared in the center of the cavern and opened it.

As the lid opened, Jayce hit level thirteen.

"Holy crap!" he yelled.

"What?" John queried.

"I leveled again!"

John shrugged. "Freddy Mercury musta liked your song," he said. "Ok, I think this one is a good one for you, Jayce."

Jayce turned and saw John holding up a leather helm. "Ugh, I'm so not a hat person!" he said. "Never looked good in them."

"Then this is perfect for you," John replied. "Check it out," he said, tossing the leather cap to Jayce for inspection.

Jayce caught the hat and inspected it.

> *YOU HAVE FOUND: LEATHER CAP OF THE BARD
> THIS CAP CAN TAKE ON THE APPEARANCE OF ANY HEADGEAR THE BARD WISHES OR TURN INVISIBLE WHILE STILL OFFERING THE SAME PROTECTIONS.
> +5% HEALTH
> +2 CHARISMA
> +2 INTELLIGENCE

Jayce smiled and put the hat on. He focused on the hat being invisible, and then he turned to the others. "Did it work?"

John smirked. "Sure did, but I didn't think you would pick vanity over protection."

"In general, I wouldn't, but I have a thing about hats," Jayce told him.

The second time through the dungeon went much easier with Jayce two levels higher and having more experience with the team. He didn't level from that run, but right after the last boss, his bond with his sword increased.

> *YOU NOW HAVE A LEVEL-TWO BOND WITH SHADOW.
> SHADOW GRANTS YOU THE ABILITY: SHADOW DANCE.
> YOU MAY NOW COMBINE UP TO NINE SHADOW STRIKES

INTO A SHADOW DANCE, ALLOWING YOU TO STRIKE UP TO NINE TARGETS WHILE RAPIDLY FLITTING THROUGH THE SHADOWS.
THIS ABILITY HAS A ONE-HOUR COOLDOWN.

"Saaa-weeet!" Jayce exclaimed.

"What happened?" Kull asked

"I got an attack that can hit up to nine people. It's kinda single target, kinda AOE. I get to bounce around the fight stabbing enemies in the back once an hour!"

"Nice!" said Morri. "Just remember your main job is support."

"I've actually been having fun in the back," Jayce said. "Once I got used to it, I love heckling the monsters, too. Sooo much fun!"

Tim laughed. "You need to start coming up with better things than 'Nanny nanny boo boo.' I mean, come on."

John looked at Jayce quizzically. "No level this time?"

"Nope," Jayce said. "I guess two in one run last time was all the luck I was gonna get."

As they exited the dungeon and John reset it, they all looked around surprised. It was much later than they expected. Jayce frowned. "Guess carrying me took longer than we thought."

"It seems so," John told him. "Might as well stop for the night and try to get three runs in tomorrow."

They set up camp, organized watches, and settled in. Jayce took the first watch, and in his best Samuel L. Jackson impression, he recited Adam Mansbach's book, *Go the Fuck to Sleep,* while strumming quietly on his guitar. Before he got to the end of the second page, everyone was passed out.

When he woke up Peri for the second watch, she got straight up and stretched. "That was the best rest I've ever gotten," she said. "You should tell bedtime stories more often."

In the morning, Kull cooked some fresh meat and eggs. Jayce did not ask where the ingredients came from, but it was a nice change from the travel rations they had been eating on the road.

"Thanks, Kull," Jayce said. "This breakfast is amazing."

"There is a reason John always calls me up for these adventures, and it's not because he can't tank without me."

"Aww! Hey now!" Peri quipped. "You're more than good food; you make an amazing pack mule, too!"

Jayce hit fourteen after the first boss, dropped a point into Strength, bringing it up to nine, and banked the ability point. He now had two ability points but decided to wait a while before spending any more.

The second run of the day went smoothly, and after finishing the third run, Jayce leveled again. To his surprise, so did Kull.

"Didn't think you guys were getting anything from this," Jayce said.

"Even Mr. Twenty-one over there is getting a tiny bit from it," Morri said. "I'm hoping to hit twenty in the next run or two."

The next day saw three more runs. Jayce got to level sixteen, and Morri hit twenty.

"Time to head back," John said. "We have double the number of pristine hides we need, and I'm sure even Jayce's crafting bag is getting full of regular cave drake hides at this point."

"You're not wrong," Jayce replied.

With a more powerful Jayce singing them on their way, the trip home only took two days. They slowed down a little while going through Fiona's swamp so Jayce could sing and play the entire *Shrek* soundtrack—or at least as much of it as their combined memories could muster. They were all actively looking for Fiona so that Jayce could fulfill his promise, but she never showed her face, even when they called out to her. Jayce was sure she was listening.

Chapter Eighteen

Back at the manor house, Jayce looked over his ability menu. He had four points banked. He had already attained Charm Person, Heal, and Inspire Party. No new abilities had shown up as he leveled, so he went with Folie à Deux.

> FOLIE À DEUX:
> YOUR MELODY OF MOCKERY IS NOW CAPABLE OF AFFECTING TWO TARGETS AT ONCE.

With that done, Folie à Foule appeared in its place but greyed out. Jayce stared at the choices. He could get Heal Party or Charm People with his remaining two points or save up for Folie à Foule, which he could only assume would let him mock even more people. Having no reason to charm people or heal the party, he decided to wait.

After spending the night in comfort at John's manor, John and Jayce headed for the mercenary camp. John was super excited to get started on "bulletproofing" his carriage. The rest of the party decided they would take a few days to rest at the manor, and if no other adventures came up, they would go their separate ways again. As much as the party enjoyed adventuring, and each other, they had all developed their own lives and were ready to go back to them.

Marshal Harley was thrilled to see them back so soon and even more thrilled at the abundance of the rare leather they had brought back. "Wow!" he said. "You guys musta killed every cave drake on the planet to get all of this!"

"Sure felt like it," John replied.

"I've never worked with drake hide before," Jayce said. "Mind if I assist you and learn a few things? I'll throw in some free runes on your work in exchange for the training."

"Now that sounds like I'm robbing you blind," Will said, "but I'm not going to argue! The best thing about drake hide is the complete lack of hair or scales. It's just a super thick and durable leather."

"Oh, I almost forgot. I collected a whole bunch of drake brains as well if you need them for curing the leather."

"Well, that's super gross of you, but we can definitely use them," Will told him.

"The Master Leathersmith I worked with before told me brain was the best substance for tanning. Is that not true?" Jayce asked.

"Well, it certainly works, and if you don't mind collecting them while you gather the hides, it is definitely the cheapest. I mostly use rendered fats and egg yolks, or I just buy leather already prepared."

Jayce took all the hides over to the scraping bench and started the long process of scraping and cleaning the hides. Like Will had said, this was many times easier than hide with hair on it, but the fat still needed to be scraped off and the skins cleaned. Once that was done, Will came over to help with the braining. "Don't worry about it," Jayce said. "I got this. Just watch to see if I do anything wrong or differently from how you would do it."

With forty pristine hides and hundreds of regular drake hides to work with, it took the better part of two months to get all the hides turned into leather. John had headed back home to say goodbye to the rest of the party, but

Jayce stayed and worked. He also trained with his sword and bow when he wasn't working the leather. His rapid level progression, combined with his role being mostly support, had left his weapon skills lagging.

When all of the pristine hides that were going to be used on John's carriage were prepped, cut, and punched for sewing, Jayce took the largest piece and set it on a table in front of him. He took out his grimoire and studied the runes. After a while, he chose Strength, Rigidity, and Resilience. One after another, he slowly imbued every piece individually. When they were all imbued, John showed him how to sew them into the shape needed to cover the carriage, and when that was done, Jayce finished the creation with a single join rune that made the seams disappear, and the whole cover turned into one piece.

Next, they pulled up the carriage, which was already complete. There were no open areas where the hide would go; rather, it would be stretched over the existing wood body of the carriage. It took hours of tugging and stretching to get the leather covering on just right, but once it was done, Jayce took out a carving tool, and in one door frame where the leather met the wood, he imbued another join rune. The already nearly impenetrable drake leather was now significantly reinforced and permanently affixed.

Before they delivered the carriage, Jayce imbued several other items that the guild had been crafting. He kept five of the largest remaining pristine leathers and several of the regular drake leathers.

"Thanks, Will," he said. "I learned a lot from you. Master Thorne mainly made armor, bags, and clothing. It was fun seeing more ways to use and work with leather."

"Well, you are definitely quite advanced for a journeyman, and if there were an upholsterer's guild, I would give you your journey papers for that, too. It's unbelievable how fast you learn. The guys all say that you have become one of the best archers and a damn good swordsman over the last two months, as well. You sure you don't want to stay and join the Free Company?"

"That actually sounds like fun," Jayce told him, "but I haven't seen much of the world yet. I really want to explore before I settle down. I was going to head into Seabeck next and see what a port city is like."

"Well, lad, if ya get tired of wandering, we would be glad to take you in here."

"Thanks, Will, but I'm not really a lad, just short like one. I must be twenty-seven by now. I've lost track of time."

"Yer still young yet, lad, and no, your height's got nuthin' to do with me callin' ya that. Just hate seeing young ones with so much potential go is all."

"That means a lot, man," Jayce said. "I'm pretty sure I'll be back someday. I'll deliver this carriage for you and see if John wants to take his new ride into town and drop me off."

As Jayce was approaching John's manor, he saw John riding toward him at top speed. He stopped the carriage and waited.

When John showed up with his horse all in a lather, he leaped off the mount, tied it to the back of the carriage, and jumped in.

"Head back to the manor," John said. "I should have added you to my guild so you could get messages from me."

Jayce got the wagon moving and asked, "What's got you all worked up?"

"World boss just spawned near Fiona's swamp; gonna be dozens of people there to fight it. The rest of the party are on their way to the swamp now."

"First, awesome. I will get to try to say hi to Fiona again. Second... wanna explain all that for me?"

"We are going to stop off at the manor and get some supplies and then head for the swamp as soon as possible. There are hundreds of world bosses. They are sort of like immortal badasses or some kind of demigod. Who knows?" John shrugged. "They spawn randomly around the world and wreak havoc until they are defeated. When their mortal form is destroyed, they leave this realm and go back to wherever they come from to gather strength again. Then, they return to some random place in the world. So far as I know, we never have more than one world boss alive at a time, and this is the first time one has spawned around here in years."

"Nice," Jayce replied. "That is very MMO. It still seems crazy that this world is much like a video game, but I'm down. And what was that you said about joining your guild?"

> *Bloop*
> You have been invited to join the guild "Spatium Vacca Pueri."
> Accept [yes] [no]

Jayce immediately selected yes.

Green text began to scroll in his peripheral vision. John grabbed the reins and said, "Go ahead and check out guild chat."

Jayce thought, *Guild chat,* and a text window appeared in his vision. He focused on the text:

Kull: *Welcome Jayce.*

Pericardium: *Welcome.*

Tim: *Sweet, good to have you in the guild, bro.*

Morrigan: *Awesome! Welcome to the space cowboys!*

Jayce: *Thanks guys! I was wondering what the guild name meant. Lol. Space cowboys. That's good!*

Morrigan: *Yeah, we formed up years ago when we decided to go our separate ways.*

Jayce: *That seems the opposite of when you should form a guild...*

Tim: *Yeah, I guess, but we didn't need it when we were always together, and we didn't really know how to do it.*

Jayce: *How does it work?*

Pericardium: *We initially went to a town council and asked to form a guild because guilds like the Mercenaries Guild can send messages through the mail and it gets to wherever the guild is established.*

Tim: *We just wanted to be able to keep in touch, you see.*

Kull: *But after we formed the guild, we got guild chat. It's really nice.*

Kull: *How far out are you guys?*

Jayce: *Almost back to the Manor. When we grab some supplies, we will head back to the swamp.*

Kull: *Awesome. You will probably be the first ones there, so you have some time to brew more of the potions. *hint hint*

Jayce: *No sweat, provided John has the ingredients on hand.*

John: Oh, yeah, I stocked up as soon as I got back. Was gonna ask you to make some before you headed out again.

Jayce: *Looks like we are here, guys. I'll let you know when we are on our way.*

No sooner did the carriage pull up to the manor house than John leaped out. There were several packs of supplies staged by the door, and John threw them into the carriage. Motioning Jayce to follow, he went into the kitchen and pointed at several bushel baskets of herbs. "I think this is everything you said you need for health potions. No idea what quantities it takes, so I bought as much as I could."

Jayce pulled his alchemy kit from his crafting bag (which was actually beginning to fill up) and got to work. After making several potions, he had a thought. Rune crafting and alchemy shared a component. Neither of them worked until he focused his magic and imbued the potion or rune. Both had a physical and a magical component. The magical component was simple: concentrate on the desired result and focus mana on it. If the physical component were crafted properly, the magic would be held. If it wasn't, the spell failed. Something was niggling at the back of his mind, but he couldn't quite put his finger on it.

Before making another potion, Jayce pulled out his runic grimoire. After studying for a bit, the runes for mend, join, strength, defense, and resilience seemed to jump off the page, and he saw how they would all fit together. Was it possible? Could five runes be joined? If it did work, what would it do? He could tell this was completely different from the combination work he had done before. Excitedly, he took out his rune crafting tools and set to work drawing the vision he had before it fled his mind.

When he was done, he inspected his work. It looked right; when he focused mana, the new rune glowed brightly. He knew it was black ink on a pale vellum, but it seemed to take on a life of its own. Jayce let his body move on its own, seemingly guided by the magic of the rune. He cleaned and dried his alchemy cauldron and placed it over the flame. He then placed the rune into the cauldron and poured the purified water over it. When that was done, he ground the herbs for the healing potion into the water and let it simmer. Looking through the herbs on the bench, he plucked out two more, but he wasn't even sure what they did. *Musta been mixed into the bulk purchase that John had bought,* he thought.

He focused on the first as he ground it in his mortar. As it turned to powder, it took on a grey metallic hue. He dipped his finger in, getting a small amount on the tip, and tasted it.

> *BLOOP*
> YOU HAVE DISCOVERED IRON WEED, AN ALCHEMICAL INGREDIENT.
> USE: UNKNOWN

He dumped the Iron Weed powder into the mix and grabbed the second, following the same procedure.

> *BLOOP*
> YOU HAVE DISCOVERED SLIPPERY BLOOM, AN ALCHEMICAL INGREDIENT.
> USE: UNKOWN

Hmm, well, at least his herbalism let him identify the names of the things. He was hoping for more information, but he supposed he would just have to trust his magic to guide him.

After adding the Slippery Bloom, Jayce stirred the mixture counterclockwise. As he stirred, he brought up a mental picture of the rune and focused on it. It glowed brightly in his mind as he gathered mana into the image. He then focused on a feeling of unbelievable vitality and strength, the feeling of indestructible immortality that only the very young ever seem to possess. He connected the feeling to the rune glowing in his mind. He then reached out with his mind and found the physical rune and the tea that was brewing in the cauldron. He mentally bound both images to both physical entities and gathered more mana, more than he had ever gathered before. When he knew he could hold no more, he pushed it from his mind to his belly and back up to the top of his heart. It rushed out of his heart in both directions and into his hands. He held it back as long as he could, focusing on concentrating the mana in his hands. It soon took on a thicker feel, almost like a gas condensing into a liquid. Still, he held it and compressed it; it took on a gel-like feel, and the huge amounts of mana became handfuls of what he could only describe as mana jelly.

He let the mana jelly drop into the mixture, shocked when it actually made a physical plop-plop as it fell into the tea. After checking his hands and seeing no evidence that something had been there, he stirred the cauldron counterclockwise some more, watching as the liquid thickened and turned a deep forest green.

This was definitely something new. The health potions he had made before turned out red and were very watery.

John cleared his throat. "I didn't want to interrupt 'cause it seemed like you were having some sort of breakthrough, but after taking less than ten minutes per batch, this one has taken you over an hour. Is everything ok?"

Jayce jumped a little as he was pulled out of his reverie. He looked at John and held up a finger in the universal sign for "wait a minute." He filled a vial with the new mixture and sniffed it. No smell could he detect. He swirled it around in the glass vial, and it moved like mercury, staying in a ball and not leaving any residue behind.

"What is it?" John asked.

"'Bout to find out," Jayce said, gulping the fluid down.

> *Bloop*
> You have created Elixir of Health: Provides the imbiber with extra health for two hours, heals one percent of health per second for two hours, and slightly increases the imbiber's natural defense for two hours.
> *Bloop*
> You have discovered a new branch of magic: Runic Alchemy

DING
YOU HAVE REACHED LEVEL SEVENTEEN.
DING
YOU HAVE REACHED LEVEL EIGHTEEN.

Jayce dropped to the floor.

"Are you alright?" John asked as he rushed over to help Jayce stand.

"I'm good, I think," Jayce said, wiping blood from his nose. "I think I just invented a new recipe and a new form of magic. I also leveled twice. Wiped me out, though."

"Damn!" said John. "Never heard of someone getting two levels at once before. Then again, I've never heard of someone inventing a new form of magic before."

"I need to rest," Jayce said. His eyelids felt like lead weights; he struggled to keep them open. He started to fall again, and John caught him.

When Jayce woke up in the morning, his head was pounding, his eyes were burning, and his throat was dry. He stumbled to the kitchen where John was waiting.

"Good, you're up and moving," John said. "I was gonna message Peri to come and heal you if you didn't get up this morning."

Jayce took one of his healing potions and started brewing a restorative tea. "I think it was the breakthrough in my crafting and runic magic that did me in."

"I'm sure it was," John told him.

Jayce checked his character sheet and dropped his level seventeen stat point into Intelligence, bringing it up to 15, including the bonus from the helm. He then sank four points into Heal Party, and it was replaced by a greyed-out Heal Raid.

With that done, he explained to John what his new magic was and what the elixir did.

"Think you have it in you to make more?" John asked.

Let me make some more of this tea, and I'll give it a go," Jayce said.

Sifting through the herbs, Jayce only found enough Iron Weed and Slippery Bloom for two more batches, but in the end, the three total batches yielded twelve more vials of the elixir. Each batch took less time to brew and grew easier to manage. He felt as if drawing on and pooling the mana the way he did had somehow increased his mana pool and regeneration rate considerably.

"I need to rest again," Jayce said. "It's not like yesterday, but I don't think I can stay conscious much longer."

"Hang in there a little bit, if you can," John told him. "You can rest in the carriage on the way. We really need to get going."

Jayce was pretty sure something had changed. He checked his character sheet to see if his stats had changed. Sure enough, his Wisdom had gone up five points and was thirteen, while his Intelligence had gone up two points and sat at seventeen.

When he filled John in on his results, the man was floored. "Once again, breaking the mold," he said. "You are officially the baddest level eighteen in history. Your overall stat points are higher than mine. Sure, mine are allocated differently, but total point count, you win, man."

CHAPTER NINETEEN

As they finished loading the carriage, an old man showed up on horseback. "Gandolf!" John yelled. "Good to see you, old man!"

Jayce rolled his eyes, glad that he had decided to keep his own name. He might have been tempted to call himself Bilbo; how awkward would that be now?

"I saw in guild chat that you had your new carriage and were going after a world boss," the old man said in a shaky baritone.

"True enough," John replied.

Gandolf turned to Jayce. "And you must be Jayce, the new guild member."

"That's me," Jayce said in confusion.

John spoke up. "Jayce, Gandolf, here, has retired from adventuring, but he was a mentor for us, so he stays in the guild and occasionally offers his wisdom."

"Well met," Gandolf said.

"Nice to meet you," replied Jayce.

"Figured I'd come drive your wagon for you so you don't leave it in the wilderness like a fool," Gandolf groused. "My old bones won't get anywhere near the world boss, though. I'm too old for that shit."

"Well, hop on up and drive then," John said. "Always glad for your company. I'll tell them we are on the road."

Jayce promptly fell asleep.

John: *Leaving the manor now. Gandolf is driving!*

Morrigan: *Wooo Hooo! Gandolf, nice man! Gonna join us for one more huzzah?*

Kull: *Hell yeah.*

Gandolf: *Nope, just playing chauffeur.*

Tim: *Damn.*

Morrigan: *It'll be good to see you anyway.*

Pericardium: *Finally, some good company!!*

John: *Lol.*

A few hours later, Jayce awoke to the bouncing of the carriage down the road. He summoned his guitar. "Any requests?" he asked.

Gandolf requested country music for the trip. Not his usual fare, but Jayce whipped out all the John Denver, Charley Pride, and Merle Haggard he knew. He even threw in some Tracy Chapman before ending his set with "Son of a Sinner" by Jelly Roll and Johnny Cash's cover of "Hurt" by Nine Inch Nails. The miles flew by, and before they knew it, they had gone as far as the carriage could take them.

"It's on foot from here," John said. "Intel has it that the world boss is headed into the swamp. It should be four hours or so on foot; I can't afford to have you playing, though. If the boss attacks before we are ready, it will be a disaster."

Gandolf helped unload the supplies they would carry with them and then started to set up camp. "I'll be here when you whippersnappers are done," he said.

John and Jayce shouldered their packs and started walking back toward Fiona's swamp. As they walked, they met up with a few other adventurers.

"Ok, Jayce," John said, "I know it's been a while since you were out there playing games in the real world, and I don't want you to be confused or lose focus while we fight, so I'm going to refresh your memory; we all need to be on the same page with terminology."

"Ok," Jayce replied.

"Rez is short for resurrection; some of our healers can resurrect people when they die, so it is important to keep them healthy and alive. If we all die, there will be no one to rez us. That is called a wipe, and we are stuck until one of the healers can self-rez and bring us back up, provided the boss doesn't stick around and prevent that."

"We can be resurrected?" Jayce asked. "Meg told me she knew someone who died."

"It is really hard to kill an adventurer permanently," John told him, "but it happens."

"A regular rez can only happen outside of battle. It takes too long and causes the boss to focus on the one attempting it, making it impossible to concentrate on the spell. An even rarer version is called a battle rez or brez; they tend to have longer cooldowns, and not as many healers can do it."

"Standard MMO fare, I guess," Jayce said. "I'm following ya."

"Great," John told him. "For the most part, focus on your support role. If you see a healer taking a beating, then try to heal them. If anyone calls out something you don't understand, just ignore it and ask questions later. As a support role, you should be fine keeping to the back."

"Got it," Jayce said as more people joined them.

"Good to see people are trickling in already," John said. "Our guild is too small for a world boss raid, and pickup groups can sometimes be hard to form. I would hate to have to wait for days before we had a raid together." John formed a group, and Kull, Morri, Peri, and Tim joined immediately. Next, John converted the group to a raid and began inviting each person they came across.

One of them was Fatty, the kill-stealer.

"Ugh, I really don't like that guy," Jayce told John quietly.

"What's up?" John asked.

Jayce told John about the hunting trip and Fatty stealing his loot. "And when I confronted him about it, he just told me, 'That's what you get for being too slow,'" Jayce said. "Then he told me he was gonna sell my loot in Seabeck."

"That sucks," John told him. "Unfortunately, some people are like that. Luckily, it's the exception, not the rule."

"Can we boot him from the raid?" Jayce said.

John gave him a sideways look. "That doesn't sound like you," he said. "You're not usually petty and vindictive."

"The dude really got under my skin," Jayce told him.

"I guess he did," John replied, "but we can't boot him. If we did, he would follow us and try to kill-steal. If someone outside of the raid delivered the killing blow, they would get the credit, not us."

"Oh," Jayce responded, "best to keep him in the group then."

By the time they saw the head of the giant world boss poking out above the trees ahead, they had thirty people in the raid group.

RAID Fatty: *Pass lead.*

RAID John: *??*

RAID Fatty: *I am the best raid leader in Seabeck.*

RAID Kull: *I'm good with John keeping lead.*

RAID Morri: *Yeah, sorry Fatty. John's got this.*

RAID Fatty: *All call; John or Fatty for lead.*

When the votes were in, John was voted as raid leader twenty-five to five.

RAID Fatty: *Fine, but don't blame me when we wipe.*

The group slowed and trailed the giant crab-looking beast from a distance as they waited for ten more people to show up. Once they had a full forty-man raid group, John sent out a message.

RAID John: *OK, if you're here, I assume you know what you're doing. If this is your first world boss, be careful. These things are no joke. It is not uncommon to lose half the raid before the end.*

Having said that, I'm not going to micromanage forty people.

I've put the tanks and healers in their own groups. Kull will take the initial pull.

Tanks: work it out and set up a rotation.

Healers: decide amongst yourselves who is on tanks and who is on raid.

We pull in five minutes.

RAID Fatty: *Brilliant leadership, man.*

RAID Kull: *Just shut up and do your part, Fatty.*

RAID Fatty: *Yeah, you guys would fail without me.*

RAID John: *Focus people and get ready.*

The area erupted in low chatter as people found their group members and worked out what they needed to do. The excitement was palpable as people worked themselves up for the challenge.

After four minutes, John sent out a message again.

RAID John: *T-minus one minute, folks. Make your final checks and preparations. Just one person unprepared can wipe the whole raid.*

RAID Fatty: *Ugh, amateurs.*

-Forty seconds later-

RAID John: *Kull, give us a fifteen-second pull timer.*

A fifteen-second countdown appeared in front of Jayce.

RAID John: *Pop your consumables, folks. Here we go!*

Jayce downed an elixir and saw each of his party members do the same.

When the countdown hit zero, Kull rushed the boss, screaming, "Leerooooy Jeeenkiiins!"

Jayce laughed and strummed his guitar, belting out "That Thing You Do" by The Wonders.

Peri was standing next to him and yelled, "I love that movie!"

With forty people all doing their thing, the raid was loosely organized chaos. Kull had turned the boss's back to the raid. The melee was in a semi-circle around the back, hacking at one giant chitinous leg. Before long, Kull yelled, "Switch!" and another Tank stood next to him and pounded at the monster. Kull stopped swinging and waited until the new Tank had aggro before stepping back to join the melee hacking at the leg.

Suddenly, the huge crustacean-looking monstrosity spun and smashed both claws into the melee. Before it could do more, another Tank grabbed its attention and spun it back around.

RAID Kull: *Random aggro drops and a cleave.*

RAID John: *Healers, get 'em up.*

Jayce saw several downed people get back to their feet while some of the healers looked completely stressed. He switched to Heal Party and Taylor Swift's "Shake It Off." Immediately, the members of his group seemed to perk up and redouble their efforts.

Switching back to Inspiration, he shouted, "Who lives in a pineapple under the sea?"

About two-thirds of the raid shouted, "SpongeBob SquarePants!" while the rest looked confused. It didn't take long before those who had never seen the show caught on to the concept. By the time he went back for a second run-through, the entire raid was shouting "SpongeBob SquarePants!" like a battle cry.

RAID Fatty: *OMG, you're so stupid.*

One of the legs finally went down.

RAID John: *One down, five to go. Watch for a phase shift.*

Krusty, as Jayce had decided to call it, whirled again and cleaved. Ready for it, the next Tank picked up the aggro, and many of the melee were able to mitigate the damage.

RAID John: *Healers, keep 'em up.*

Jayce switched to a punk rock version of Katy Perry's "Roar" and shouted, "I'm hungry for some Krabby Patties!" between verses.

After the second leg went down, Krusty lifted both pincers in the air.

RAID John: *Phase shift; be ready.*

Everyone seemed to pause in anticipation as bright lights burst forth from Krusty's claws. It slowly brought them down to either side of itself. Most everyone managed to move away before the beams leveled themselves about waist-high to the average human. The few that didn't move in time went down immediately.

RAID John: *Stay out of the beams and hold rezzes until the mechanic is done.*

Krusty slowly spun three-sixty, forcing the raid to move the dance away from the moving beams. After the spin, it switched directions. The direction change dropped another melee. This time, it spun one-eighty before changing directions yet again, spinning ninety degrees before the lights faded.

Kull quickly grabbed aggro, and the raid began hacking at a third leg. After two more legs went down, they were subject to the laser beam dance again. Most of the players were rez'd by the healers.

RAID John: *Any Brezzes left? We still have three down.*

No one responded.

RAID John: *Looks like we are out of Brezzes, folks. Call out if you have one. Come off cooldown.*

One more leg dropped.

RAID John: *One leg remaining; watch for phase shifts.*

Krusty once again raised its claws to the sky. This time, instead of laser beams, shadowy circles appeared around the raid. Anyone in the shadows dove out of the way as huge lichen-encrusted rocks fell from the sky. Four people didn't move in time, and the raid was down to thirty-three. The mechanic repeated, and two more were lost, including Kull.

RAID Pericardium: *Brez up.*

RAID John: *Kull.*

Peri cast her spell, and Kull got to his feet. Jayce targeted him for healing and belted out Matthew Wilder's "Break My Stride."

As Kull's health rose, he grabbed aggro.

RAID John: *Everyone on that last leg.*

As the last remaining leg cracked, Krusty slammed to the ground, and most of the raid was knocked back and off their feet. Krusty began pounding the ground, causing the earth to shake.

RAID John: *Blow all cooldowns.*

Jayce immediately got to his feet, summoned Chuck Berry's guitar, and swung into "Johnny B. Goode." The shaking ground made it difficult to concentrate, but he focused all his energy on the song. Everyone in his group got the full buff, but everyone that could hear seemed energized. Two more people went down under the cataclysmic shaking and didn't get back up. The rhythm of the pounding claws increased, and people began dropping fast.

At long last, the claws slowed, and the movement became twitchy. Jayce switched to his best James Morrison impression and slowed it down with the Doors' "The End."

When Krusty at last stopped moving, fifteen of the forty-man raid were left standing.

RAID John: *GJ, everyone. Healers: get your mana back and start rezzing. Loot will be distributed by roles.*

Jayce stopped singing, his throat sore. He wouldn't be singing again for a few days, at least, after all of that.

Bloop Your share of the loot is one gold, eight silver.

RAID John: *First up.*

[Chitinous Shield Epic] This teardrop shield is tough and lightweight with sharpened edges.
+8 Toughness
15 Stamina
+10 Block
400 Armor
May be wielded as a melee weapon. Chance to apply bleed effect when used to attack. Requires level 20+. Requires Shield skill expert+.

RAID John: *Tanks, link your skills to roll.*

RAID Kull: *[Shield specialty] [shields: profound]*

RAID Boudica: *[shields: expert]*

RAID Attila: *[shields: expert]*

RAID Conan: *[shields: expert]*

RAID Fatty: *[shields: profound]*

RAID John: *Kull, Boudica, Attila, Conan, and Fatty Roll*

RAID Kull: *89*

RAID Fatty: *12*

RAID Attila: *89*

RAID Boudica: *88*

RAID Conan: *42*

RAID John: *Kull, Attila Roll*

RAID Kull: *37*

RAID Attila: *1*

RAID John: *Congrats Kull!*

RAID John: *Next up.*

> [Serrated Blade Epic] Made from the serrated claw of a giant crab, this sword is sharp, extremely durable, and lightweight.
> +4 Strength
> +4 Agility
> Damage x2
> Chance to apply bleed (stacks up to 5 times). Requires level 20+. Requires swords expert+.

When all the loot had been doled out, John disbanded the raid.

John: *Grats again, Kull and Morri. Great drops. Sorry for the rest of us not getting anything new, but damn, that was a good fight.*

Morri: *I leveled.*

Kull: *Me too.*

Tim: *As did I.*

Peri: *Yup.*

Jayce: *Not me.*

John: *Looks like you were the only one not to level then Jayce, but you got two levels just before the fight, so I wouldn't feel bad.*

Morri: *That means you're Mr. Twenty-two now?*

John: *Yuppers.*

Morri: *Grats, man.*

As the raid was breaking up, Fatty yelled, "Anyone wanna go kill that ogre in the swamp while we are here?"

Jayce stood still in shock.

A couple of other adventurers began to walk toward Fatty.

Peri spoke up. "Leave her alone."

"Screw you. You were lucky I was in that raid, or you would have wiped. I don't want to carry you anymore anyway," Fatty yelled.

John stepped up to Fatty. "I suggest you listen to the lady."

"Or what?" Fatty said.

"Fiona is actually kinda sweet," Jayce said. "What has she ever done to you?"

"Same thing Mr. Krabs here did: exist," Fatty replied. "Besides, I bet she has some awesome loot."

"Leave it alone, Farquat," Kull said. "She is one of us."

"I don't care who she is," Fatty said. "Ogre's gonna die. Come on, guys."

The people who had gathered to join Fatty looked from

Fatty to John and back again, shrugged their shoulders, turned around, and walked away.

"You cowards!" Fatty yelled after them before turning back to John. "This isn't over. I'll be back to get that ogre and whatever loot she has; she wouldn't be holed up in that swamp if she wasn't hoarding something."

Chapter Twenty

"Damn it," Peri cursed. "This is bad."

"I agree," John said. "We have to help her. Peri and Morri: go to her and convince her of the danger and that we want to help. Kull and Tim: get to Gandolf and be prepared to defend or lend assistance. Jayce, you and I are going to Seabeck."

Jayce pulled out his guitar and began to strum some traveling music. "I'll speed us up so we can beat him to Seabeck, but it'll have to be instrumental," he said. "My throat is shot after that fight."

"So long as it works. You can slap some spoons together for all I care."

Jayce immediately began an instrumental rendition of Soundgarden's "Spoonman."

As they sped off toward Seabeck, Kull and Tim turned toward the wagon and Gandolf while Morri and Peri headed deeper into the swamp.

Peri smiled to herself; she knew they were being watched.

As Morri and Peri hurried toward Fiona's home, Fiona trailed them from a distance. She had come out to the edges of her swamp to watch the fight with the world boss. She had also heard the whole thing with Fatty and the conversation after that. There was a warmth deep inside her that she hadn't felt in many years. These strangers wanted to help her. She was determined not to leave her swamp, but still, something about the way they seemed to care pulled at a part of her soul she had long thought withered and dead.

Peri had healed her a few years ago when she had been caught in a trap set by some ne'er-do-wells who had wanted to kick her out of her swamp. She felt she could trust that one, maybe, but the others? A few pretty songs didn't make a strong foundation for trust. On the other hand, they hadn't known she was listening, and they genuinely seemed to want to help.

Jayce played until his fingers bled, and then he pounded out a rhythm on his thighs until his hands were sore. Finally, he hummed them through the last bit of the way to Seabeck. Two days nonstop after that insane world boss battle left the two of them exhausted, but they had to have beaten Fatty here by a long way.

Barely able to move, they stumbled into the Mercenaries Guild and asked to speak with the local Guild Master. The receptionist told them he was not in residence but was expected back the next day.

Jayce showed his membership token and got them rooms at the guild. Before turning in, they headed to the nearest inn for some food and gossip.

It was still relatively early in the evening, but the inn was busy. There were no tables available, but they found a couple of seats at the bar.

"What'll it be, gents?" the pleasantly rounded barmaid asked.

"Couple of the local best," Jayce replied before John could speak, "and two plates of whatever's hot."

The barmaid eyed their disheveled, road-worn appearance and hesitated. Jayce took the hint and piled some silver on the bar in front of him. "Keep the drinks coming until that's all gone," he said.

The barmaid nodded, poured a couple of frothy drinks, and handed them over the bar before turning toward the kitchen.

Jayce and John turned their backs to the bar and looked out at the dining room. They quietly sipped their drinks and listened to the low hum of conversation.

Two heaping plates of dinner and three drinks each later, they headed out to turn in for the night.

As they walked back to the Guild Hall, they compared notes. "No mention of Fatty or Fiona," Jayce said.

"Agreed," replied John. "We should have at least a couple of days, then. Even if Fatty is able to rally some people to go with him, no one will take that trip without a day or two to prepare."

Satisfied that they were perhaps ahead of the situation for now, they went to their rooms. Jayce didn't even have the energy to undress before he flopped on the bed and passed out.

Jayce and John were waiting in the lobby when the Guild Master came through late the next afternoon. "Sir John! I wasn't expecting you; should I have been?" he said, eyeing his receptionist.

"No, no," John placated, "only just arrived last night. I do have a matter I would like to discuss with you, though. Should only take a minute of your time."

"Follow me then," the Guild Master responded as he led them through the door to his office. He motioned for John to take the seat across from his desk. "I'm afraid I don't have an extra chair for your man at the moment. Would you like me to send for one?"

"Don't trouble yourself," John said. "We won't be but a moment."

"Very well, Sir John, what is it that you need to discuss?"

"Do you have a man who goes by the name of Fatty in your guild, Jack?"

"Ahh, yes," Jack said. "Obnoxious prat, but he is a member in good standing. Why do you ask?"

John sighed. "I was hoping he wasn't a member. Woulda made this easier. Do you know of Fiona, the ogre out in the swamp?"

"Of course," Jack replied. "People have made talk about flushing her out for years, but she don't bother no one really, so it has never gone anywhere."

"Well, we were out that way taking down that giant crab world boss that popped up a few days ago. When we took the boss down, Fatty tried to get a group together to kill Fiona. We talked the rest of them out of it, but Fatty swore he would gather a group and go back for her."

"Unfortunate," Jack said, "but not surprising, really. What's the problem?"

"The problem," John said slowly, "is that she is a friend of mine, and I would rather not see her harmed."

Jack, who had just taken a sip of his coffee, spit it back out in true sitcom spit-take fashion. "An ogre, a friend of yours?"

"That's right," John said, enunciating carefully. "She. Is. My. Friend."

"Ok, ok," Jack backpedaled, "I was surprised, is all. Didn't know they were smart enough to make friends. Figured they were more smash and bash than talk and tea."

"Can't speak for all of 'em," John said, "but this one is plenty smart, and like I said, I would rather not see her harmed."

"I see," Jack said. "I can certainly do my best to discourage anyone from going after her, but surely you realize that I can't forbid a contract on an ogre. I'd lose my position, and my replacement would lead the charge himself."

"All we ask is that you do your best to protect her," John soothed.

"Very well, I'll do what I can, Sir John, but it'll likely only buy you a few days if Fatty really puts his mind to it. He has a few cronies that toady to his every whim. The problem with loudmouths like him is that they tend to gather the mean kids around them."

John stood, pushing his chair back. "Best we be off then. Thanks for your time, Jack."

Chapter Twenty-One

John - *No luck in the city. Guild Master Jack is going to try to dissuade people from joining Fatty but isn't hopeful that he will do more than buy us a few days.*

Morrigan - *We finally got Fiona to talk to us, but she is adamant about not leaving her swamp.*

Gandolf - *Tim, Kull, and I have moved the carriage as close to the swamp as we can. If you convince her, we can make haste out of here.*

Jayce - *We can take her to Meg in Fleet. I think Meg and her young ward Emily would be good for her. Not to mention Jack, Emily's dog. That little guy is pure love with a waggly tail.*

John - *Jayce and I are about to head back your way. Let Fiona know we are coming so there are no surprises. Remind her she likes Jayce's singing.*

Pericardium - *Lol. She actually asked if he was going to come by and sing again. I think she may actually be pleased to see him. Be careful though, guys. From what I've been able to gather, her trauma runs deep.*

John - *Well, that certainly won't help her trust us. Thanks for the heads up.*

It turned out Fiona had a pretty nice place. It was still a cave in the swamp, but she had sectioned it off into several rooms with wooden partitions. She had a sturdy table and a very comfortable chair, and she had shelves upon shelves of books. Along with original titles, travelers from Earth had recreated loads of books from their memory and published them here. She had JRR Tolkien, Ursula K. Le Guin, Terry Brooks, Octavia Butler, Michael Moorcock, Frank Herbert, Steven R. Donaldson, Mary Shelley, Anne McCaffrey, Patricia A. McKillip, and more. Her library was AMAZING! If it wasn't for the urgency of the situation, Jayce may have asked if he could stay for a while.

"I don't care how many come," Fiona was saying, "they won't chase me from my home. I haven't done anything to anyone."

"I know you haven't," John told her, "but that won't stop them from hunting you. This guy has it in his head that he is going to do it, and from what I've heard about him, nothing will change his mind."

"I know a great place where you can stay," Jayce said. "My friend Meg is a swamp witch, and she has a place in Fleet. She is like us from Earth, and she has dedicated her life to helping Earth's people in this world. She knows Themiscura, too, if that helps."

"Oh, I do like Themiscura; she brings such lovely books. But I can't live in a city," she said. "I don't like being around all those people."

"Enough!" Peri exclaimed. "You are not going to convince her. Fiona, just know that you have a place to go if you need it, and we are here for you."

Fiona's eyes glossed over a little, and she sniffed before bowing her head. "Thank you," she whispered. "I don't think I've ever had anyone look out for me before, at least not without an ulterior motive."

"Rest assured," Morri soothed, "no one here wants anything except for you to be safe and happy. Do you have any requests? Jayce is dying to play you a song," Morri said, winking at Jayce.

Jayce took out his guitar and tuned it as Morri thought he would.

"Could you play 'True Colors' by Cyndi Lauper?" she asked.

"I would love to," Jayce said as he began strumming the song.

Guild: Gandolf - *I hope you guys are ready. You have a big ole crowd headed your way. I counted seventeen of them.*

Guild: Jayce – *Thanks, Gandolf.*

Guild: Peri – *Got it!*

Guild: Kull – *Tim and I are on our way. Meet you outside the cave.*

"Damn it," John cursed.

"What?" asked Fiona as Jayce put away his guitar and grabbed his sword in a strong two-handed grip.

"They are almost here," John told her. "Stay in the cave. Everyone else, outside. We have work to do."

They arrayed themselves outside the mouth of the cave. John was in the center with Morri and Peri on either side of him. As Kull and Tim showed up, they took the outside, and Jayce stood just behind the line, guitar in hand.

It didn't take long before Fatty and friends showed up. As soon as they saw the guild defending the cave, Fatty stepped forward. "Get out of the way, or we will get you out of the way," he said.

"Not gonna happen," John told him. "We told you; she is one of us. Leave her alone."

"And I told you I'm not going to let people like you tell me what to do." He drew his sword. "Now, get out of our way."

Tension was high, and Jayce was sure this was going to end with several people dying. Sure, maybe they could be rez'd, but people from Earth killing each other? He couldn't let that happen.

Suddenly, he knew he *could* stop it, at least delay it anyway. "I got this, guys," he said as he shuffled to the front of the group and stood right in front of Fatty.

"And what do you think you're going to do, little man? I got an ogre to kill and loot to pillage," Fatty laughed.

Jayce didn't respond. He mentally turned his hat into a fedora. He reached up with his right hand and pulled it down over his eyes. Head bowed low, he stood on his right foot and bent his left leg, toes on the ground, heel pointed toward his right leg.

Everyone just stared.

"What the fuck do you think you're doing?" Fatty spat.

Jayce focused his mind on Charm Person and Folie à Deux. He brought in some Inspire Person and focused his mana like he was going to imbue a rune. He brought a crystal-clear picture into his mind and filled it with all the spells he had conjured. He then began to fill it with his desired outcome. When he was ready, and Fatty was about to explode in anger, he began to sing "Beat it". When he got to *"Don't wanna see your face, you better disappear."* Fatty was staring daggers at him.

He swung his left leg up, knee toward his chest, and waved his foot from side to side before putting it down and going up onto the toes of both feet.

Everyone was staring at him in shock.

"You better run. You better do what you can..."

He summoned his electric guitar and focused all of his magic as he went into the next part.

Just beat it, beat it
Just beat it, beat it
Just beat it, beat it
Just beat it, beat it, ooo!

With that, he swung the guitar around to his back on the strap and began to Moonwalk.

Fatty took off running, and his posse was right behind him. They ran like they had never run before; pure mindless terror fueled their feet.

Jayce looked around and exclaimed, "Who's bad? Hehe!"

> *Bloop*
> You have learned a new skill.
> **Inspire Fear**: Upon successful use of this skill, all enemies within ten yards will run in fear for up to three minutes.

"Umm, Jayce, what the hell just happened?" John asked.

"I just gave myself a new skill: Inspire Fear. They will run for up to three minutes. Never underestimate the power of the King of Pop. If he was British he would have been Sir Michael Jackson."

"Hmm," Kull said, "that's useful. I doubt that Fatty will gather that particular bunch again, but he will be back. I'm afraid all you have done is buy us some time."

"It's ok," came a timid voice from behind them. "I'll go."

"What? Really?" Jayce asked. "What changed your mind?"

"Seeing you guys prepared to fight and maybe die for me," she replied. "I don't want you to die for me. I'll go." She turned to Jayce shyly, only briefly looking him in the eye before looking down at her own feet. "Uhmm, I just wanted you to know: I really love MJ."

It took a full day to get the carriage through the swamp to the cave and another day to pack Fiona's books and other things she wanted to keep. But the next day, they were crowded into the carriage, the luggage having been loaded into crates and strapped to the top.

The first stop was with the Free Company and Marshal

Harley. "Ho there, Will," John said. "We need to hire an escort."

"Why hire an escort when your friends will do it for free?" the Marshal asked. "What's going on?"

"Remember the ogre in the swamp, Fiona?"

"Yeah?"

"Well, she is a friend of ours and is being hunted by some jerks from Seabeck. Fair warning: they are Mercenaries Guild members, so we should hire you to ensure we don't want to cause a conflict with your team and the rest of the guild."

"I'll draw up a contract for one silver plus expenses," Will replied, "but you're going to have to tell me the story. This has got to be quite the tale."

After filling Will in on the whole story (at least as much as you could tell a non-Earther), preparations were made to set off the next day. They had kitted out two more carriages modeled after Sir John's armored behemoth of transportation. Jayce set about creating and imbuing all the same runes, and by the time they were ready to set off the next day, it was a train of three battle-hardened carriages. The front and rear carriages contained men of the Free Company. They each had a mounted ballista on the roof with a "gunner" seated at it and two crossbow-wielding mercenaries on either side of the driver. All the supplies and luggage had been transferred into these carriages.

The center carriage held Fiona, Peri, and Morri. Kull, Tim, John, Will, and eight of Will's best men rode escort. Jayce was seated on the roof of the center carriage. He had a mounted chair and desk with an amplified hurdy-gurdy. He would provide traveling music for the train.

The hope was they would make it to Fleet and Meg before Fatty or anyone else even knew that they had left the cave, but they were taking no chances.

They set off, and Jayce stuffed his ears with cotton before turning the drone on the hurdy-gurdy; not a subtle instrument to begin with, this one was amplified to be heard by all three carriages and the men on horseback. Going deaf on the trip was not a part of the plan.

They made such good time that they passed the first roadside inn before midday. As they got close to the second inn that evening, John called a halt.

Group Chat: John - *These inns treated Jayce pretty poorly on his trip out here. You guys wanna have some fun and sleep in comfort tonight?*

Group Chat: Will - *I'm always ready to stir some shit up. What's the plan?*

John walked into the inn. The innkeeper, a large middle-aged man with red cheeks, looked up from behind the bar.

"Sir John!" he exclaimed. "On your way to visit the Master Luthier?" he asked.

"I may well do that while I'm in Fleet," John said, "but I'm on escort duty for this trip."

"Must be someone very special to have one such as you for an escort," the innkeeper whistled.

"I am escorting Master Jayce and Lady Fiona to visit with the Lords of Fleet," he replied. "I require your two best rooms for the Master and Lady. I also need to accommodate myself, Marshal Harley, and twenty-two others."

"That will take every room I have available, and even then, some of your men will have to double up," the innkeeper mewed.

"Not a problem," John said, pulling out a handful of gold coins. The innkeeper's eyes widened, and his jaw dropped before he recovered and plastered the widest grin he could on his face.

Group Chat: John - *Cue Jayce.*

Just then, the door opened, and Jayce walked in. The innkeeper's smile vanished. "Your closet will cost you double *halfling,"* he sneered.

Sir John bowed deeply. "Master Jayce, sir, I was just making arrangements for your stay." He walked over to the table nearest the fireplace, wiped it off, pulled out a chair, and held it for Jayce.

Jayce sat down. "Very well, Johnny, good of you to do so. Let me know when the accommodations are ready."

"Yes, sir," John said in his most obsequious manner.

The innkeeper stood stock still, his red face frozen in shock.

"Is the Lady Fiona with you?" John asked.

"She will be along presently," Jayce said imperiously.

John returned to the bar and gave the innkeeper a quizzical look. "You were saying?" he asked.

"Uhh, n-nothing," the man stammered. Clapping his hands, he turned to a barmaid. "Get the rooms ready for our VIP guests," he said, "and make it quick!"

"Yes, sir," the maid nodded, bobbing a curtsy to John.

Group Chat: John - *Cue Fiona.*

Will opened the door, walked in, and held it while bowing. Fiona nervously stepped through the door behind him.

"Now see here," the innkeeper began, "we don't serve..."

"You don't serve WHAT?" John cut him off, taking Fiona's hand and leading her to the table.

The flummoxed innkeeper's red face turned crimson, and sweat began to bead on his forehead. "Sh, uh, sh-shellfish, Sir John. We don't serve, uhh, shellfish, uhh, anymore. T-too many people, uhh, allergic, yeah. Had to take it off the menu."

"Is that ok, Lady Fiona," John asked, "or should we move on to a place with a larger menu?"

Fiona looked down at the table and mumbled something to Jayce. "This will be fine," Jayce said. "We will eat whatever humble fair these people have to offer."

The rest of the company had finished stabling the horses and began to haul luggage into the inn.

In a timely turn of events, the barmaid came down the stairs and showed the men where to take Fiona's luggage.

"While we wait for your rooms to be prepared," John said, "would the Master honor us with a song or two?"

"Certainly," Jayce responded. "Will there be more of a crowd tonight?"

John looked at the trembling innkeeper questioningly. "Certainly," the man stammered, "but wouldn't the little Master and the, uhh, the Lady be more comfortable in their rooms?"

"The *Master,*" John said, emphasizing the fact that he did *not* use the word "little," "is the most accomplished Bard of our time, not to mention a Master Luthier, rune crafter, and one of the most fearsome warriors I have ever met. He will do as he pleases."

"I think I shall save my voice for the crowd," Jayce said. "For now, I will go check on the rooms and wash up." He stood and extended his arm to Fiona. Fiona grasped his arm and stood. Standing, she towered over him, so she placed a hand on his shoulder instead. Even then, she was forced to slouch. As they walked toward the stairs, she straightened and walked on her own. She had pulled her cowl up and kept her head bowed as she navigated the narrow staircase.

When they came down a couple of hours later, the common room was fairly full. John had cleared the area in front of the fireplace and reserved a seat for Fiona.

Fiona kept her cowl up and head down, but she was hard to miss. She was the tallest person in the establishment, walking with the shortest, and people got out of their way, but the stares weren't especially friendly.

John pushed a table in front of the fireplace and helped Jayce get on it before passing him a chair.

Jayce pulled out his twelve-string classical guitar and, using all the skill of his Master's in Stringed Instruments from the Boston Conservatory and years of experience he could muster, he played the most difficult technical and hauntingly beautiful song he could manage.

The entire crowd was silent. Not a single noise was heard during the performance. When the song was done, the stunned and silent crowd stared on. Jayce stood. "Now that I have your attention," he said, "let's have some fun!" and he burst out with the rockinest, most raucous rendition of "The Bear and the Maiden Fair" he had ever done. The crowd was transformed. Several people left, only to reappear shortly thereafter with friends in tow. It was the busiest night in the innkeeper's memory.

Much to the crowd's dismay, Jayce wrapped up the performance around midnight so he could get a few hours of sleep before the early start the next day.

Chapter Twenty-Two

After a long day of Bard-augmented travel, they decided to continue into the night. People took shifts sleeping in the wagons as they rode, and the pre-dawn grey sky saw them pulling into Cheapside.

Jayce knocked gently and entered Meg's house. Meg was seated behind the kitchen island, nursing a steaming cup of coffee. She looked up at the knock and leaped to her feet when Jayce opened the door.

She ran to him and wrapped him in a big hug. "Jayce!" she cried jubilantly. "I didn't think you would be back for a long time yet! What brings you by, or did you just miss us that much?"

"I have some friends outside," Jayce said, "and one very special person you need to be reunited with. I was hoping she could stay with you for a while. Meg, I have Fiona with me."

Meg walked back to her stool at the island and wiped the tears that were brimming from her eyes. She sat in silence.

"What's wrong?" Jayce asked. "Was I wrong to bring her here? Are you ok?"

"These are tears of joy, Jayce," Meg said. "I had hoped you could help her, but this is beyond my wildest expectations. How did you get her to come here? She never showed any inclination to leave her swamp."

Jayce filled Meg in on everything that had happened since he left Fleet. Meg nodded along, and when he came to the end of the tale, she spoke. "Well, we have left them waiting outside long enough. If the men decide to stay, they will have to find rooms in Fleet, but Fiona can have Dru's room. Dru has moved into the apprentice quarters at Thayer's place. Thayer is going to want to see you and hear your story anyway."

Just as they were getting ready to head outside, Emily came rushing into the kitchen with Jack at her heels.

"Jaaaaaaaaayce!" she called as she threw herself into his arms.

Jayce barely managed to catch her in time, and before he even had a chance to respond, Jack started bouncing around Jayce on his hind legs in true Jack Russell style. Jayce dropped to the floor, sitting cross-legged as he played with Jack and Emily in a great big, joy-filled reunion. Jayce felt his heart blossom as he realized just how much he had missed the pair. He felt a feeling of belonging that he just now realized he had never felt before. Meg left and brought Fiona in while Jayce played with Emily and Jack on the floor.

Fiona stopped and watched for a while, and Jayce looked up, startled. He was having so much fun that he hadn't even noticed when she came in.

"Fiona, this is Emily and Jack," Jayce said. "They are family, like Meg. I really think you are going to enjoy staying here."

Meg requested everyone leave the house while she got Fiona situated. John, Will, and the rest had to get situated at the Mercenaries Guild for the night anyway, so Jayce went with them. On the way to the Guild Hall, they passed Thayer's shop, and Jayce decided to part ways for a little while and visit his old friend.

"Ask Gerault to save me my old room," he told them. "I'll see you guys later. I want to go see Thayer and Dru."

"No problem," Will said. "Tell Thayer I'll stop by before we leave again."

Walking into the shop gave him another wonderful feeling of home and belonging. Dru was very excited to see him and hear the tale of his wandering. Jayce spent a couple of hours catching up with the boy and admiring how much he had learned. Dru had really taken to the craft and had a promising start. Jayce felt like a proud older brother. Eventually, Thayer put the lad back to work, but not before Dru made Jayce promise to give him some guitar lessons while he was in Fleet.

Thayer took Jayce into his living quarters for a chat.

"It was well done, what you did for Fiona," Thayer began. "When I sent you out, I had no idea where your journey would take you, but I'm glad it went as it did. I was particularly proud of how you handled the situation with Fatty."

"Wait," said Jayce, "I've only just told Meg the story, and she is busy with Fiona right now. How do you know what happened?"

"Have a seat, Jayce. There is much for me to tell and more for me to ask of you."

Jayce sat in a chair at the kitchen table. Thayer poured each of them a drink and sat opposite him at the table. "I am not what I seem," he started. "Well, I am, but I am also more. I came to this world from Earth a very long time ago."

"You're from Earth?" Jayce said, stunned.

"Everyone on this plane was once on Earth," Thayer said.

"But how is that possible? Most people say they were born here. They don't have the leveling system; we do. If they were all from Earth, at least a few of them would get my jokes!"

"Be still, and I will explain," Thayer continued. "I was what you might call a shaman back on Earth, though that term was not yet invented. The language I spoke was extinct before the Sumerians and Mesopotamia."

Jayce looked at Thayer wide-eyed. His thoughts were racing. He took a sip of his beer and rubbed at his face before looking up again. He realized that Thayer was waiting for him to focus before he continued.

"I believed in magic when I was on Earth; I believed in my abilities with magic. So, when I came here, and my powers manifested in more physical and tangible ways, I was not surprised—everyone who was here at the time believed in them as well. Earth was a very different place back then. Science had not taken the wonder out of life yet."

"You have magic?" Jayce asked.

"Yes," Thayer told him, "I will explain more if you let me continue."

"Sorry," Jayce said, "I'm just trying to wrap my head around all of this. This is just as shocking as arriving here was to begin with."

"When I arrived, this place was an endless plane. It stretched farther than anyone had been able to travel. Magic was commonplace, and no one doubted what we could do. We did not need the system you are used to now."

"I never even suspected you were from Earth, let alone that old," Jayce said in awe. "How did this endless plane become the world we are in now?"

"It was about the time the Sumerians started showing up here that we got some people who, although they believed in magic, did not believe that they could do or experience magic. With that belief, they were not able to access the magic of this world. As time went on, fewer and fewer of the new arrivals could access the magic of this world. Many of those who could use magic began to take control and rule over those who could not. We wanted to find a way for everyone to access the magic we used so freely."

"Wait," Jayce interrupted, "is Meg right then? Are we all dead?"

"Most people here are dead on Earth, yes," Thayer told him, "but not all. Anyone who is not present on Earth may manifest on this plane. Those who are in a coma or sometimes those in the deepest of sleep may touch on this world. I don't know why, but it seems like this plane was intended to be a place of refuge. It may not be another world at all; it is more like another dimension. Another phase of reality, if you will."

"Wait. If you have been here so long, how do you know of comas and other dimensions?" Jayce asked.

"First of all, we were less sophisticated and technologically proficient back then, but we were not without intelligence. We had people lapse into comas. We did not know how to care for them, so they died before too long, but we were not unaware of the phenomena."

Jayce looked into his mug, a little embarrassed.

"Second, I have kept up with the goings-on back on Earth. I have followed the times and technology."

"But how?" Jayce asked. "If you are here, how do you keep up with things back on Earth?"

"Be still, and let me explain, Jayce," Thayer admonished. "Hold your questions. I will most likely answer them all before the end of my tale."

"Sorry," Jayce said again, lamely.

"As some of the more powerful of us began to take power, many of those who had suffered the most in life on the Earthly plane were forced to suffer again on this one. This did not sit well with me and with many of my older brethren. We came from a time and place where we looked out for each other, where life was valued and differences cherished."

Thayer paused to take a drink before continuing.

"A little over one hundred of us determined to section off a sanctuary. We built a magic barrier around an inland sea and the lands that touched it. We focused on natural barriers like ice flows and mountains, but we erected a magical barrier that very few would be able to pass. In so doing, we sectioned off a portion of the eternal plane about three times the size of Earth. This is where you are now."

"Why so big?" Jayce asked.

"Based on the increasing number of people arriving, we knew that eventually, we would probably need the space," Thayer told him. "And with an eternal plane, why not?"

Jayce downed another big gulp of his drink and contemplated the implications of what he had just been told. So many questions ran through his mind, but he put his mug down and gave Thayer his attention once again.

"We gathered in this land those who had a like mind to ourselves; the number were few, but that did not matter. The next thing we did was cast a magical net that would gather the souls of those who most needed our help as they transitioned to this plane: those who had suffered the most in their Earthly lives. There were many hard times in human history, and it soon became apparent that this area, as large as it is, would not be large enough for our needs. Imagine a place large enough for everyone who has ever died. We annexed more areas and gave control of them to some of those who had been with us the longest. We narrowed our net to those who fit certain personality traits while the other newly formed areas did the same for other personality traits."

"So, this land is for abused people who like swords and sorcery?" Jayce asked.

"It so happens that in your time, that seems to be a common trait of people who come here. But it is more about an open imagination: people who would be more likely to accept magic," Thayer said.

"I think I need a break," Jayce told Thayer. "I'm not sure I can process anymore right now."

"That is fine," Thayer said, standing. "I should check on Dru before he gets up to his antics."

"I'll come back tomorrow," Jayce promised. "I am excited to be getting some answers finally."

Jayce checked into his room at the Mercenaries Guild. He felt like his brain was full. So much had just been revealed to him. It was overwhelming.

After putting away his belongings, he decided to go see Thorne. As he left his room, he found Will and John approaching his door.

"Hey," John said, "we were just about to go get a drink. Wanna come along?"

"Absolutely," Jayce said, locking his door, "but we have to go to the Pig and Pony. I should say hello to Molly."

"Perfect," Will said. "That's where we were headed anyway. Inns inside the gate are too stuffy for our taste."

As soon as they entered the Pig and Pony, Molly came running up to hug Jayce. Once again, he found himself marveling at how close he felt to people here. Other than TJ, he never really felt comfortable around people back home.

The regular patrons recognized him and immediately started buying them rounds as soon as they sat down.

John and Will were impressed. "You sure are popular!" John said, patting him on the back.

"I'm all for it!" Will said. "Free drinks are free drinks!"

It didn't take long before people talked him into playing for them. He took out his guitar and started with what had become his signature song, "The Bear and the Maiden Fair."

John joined him on the songs he knew, and Thorne eventually came by and played the drums. They played late into the night. It felt good to be home.

The next day, Jayce stopped by Meg's again. Meg was in her usual spot. Emily was curled up with Jack on his bed in the corner, and Fiona was sitting at the island in his old spot.

"I see you have met Meg," Jayce said.

"Themiscura explained it all to me," she said. "Meg would have stayed as Themiscura for me, but I told her she should stay in whatever form she is most comfortable in."

"Meg is my natural form," Meg said. "The rest take effort I would rather not have to spend in my home."

"Good," Jayce said. "Meg is my favorite anyway."

"Did you talk to Thayer?" Meg asked as she made him a plate of food and poured some tea.

"Oh boy, did I," Jayce replied. "How much of what he said did you know?"

"I know everything," Meg replied. "I've been working with him as long as I've been settled in Fleet."

"It's all a bit overwhelming," Jayce said. "I get why you didn't tell me everything at the beginning."

Fiona looked confused but shook her head. "I'm happy just being here for the moment," she said. "I don't think I want in on whatever you two are talking about."

"How about a song then?" Jayce asked, summoning his guitar.

"That sounds wonderful!" Fiona said, walking over to wake Emily and Jack. As soon as Emily saw him, she had to take her place on his lap. Jack bounced around at the foot of the stool until Jayce tossed him a piece of bacon. When everyone had settled down again, Jayce handed Emily over to Fiona, who gladly took the girl onto her lap. Emily smiled and snuggled into the ogre.

"I knew you two would hit it off," Jayce said as he tuned his guitar. "Any requests?"

"Malawaina!" Emily said immediately.

Surprised by the request, he put his six-string back in his inventory and summoned the twelve-string.

"'Malagueña' it is," he said and started to play the classical piece.

Fiona had never heard Jayce play classical guitar before and sat in silence, hugging Emily to her chest while Jayce played. When he was done, he put the guitar away.

"More!" Emily said

"Yeah, more!" Fiona said reverently.

"Next time," Jayce replied. "I'm sure I'll be here at least a few days. I have to go see Thayer again."

Meg nodded in approval, and Jayce got a round of hugs before he left for Thayer's.

As Jayce walked into the lutherie, Dru looked up from the workbench. "Jayce!" he exclaimed. "Come and see my work." As Jayce walked over, he could see the boy was disassembling the neck of a fiddle. Jayce reached out and gently moved Dru's hands around to a position that would better allow him to fit the scraper under the fingerboard. "Be very careful removing the fingerboard and you may be able to reuse it. They are usually made thicker than they need to be so they can be planed and reshaped when they wear down."

Dru smiled. "I know, I just can never seem to pull them off in one piece."

"You may not be steaming them enough, or you may

just need to move slower and have patience; let me show you."

Dru handed the fiddle over for Jayce to work with. Jayce picked up a knife and tested the glue. The fingerboard was loose enough to work with, so he slid the knife very carefully into place, making sure Dru could see what he was doing, and worked it along the neck under the fingerboard. Before he was finished, he handed the instrument back to Dru. "Did you see the difference in the way I used the knife?" he asked.

"Yeah," Dru replied as he slowly tried to replicate what Jayce had been doing.

"That looks much better already," Jayce told him. "Take your time; learning this craft takes precision and patience. I'm sure that Thayer already showed you how to do this. Don't be in a rush. It is more important to get your technique right than it is to be fast. Speed will come as your body learns the right way to do things."

"Thanks, Jayce," Dru said as he turned a little red in the face. "Master Thayer says the same thing, but it's hard to go slow."

"Trust me," Jayce admonished. "It is well worth it to perfect your skills now and let speed happen later. Take all the time you need to do it right. Keep going, and I'll ask Thayer if I can teach you some guitar later."

Dru beamed. "Oh yes, please," he said excitedly.

Jayce smiled and headed back into the residence behind the shop to talk with Thayer.

"If everyone here is from Earth, why do so many people not seem to know about Earth or that this is an afterlife?" Jayce asked as soon as they were seated.

"After a long time, many of the people who had come to live here decided that they wanted to forget their former lives and just exist on this plane," Thayer explained. "They wanted to live like they had always been here, like there was no former life full of grief and sorrow. None of us had the power to make that happen. So, the oldest among us put our heads together, and for many years, we struggled with a way to make that happen. Eventually, we came up with a method that, in theory, could transport people's souls into newborn bodies.

"Like reincarnation?" Jayce asked.

"Yes," Thayer responded. "We discovered how to make reincarnation—of sorts—happen here on this plane. None of us, however, had enough power to make the spell work. Even casting together, we could not figure out how to make it work." Thayer paused, letting that sink in.

"I'm following so far," Jayce told him.

Thayer took a drink and continued. "Finally, one of my friends discovered a way for everyone to concentrate their power in the hands of a single individual. With that power combined into one, we hoped that we could grant the wish that so many people had."

Thayer trailed off, sipping absently from his mug, his thoughts turned inward to that time so long ago.

After it became apparent that Thayer was lost in thought, Jayce cleared his throat.

"Sorry," Thayer said. "It was long ago, and I don't often tell this story."

"This is a good time for a break anyway," Jayce said. "Do you mind if I teach Dru some guitar, and we can pick this up again in an hour or so?"

"That sounds perfect," Thayer said. "I need to inspect his work anyway."

The two walked out into the shop, where Dru was very carefully cleaning the glue from the neck of the fiddle.

"Good job," Thayer told the boy. "You removed the fingerboard in one piece, and you're taking your time for once."

Dru blushed and smiled at Jayce. Thayer looked between the two and laughed. "Oh, I see," he said. "When Jayce tells you what to do, you listen."

"It's not that," the boy stammered. "I guess it finally sunk in this time is all."

"Well, why don't you take a break and let Master Jayce teach you some guitar," Thayer said. "I'll inspect your work and give you some pointers after."

Dru carefully set the instrument he had been working on down, cleaned up his workspace, wiped down his tools, put them away, and ran to grab a guitar.

"Nice," Jayce said to Thayer. "Looks like you have already instilled some great habits."

"He is a good lad," Thayer said smiling. "Eager to learn and to please. He isn't the fastest learner, but once he gets something right, I never have to reteach it."

Dru came back with two guitars, handing one to Jayce.

"We are going to start by learning two very simple chords," Jayce instructed. "They are two-finger cords and go together well." He had Dru sit down and then showed him how to hold the guitar before positioning his fingers to an E minor. "When you play this, we are going to start by only strumming on the down stroke; watch me." Jayce picked up his guitar and played an E minor. "Now you try," he said.

By the end of the hour, Dru had learned E minor and D/6/9F# and could play them well while strumming on the downstroke.

"Now watch what I can do with these two chords," Jayce said as he played "A Horse with No Name" by America. When he was done with the song, he handed his guitar to Dru. "Now put these away, listen to your Master, and get this fiddle done right; I'll show you how to play that song later."

Dru ran to put the instruments away and stood eagerly at the workbench. Jayce smiled and went back into the residence.

When Thayer rejoined him, Jayce had made a pot of tea and served them both.

Thayer took a sip before continuing.

"Eighty-one of us gathered that day, and we formed a giant circle and combined our powers. Gandolf led the spell. As we poured our mana into him, he took the souls of a few of those who wanted to forget their past lives out of their bodies and helped them reform into the wombs of others who were waiting to help."

"So you made immaculate conception happen?" Jayce asked.

"Not really," Thayer responded. "More like we gave the ability to reproduce to some mothers who volunteered to raise more children. Although we had altered their bodies to be able to reproduce again, we did not have the ability to create new souls. As powerful as we are, that ability is beyond us."

"Ok," said Jayce. "So, the souls you removed from the bodies of people who wanted to start over went into the wombs of those who wanted to be mothers, then?"

"Exactly," Thayer said. "On this plane, in this space, when there is a couple who want to be parents AND a person who wants to be reborn, then and only then is conception possible."

Thayer went to take a drink and realized his mug was empty. He gathered the mugs and got up to refill them while Jayce soaked in what he had been told.

"Are you involved in every birth that happens here, then?" Jayce asked.

"Not at all," Thayer replied. "I'm not even sure how the spell worked, really. Gandolf, or Liang as we knew him then, was the only one to figure it out, the only one who truly understood what we were doing."

"The same Gandolf that I've been traveling with?" Jayce asked.

"That's him," Thayer smiled.

"Leaving that aside for now," Jayce said, "if everyone

here is from Earth and has been brought to this place to heal from their trauma, why is there suffering here?"

"That is a product of rebirth," Thayer told him. "When there were far more people with memories of life on Earth than there were reborn, we continued to take care of each other and shepherd those who no longer knew. Soon, though, rebirth became very popular, and the reborn began to outnumber the Earthborn. The same societal pressures and failings began to creep into our plane."

"But aren't you all-powerful?" Jayce asked. "Couldn't you stop it?"

"Some say I am the god of this world," Thayer said, "but the definition of a god has changed drastically since my time on Earth. We did not believe in all-powerful and all-knowing perfect beings, only in more powerful and more knowing than us mortals. I am not omniscient, nor am I omnipotent. I do try to influence the world and correct injustices. But I do not have the power to be everywhere at once, to see and affect everything in my domain at all times. From time to time, I recruit helpers. You know one of them."

"Meg," Jayce said.

"Precisely," Thayer replied. "Gandolf is one of the few remaining from my time, and he is tired. He wishes to be reborn himself but has agreed to hold off until we can recruit a replacement."

"A replacement for someone so ancient? How does that work?" Jayce asked.

"No, a replacement to help shepherd this world," Thayer told him. "It is already too much. It would be that much harder with one less of us. So, we cast a specific net, looking for one with extraordinary abilities. Someone who could help us find the lost and repair the damage done in this world in a way that no other has before, but one who still belonged. Two hundred years have passed since we cast that net. You, Jayce, are the first that has met our criteria."

"Me?" Jayce asked. "But I'm no one special, and I don't have a tragic backstory. How do I fit your criteria?"

"You underestimate yourself, Jayce. You graduated top of your class in high school, undergrad, and graduate programs. Although you worked hard, you worked no harder than many of those you surpassed. You were one of the most sought-after studio musicians in a very competitive market. You could have easily been a painter, sketch artist, or sculptor. Or, with your math skills and analytical ability, any number of other occupations. You would have excelled at anything you chose."

"I suppose," Jayce hedged, "but I grew up in a stable home. I had no real drama or trauma."

"That is true, to an extent," Thayer said. "You more than met the criteria for open imagination and the ability to accept what we created here. While you don't fit the usual view of trauma that brings most people here, you still needed to heal and grow, and it was enough for us to bring you here; we made the rules, after all. I think that this is enough for today."

"There is more?" Jayce asked.

"Spend time with your friends and come back in a few days," Thayer said. "You know everything now. We just have to discuss how you can help."

As Jayce walked back through the workshop, Dru looked up. "You going to the Pig and Pony tonight, Jayce? Can I come?"

Jayce smiled. Some things, at least, were the same. "That's not up to me, buddy. You're an apprentice now."

Dru looked at Thayer hopefully. "Can I go? I'll work

extra hard. I'm getting faster. I will make up any work I miss, I promise. Please, can I go?"

Thayer laughed. "I tell you what. Finish the tasks I have set for you already, and you can have the night and tomorrow to spend with Jayce... if that's what he wants."

"Yes!" Dru whooped excitedly, looking over at Jayce.

"That sounds good to me," Jayce said, then he looked at Thayer. "Join us at the Pig and Pony tonight? Maybe bring Thorne and your instruments?"

"Wouldn't miss it," Thayer told him.

With his head full of all the new information from Thayer and his heart full from Dru's enthusiasm, Jayce decided to head back to Meg's; his surrogate mother always had a way of helping him work through his thoughts. Besides, it would be good to see Emily and Jack... and Fiona. He was growing rather fond of Fiona.

Giving the door a quick knock, he opened it to see Peri seated at the island with Meg and Fiona. Emily and Jack were nowhere to be seen. The familiar sight of herbs hanging from the ceiling, friends seated around the island, and Meg making tea was nearly overwhelming. *This is what a home should feel like,* he thought. I guess I never knew what I was missing.

"Ears burning, were they?" Peri asked.

"What?" Jayce said.

"Oh, we were just talking about you," Meg said flatly.

"Uh oh," Jayce said. "Am I in trouble for something?"

Fiona looked down. "No," she said, blushing.

"Meg was just telling us about your many accomplishments last time you were here," Peri chimed in just as the silence was growing awkward.

It was Jayce's turn to blush. "All exaggerated, I'm sure,"

Jayce said. "Meg is more like a mother than my own mother was. Never take a mother's word when she brags about her son."

"Oh, you stop that," Meg chided. "None of that self-effacing nonsense today."

"Ok, ok," Jayce said chastised. "Just makes me uncomfortable, is all."

Peri reached over and patted him on the head like a dog. "Aww, he *can* be taught!" she joked.

Looking around, Jayce went to the kitchen side of the island and grabbed a stool. Peri moved over, making room between her and Fiona for Jayce to sit. He set the stool down and sat, briefly making eye contact with Fiona before clearing his throat. "So," he said, "how about those Mets?"

Everyone chuckled, but the quip worked, and in no time, they were all chatting around the island, and Jayce realized that this was truly where he belonged. Suddenly, he didn't care what had brought him here or why. This was right, and he was home.

Acknowledgments

First, I need to acknowledge my Kickstarter backers in backing order:

Tommy Pucket, Ryan, Eva Dennis, Jace the Ace, Josh G, Ariquelle, Brent Longfellow, Kenneth, Ben Zumwalt, Jennifer Williams, Nichol Hines, Michael, Esther van Veghel, Russell Ventimeglia, Nicholle Taurins

Thank you for your support! Self-publishing can get very expensive, and you guys all made this possible. I cannot express my appreciation enough.

The AMAZING artist Kat Miller (@Kathumanart.bsk.social) for the cover art, Kickstarter campaign art, and sword for scene separation.

A very special thank you to Andy, my editor at Cup & Quill. Your criticism is the very definition of constructive. If there are parts of this book that suck, it's only because I didn't make all the changes you suggested.

I must acknowledge all the music and musicians in the world. You make the world a better place, and your efforts mean everything.

I probably shouldn't, but I will acknowledge Jared H. and Dan P. You made my life a living hell to the point where I no longer wished to live it. This has made me examine the way I treat the people around me and ultimately makes me a better person.

And, of course, all of the authors out there sharing their visions with the world. Thank you for doing what you do. Lately, I have been following John Scalzi on Bluesky, and his comments are usually gold, so thank you John Scalzi.

Song List

Pearl Jam, Jeremy; Temple of the Dog, Hunger Strike; Beastie Boys, She's Crafty; CCR, Travelin' Band; The Band, The Weight; Supertramp, Bloody Well Right; Fleetwood Mac, Go Your Own Way; Ted Nugent, Cat Scratch Fever, Wango Tango; Simon and Garfunkel, Parsley Sage Rosemary and Thyme (album); Drowning Pool, Let the Bodies Hit the Floor; Linkin Park, One Step Closer to the Edge; The Bear and the Maiden Fair (from HBO's *Game of Thrones*); Toss a Coin to Your Witcher (from Netflix's *The Witcher*); Twisted Sister, We're Not Gonna Take It (Dee Snider Cancer Version); The Beatles, A Hard Day's Night; Flogging Molly, Drunken Lullabies; Dropkick Murphys, Barroom Hero; Elton John, Saturday Night's Alright (For Fighting); *Carmina Burana*; Led Zeppelin, Immigrant Song; Oingo Boingo, Dead Man's Party, No One Lives Forever; Danny Elfman, This Is Halloween; La Malagueña; John Butler, Ocean; John Butler Trio, Wade in the Water; The Hold Steady, The Bear and the Maiden Fair; Tones and I, Dance Monkey; Lynyrd Skynyrd, Free Bird; Chuck Berry, Johnny B. Goode; Willie Nelson, On the Road Again; Tom Cochrane, Life Is a Highway; Red Hot Chili Peppers, Road Trippin'; Frank Sinatra, It's Nice to Go Traveling; Johnny Cash, I've Been Everywhere; The Proclaimers, I'm Gonna Be (500 Miles); Metallica, Turn the Page; Simon and Garfunkel, I Am a Rock; Lily Allen, Fuck You; Queen, We Are the Champions, Another One Bites the Dust; the *Shrek* movie soundtrack; The Wonders, That Thing You Do! (from the movie); Taylor Swift, Shake It Off;

SpongeBob SquarePants; Katy Perry, Roar; Matthew Wilder, Break My Stride; The Doors, The End; Soundgarden, Spoonman; Cyndi Lauper, True Colors; Michael Jackson, Beat It; America, A Horse with No Name.

I would list the Movies, TV shows, Books, Comics, and other pop culture items that influenced this book... but there are way too many, and I made a huge effort to give credit where it was do in the book. I do know that I never said "Suck it, Shawn" was from *Psych*... but if ya know, ya know!

www.ingramcontent.com/pod-product-compliance
Ingram Content Group UK Ltd.
Pitfield, Milton Keynes, MK11 3LW, UK
UKHW020653200225
455358UK00009B/407